Seduction

And while seduction should prove a simple task—a job, nothing more—Blyss knew once she stood in Stryke's arms again all bets would be off. She'd fall into his beautiful brown eyes and sexy smile and wish only for his masterful kiss. A kiss that had left her breathless in the gallery office.

A kiss she wanted to taste again.

Shaking her head furiously, she battled with the devil and angel hovering above each shoulder. She would never be an angel. She tried not to be so devilish. But this afternoon she had to be a temptress and seduce.

Because if she did not, she would then have to face her beast. And that was something she could not be

MOONLIGHT AND DIAMONDS

MICHELE HAUF

Published in Great Britain 2015
by Mills & Boon, an imprint of Harlequin (UK) Limited,
Eton House, 18-24 Paradise Road, Richmond, Surrey, TW9 1SR

© 2015 Michele Hauf

ISBN: 978-0-263-25409-9

89-0415

Michele Hauf has been writing romance, action-adventure and fantasy stories for more than twenty years. France, musketeers, vampires and faeries populate her stories. And if she followed the adage "write what you know," all her stories would have snow in them. Fortunately, she steps beyond her comfort zone and writes about countries and creatures she has never seen. Find her on Facebook, Twitter and at michelehauf.com. You can also write to her at PO Box 23, Anoka, MN 55303, USA.

Chapter 1

Paris

"Achoo!"

Stryke Saint-Pierre chuckled at the power sneeze that had blown out of Summer Santiago's two-year-old mouth. Her dad, Vail, instead of wiping his daughter's nose and cooing reassurance, lifted his head and fiercely scanned up and down the Parisian street. They stood before the Hawkes Associates building, along with Rhys Hawkes, Vail's stepfather. The trio were enjoying the cloudy day and discussing Rhys's need for help.

"See any?" Rhys, a tall, salty-haired half vampire, half werewolf, asked his son.

Vail, full-blooded vampire, nodded across the street.

Stryke followed the vampire's nod and spied a lanky man wearing a blue hoodie, tattered jeans and combat boots who strode down the sidewalk. The stranger glanced toward them. Red eyes glowed.

"Demon," Vail confirmed. "He's cool, though. Doesn't appear as though he means any trouble. Does he, sweetie?" He kissed his daughter's curly blond hair.

"Demons are not my favorite breed," Rhys muttered. "But he looks harmless. She still allergic?" he asked Vail.

Vail, with coal-black hair and silver rings on his fingers that glinted even with the lacking sunlight, nodded. He explained to Stryke. "Ever since Summer had a little run-in with Himself last year she's been allergic to sulfur. Good demon alarm, though."

"How does a baby have a run-in with Himself?" Stryke had been in Paris all of two days and was staying in an apartment owned by his grandfather—the rest of his family was, as well—and what he'd learned since arriving was that paranormal breeds of all varieties were in abundance here as compared to Minnesota, which he called home.

"Himself kidnapped her," Vail provided. "Long story. She's good. Wasn't hurt. But you know. Allergic now. I have to head out. Lyric is probably already at the tailor's waiting for me. I have to try on the tuxedo again. I hope the tailor got the studs right this time."

Stryke smirked. Vail wore black velvet jeans and a crisp black shirt with black lace around the wrists. And there was enough silver and diamonds on his wrists, ears and rings to flash signals to the moon. The vamp defined glamour rock, but with a bite.

"I sent a suit to your apartment, Stryke," Vail said. "Your mother reported to my wife that her sons hadn't properly packed. Ha! Anyway, not sure if they'll fit you with a tux for the wedding. But in case not, I thought you could borrow one of mine. I sent one to your brother Trouble's apartment too, but that guy is a block. Not sure my stuff will fit him."

Indeed, Stryke hadn't packed anything fancy for the family wedding. When he'd learned it was black-tie, he'd shaken his head and tried not to moan too loudly. Suits were not his style. But it was generous of the vamp to send him a loaner. Stryke's shoulders were broader than the vampire's and his biceps were definitely bigger, but he figured he could make it work. Unless it was velvet. It was probably too late to specify a more subtle fabric choice, so he'd keep that worry to himself.

"Thanks, man." Stryke met Vail's fist bump and then tweaked Summer's button nose. "See you at the wedding, Summer."

The shy toddler tucked her face against her dad's neck yet, with a giggle, peeked back at Stryke.

"Hug?" Stryke held out his arms.

Surprisingly, she stretched out her arms and he took her into a bear hug. A hug from a kid defied explanation. Stryke wanted a pack of his own. Soon. The urge to raise a couple of sons, and heck, why not a few daughters too, was strong. Hugs seemed a very necessary purpose to life.

"She likes you." Vail retrieved his daughter.

Summer said, "Puppy?"

"Ha! She's already got a nose for the wolves," Vail said.

Stryke playfully barked at her, and Summer giggled.

"See you at the wedding!"

The vampire strode off toward the red Maserati convertible parked down the street. Stryke and Rhys waved to Summer in the front car seat as the twosome rolled by.

"That's the third Maserati in so many years," Rhys commented on the sleek vehicle that sported a noticeable dent on the passenger door. "That boy needs to take a driver's course."

"Wow." Stryke shoved his hands in his front jeans pockets. He couldn't imagine having the kind of disposable income to afford a six-figure car—three times over. While set for life, thanks to investments, he lived a middle-class existence in a small town. He gladly claimed the title of redneck. Happiness to him was living simply.

Though he wouldn't mind hooking up with a pretty Parisian werewolf while here. The available females back home were slim-pickings, and his werewolf had never had the pleasure of dating another of his breed. It was what he most desired. That, and starting a family that he could call a pack.

Finding a woman had actually become necessity since Stryke's father had given him the task of starting a new pack. Malakai Saint-Pierre was ready to retire and travel the world with his wife, Rissa. The Saint-Pierre pack consisted of only family. They needed a strong new pack in the area. A diverse pack made up of many families. It was how the werewolves in Minnesota would finally grow their numbers.

The Saint-Pierre pack's scion was currently Trouble, Stryke's eldest brother. Trouble hadn't the calm control to step into his father's position as principal and lead others. Malakai had said as much to Stryke. His oldest brother was a loose cannon, who picked fights at the drop of a shifty glance and reveled in partying all night. Slightly ADD? Always possible with Trouble.

Stryke was eager to head a pack and had the confidence to do so. But to grow a pack a man needed a good woman at his side.

"So you said you were going to stay on a bit after your family heads home?"

"A few days, for sure." Stryke returned his attention to Rhys, who owned Hawkes Associates, a sort of bank/savings/storage conglomerate that catered to all paranormal species. "My parents and brothers and sister are here for five days. But Grandpa Creed said we could stay in the apartments as long as we like, so I'm going to fit in some touring when the wedding is over."

"When you're not wandering and checking out the sights I'd love it if you'd consider helping me out. I'm shorthanded and have a lot of work in the office. My assistant is out of town on his honeymoon. I've a pickup with the Order of the Stake. It would be simple. You'd meet Tor and he'll hand over the artifacts."

"Is the Order of the Stake what I think it is?"

"Yes, they are an ancient order of mortal knights who hunt vampires. But they're cool. Vail informs for them on occasion. Torsten Rindle does their spin. He also handles exchanges with Hawkes Associates. Sometimes the knights in the Order come upon treasure or, let's just say…their victims' belongings have to be cataloged. They've recently acquired a demon artifact that I bought for my own collection. It wouldn't take long. But I don't have the time to run over there myself with all this wedding stuff."

"I can do that. Doesn't sound too difficult. Tomorrow?"

"Yes. I'll text you the information and provide Tor with your name. Thanks, Stryke. I appreciate it. Oh, and now that I think of it… Here." Rhys tugged out two tickets from his jacket pocket. "You have any interest in gallery showings?"

Stryke shrugged. "I do hope to catch some of the museums and culture while I'm in town. Always willing to put new ideas in my brain and learn what I can about art and history."

"I think this is a seventeenth-century jewelry collection on display. I got the tickets weeks ago, but won't be able to make it tonight. As grandparents of the groom, my wife and I have to attend a rehearsal dinner tonight. Tedious."

Stryke accepted the tickets. He wasn't much for jewels, but he'd made the decision to take in as much of the city as he could while here. This was the first time he'd been overseas. He wasn't sure he could survive being cooped up in an airplane for nine hours to ever make the return visit, so while on land he would do the town up right.

"Maybe one of my brothers will go along with me. Do I have to dress up?"

"You'll probably want to wear the suit Vail sent to your place. Thanks, Stryke. I'll call you in the morning with details on the job."

Rhys clapped a hand across Stryke's shoulder then wandered back inside the six-story black granite building where he did business.

Stryke tucked the tickets in his back pocket and shook his head as a bright pink Vespa scooted by. A gorgeous woman wearing a skirt commandeered the scooter. She even wore high heels. The women here were so different from back in the States. They liked to look good, no matter what the activity.

He didn't understand a single word of the language, so he had gotten more sneers and snide side glances than he'd experienced in a lifetime. He was taking it in stride. He wasn't the sort to anger easily. That was his brother Trouble's forte. Maybe by the time he boarded the plane for the return trip home he'd actually know a bit of the language and have found that fantasy werewolf he dreamed about meeting?

Then again, he'd be thankful to not starve—because he couldn't ask for what he wanted in French—not get arrested, and not make a fool of himself if a pretty woman *did* glance his way.

And if he was lucky he might happen upon some danger. Because before he started the dream family and pack, he needed to satisfy a soul-deep craving for adventure. His brothers always seemed to find danger and excitement in spades.

Stryke had survived a near-death experience last winter. Time to live his life and make the most of it.

Private gallery, 10:00 p.m.

Two hundred people wandered about the airy gallery off the Rue de Rivoli. Excellent turnout. The champagne flowed, and the silver-dusted vanilla macarons catered from Pierre Hermes were nibbled even by those women who would never deem to smudge their lipstick. It wasn't the calories, *chéri*; it was the humility of being seen chewing in public.

Blyss Sauveterre had owned the gallery for two years and it wasn't so much a labor of love as her means to keep tabs on society. By featuring a new exhibit every month she ensured the flow of the rich and famous in and out of the gallery doors never ceased. The diamonds on display this evening were once Marie Antoinette's prized possessions. Gifts from her lover, Count Axel von Fersen.

Blyss wasn't sure she believed the provenance. Axel Fersen had been a rake, a solider, an opportunist. Had he really garnered enough wages to afford such elaborate diamonds for the queen? History painted him more a lover than a businessman, which she was inclined to agree with. Whether or not he'd had an affair with the doomed queen? She certainly hoped that part was true.

The fantasy of it all intrigued her, and no one this evening had questioned the story behind the beautiful gemstones glinting within their rococo silver-and-gold settings.

The exhibit tonight was a preshow to the grand event Blyss and her assistant planned to feature perhaps next month—the unveiling of *Le Diabolique* to the public.

Le Diabolique was a fifty-carat black diamond that glinted red from within. History told that it had been given by a seventeenth-century Belgian duke to the French Queen Anne. It had been stolen less than a week after she'd taken it in hand. The diamond had been recovered and stolen throughout history many times over, and rumor told that anyone who possessed it faced great torment, wickedness and terrible evil. If not the ultimate misfortune of death.

Blyss believed the rumors. The diamond would prove her greatest torment should she not pull off the heist properly this evening. Part one had already been accomplished. Now the handoff.

"Blyss!"

Her assistant, Lorcan Price, was bedecked in a pink bespoke suit and bright purple bow tie. He adjusted his thick black-rimmed glasses and crossed the room, weaving between patrons and wielding champagne flutes in each hand. He gained her side and pressed a cool champagne glass into her hand.

The man seemed to possess a sixth sense about how to please her. Bon mots uttered at the precise moment she was beginning to doubt herself, a compliment about her designer shoes, even a conspiratorially catty wink from across the room during such events as tonight.

Blyss tilted back a few sips of bubbly, eyeing the crowd over the crystal rim as she did so. Most men had a woman draped on their arm this evening and looked oh-so-bored. If they were wise, they'd pay attention to those things that attracted their partners' eyes, such as all things sparkly. Blyss's usual type, an older man who wore an expensive suit, tended his nails and hair, and who reeked money, were spread throughout the gallery. Some had even come alone. Such fortune.

But tonight she required someone different.

"The show is going well," Lorcan said in his quiet yet enthusiastic voice. "The duchess Konstantinov has suggested to me she may loan the gallery her grandmother's sapphire collection. She's from old Russian money. Wouldn't be surprised if they've a Fabergé egg stashed away, as well. Isn't that spectacular?"

"Exquisite," Blyss agreed. Yet the intrigue of whether or not the duchess did own a Fabergé egg didn't pique her curiosity. Her heart wasn't in the moment. Too much to think about. The plan must go off or she faced a horrible future.

"Is all well with the, erm…big surprise?" he whispered conspiratorially.

"Oui, bien sur." At least, not if anyone cared to study *Le Diabolique* too closely. "Soon, Lorcan. But I don't know about announcing it tonight."

"I will leave it to you, then. You do have the only key to the storage room."

Always trying to gain that access, Blyss thought. Maybe someday she would trust him to tend the acquisitions. But not yet.

"Keep working the room, Lorcan. And do be sure to introduce yourself to Madame Horchard. She's filthy." As in rich. A shorthand the two of them shared. Because if there was one thing that had drawn Blyss to Lorcan, it was his desire to climb the social ladder by means of attaching himself to money. "I must make another round through the gallery."

They bussed each other's cheeks. Lorcan knew well that Blyss abhorred getting her lipstick or her hair mussed.

Clutching the goblet, she strode slowly through the crowd, nodding in acknowledgment to those she knew. Normally she noted the flash of bling on ears, at necks, and wrists and fingers. So *she* had managed ten carats from her lover? Lucky girl. But tonight her mind was a scatter. Nerves made her tense.

Her heartbeats thundered. She inhaled and then exhaled deeply, vying for calm. She hated this feeling of desperation that had settled into her being the past few days. She'd thought to have perfected her life and that smooth sailing was all her future held.

Until her father, Colin Sauveterre, had shown up at her door a month ago, slobbering drunk and crying. His gambling debts had caught up to him. He'd needed her help. But by helping him, she had placed herself on a precipice that loomed over a dangerous fall.

Would she ever again feel safe and sure? As if her life was exactly as she had designed it? All she desired was to drop her shoulders and relax, knowing all was well. And that she fit in.

Exhaling heavily, she drew in a breath of courage. She could do this. She *had* to do this.

She managed a fake smile to a dignitary whose name she could not recall, and drifted away from the velvet-and-glass displays that featured dazzling diamonds and colored stones in gorgeous settings from the seventeenth and eighteenth centuries.

Rubbing a hand along her lace dress, Blyss cursed the fact her palm was moist. Nerves were not her thing. She could work a room peopled with hundreds and never let them see her sweat. But tonight was different. And she hadn't found the right man yet.

But she remained hopeful.

Trading her empty flute of champagne for a fresh one from a waiter's silver tray, she glided through the room and out into the large gallery that housed marble sculptures and where many had gone to chatter louder and more gregariously than the smaller room allowed.

The men were of all varieties. Old, young, middle-aged. Handsome, ugly, oddly alluring. Black ties and designer labels, mostly. Some lesser suits, of which she did not recognize the designer. The women were all dressed to dazzle and reveal.

The couture made her wish she had a credit card that wasn't maxed out. Alexander McQueen? Oh, yes, please.

Blyss revealed as much as the other women. The black lace dress was cut low in the back to expose almost everything, and the front featured a deep V that clung to her breasts yet revealed their inner curves. A thigh-high slit on the floor-length skirt showed off her red-soled Louboutins. Diamonds at her neck and ears were prizes earned on the quest for the rich and bored who hunted for a sparkling trophy to hang on his arm. But never commitment. No, she chose her men for their expiration dates—and the wanderlust in their eyes. And if they suggested something longer than a fling or a few weekends in Madrid? She quickly extricated herself.

It wasn't easy maintaining the lifestyle she enjoyed, but every kiss, every extravagant meal, every late night hookup in a lavish hotel room was worth it. Blyss adored luxury.

Most of all, she adored being adored.

Hmm, now there stood a possibility. The man chatting with the waiter over by the Rodin. She hadn't seen him at any of the gallery's previous functions. He was tall, nicely tanned—perhaps from yachting?—and wore his hair in a close shave against his head. Bright white teeth flashed beneath his blade nose. An easy stance advertised a certain laissez-faire. He didn't care what others thought about him.

Blyss could not relate to lacking concern. As well, something about him didn't quite fit him among the elite crowd. Was it the fabric that stretched at his broad shoulders? The suit had been poorly tailored. Or his seeming awestruck gaze as he took in the festivities? He was…big. Almost awkward. Like a boulder tossed into a flower garden.

Well, he wouldn't be here without an invite. And Blyss

tendered her invites carefully. He was worth checking out—if not, using.

Stryke wandered through the marble-walled gallery, taking in the sculptures by artists he'd only read about in books. Yeah, so he was probably the only one of his brothers who claimed to read. Much unlike his brothers, who hadn't the patience or interest in fine arts, he enjoyed learning new things and bulking up his cultural-knowledge quotient.

He took in the elite crowd who sipped champagne and nibbled caviar-coated crackers. He assessed every step, every gesture, every cut of fabric and deviously delivered bon mot. Diamonds glinted at ears, necks and cuff links. He was pretty sure the clothing cost a small fortune, and didn't even want to guess at how long he'd have to work to afford the diamond choker around that old lady's neck.

He wasn't currently working for a paycheck. After a short stint as a volunteer fireman—the fire station had been closed due to budget problems—he was looking for something to fulfill his need for action and danger. It didn't need to provide a paycheck; he was set for life. But as well, if it involved helping his own breed then he would be even more attracted to taking on the job.

These people were not his breed. They were human. Not his crowd. On the other hand, he was accustomed to existing among humans because that was simply life as he knew it. Wasn't as if a private werewolf haven existed on an island in the Pacific.

He wouldn't be interested if it did exist. He liked humans. They were just like him, but without the propensity to grow fur and flick out the claws when the mood struck. Poor humans.

Tonight's biggest surprise? His brother Blade had come along with him. The last of the Saint-Pierre brothers he would have guessed had an interest in art. Reclusive almost to the extreme, Blade had nodded and muttered something about "getting away from the crazy chicks and their wedding talk."

And yet, Blade had left fifteen minutes ago with his arms wrapped around sexy blonde twins wearing matching red miniskirts. So Blade's idea of art was a little different than most.

Stryke had flown to Paris with his family. His parents, Malakai and Rissa Saint-Pierre, and their children, Trouble, Blade, Kelyn and Daisy Blu. Stryke's aunt Kambriel was marrying Johnny Santiago in a few days. The Santiagos were the Hawkes side of the family, and they were vampires.

Fine by him. As with humans, he had nothing against vamps. His grandfather Creed Saint-Pierre was a vamp, and Blade was actually half faery—as well as vampire. It was all good so long as there were werewolves in the mix at the wedding.

Stryke had heard Europe's werewolf population was booming and the females were in abundance, much the opposite of his native hometown. He hoped that was true. It would increase his chances of meeting a female werewolf, falling in love and getting married.

If only reality proved as simple as the fantasy.

Stryke likely wouldn't hook up so easily as Blade had tonight. He was no slouch when it came to dating, but he did tend toward a specific type. Pretty, yet slightly tomboyish, able to embrace fun and a lover of all things outdoors, including snuggling by a midnight bonfire and long walks through the woods.

Was that asking too much? He didn't think so.

And yet he wasn't feeling attraction to any of the women. All of them were dressed to the nines with hair that must have taken hours in a salon and makeup that had probably been professionally applied. The diamonds flashing on fingers, necks and ears could light the New Year's Eve ball dropped in Times Square. He guessed none of them would even look at a man whose bank account didn't scream high seven figures.

Didn't matter. Now that Blade had taken off, he could focus on the art. He'd browsed through the jewelry display. Diamonds were just sparkly chunks of carbon, right? He couldn't figure their appeal. Here in this large open area many sculptures held court. Carved from white marble, he was awestruck how the stone looked as if it was real, warm flesh. As if he should touch one of them the statue would startle. Cool.

He glanced around. Would an alarm go off if he did touch one? He crossed his arms to fend off the compulsion but the suit coat tugged at his shoulders. Vail was definitely less broad in the shoulders than he was.

A waiter offered more champagne and he refused. "Thanks, man—er, *non, merci.*" Yeah, he'd picked up a few French words. He would be working the language like a native in no time.

Stryke heard all languages babbling about tonight. Earlier he'd listened to a couple of women chatter in English about their hemlines. Why were the conversations he could understand the boring ones?

A crew of well-suited men passed him, each with a gorgeous looker draped on his arm. Stryke tilted back his shoulders. He didn't need a woman to look important. He preferred his females a bit tussled and wilder, anyway. The princess of his pack would need endurance, patience and, hell, she must be fun, too. And like beer.

"But maybe I should reconsider lace," he muttered as his eyes landed upon a sheath of black lace caressing the most gorgeous figure he had ever seen. He felt sure he couldn't even dream up something so luscious.

Black lace caressed long legs and hugged a tight ass and narrow waist. Red-manicured fingernails glided over a hip before gesturing as she spoke to another woman. The gesture directed Stryke's eyes to the deep-cut neckline that exposed the cusps of perfect, round breasts. And up the slender neck where a single diamond glinted, yet didn't distract from the soft, pale skin.

Petal-pink lips caught his interest. Kissing those lips would be better than tasting the home-brewed beers he enjoyed and brewed in his basement. Kissing those lips, and running his fingers through that soft dark hair that was pulled up in back yet fluffed on top to frame black-lined eyes could ruin a man for other women.

After a man kissed those lips, there would be no going back. And to stroke his fingers down her neck and arrive at the curves of her breasts? Mercy.

Think rednecks and beer.

Stryke smirked and caught himself laughing quietly. He didn't do stuff like moon over a gorgeous woman. That chick was so out of his league he'd never get closer than the nosebleed seats. He bet she would never wear flannel or even consider a hike through the pine forest out back of his home.

And yet, she was something to look at. Much more

intriguing than the sculpture of a naked man immediately to his left.

So he let his gaze linger as he strolled closer, hoping to catch a whiff of her scent. It would be expensive, for sure. His werewolf senses picked up too much from the room. Perfume, aftershave, champagne, salted crackers, sweet treats, body odor. The sensory assault was overwhelming, but he knew how to turn it down and had done so within minutes after arriving.

Now he sought to home in on her scent. A piece of her to tuck into his memory and take along with him tonight. Something upon which to dream.

As he neared, she dismissed the person she was talking to and brushed close to him, not noticing him, but Stryke felt her heat pierce his borrowed suit and dress shirt. Her body heat was visceral. And her scent was sweet but not like sugar, more like a garden full of flowers with bees buzzing among the petals. Subtle yet intensely heady.

His wrist jerked as she passed, and Stryke swung to see what had happened. "Oh, shit. Uh…" He followed as she walked, unknowing, until she did realize and turned to bump chests with him.

"Sorry," he said. "My cuff link is hooked on your dress. You passed so close." He twisted his wrist, but could feel the resistance. "Uh, *parlez vous Anglais*?"

"Interesting way of picking up a girl," she said in a cultured voice that belonged in a jewelry box aside all that was precious. And on the box? A sign labeled Don't Touch. "*Oui*, I can manage English when I must. Can you get it unhooked?"

"Give me a minute. Your dress is all lace and so delicate. I don't want to tear it."

"Please do not, *monsieur*. It's one of my favorites."

He'd snagged her right over the ass, and he worked the back of his hand against her derriere, feeling guilty for the stolen touch, yet at the same time, loving the freebie. The diamond cuff link Vail had loaned him was worth a pretty penny, he felt sure. One of the clasps holding a stone had dug its clutches into the thin black lace.

He straightened, standing beside her with his hand behind her and fingers curled so he didn't blatantly cup her ass. Causing a scene was the last thing he wanted to do, so he'd act casual. Mercy. She smelled good. It was all he could do not to tilt his head against hers to sniff her hair.

"My name's Stryke Saint-Pierre, by the way."

"Blyss Sauveterre," she offered. And oh, yes, she was. "What sort of *pre nom* is Stryke?"

"The one my parents gave me. Uh, I'm from the US."

"That is obvious from your accent," she said with not even a smile.

Nope. He wasn't going to win her over this way. Damn. Way to spoil things. Worst pickup ever. Now to extricate himself without humiliating her more than himself.

"Uh, could we move over near that column where there's more light?"

He nodded toward a marble column at the edge of the gathering. Not a lot of people milling on that side of the gallery. They'd be granted some privacy to perform this delicate operation.

"If it'll deliver me of your groping hand, then *oui*."

She started toward the column and he followed, but it was easiest to let his fingers gently curl about her behind. Yeah, it wasn't cool, but what about this situation was cool?

Once at the column he pulled her around to the other side, where they found privacy and better light.

"Excuse me for what I'm going to do," he said.

Her lips pursed. Her bright green eyes were the most valuable jewels in the room tonight. And those pink lips. They looked moist and so wanting of a kiss. No chance of kissing them after this embarrassing debacle. Not as if he'd a chance with this delicious bit in the first place.

Stryke bent behind her to work at the tangle. She slid a hand down her hip, uncomfortable, he guessed. And impatient. God, she smelled amazing. All flowers covered in sugar and fluttering over him until he was buried in sweetness.

"So this is how American men meet women?" she asked over her shoulder. "Snag them like a *poisson*?"

Poisson? What was that? Poison? Hell, he didn't know. "Not generally. I like to take a less aggressive tact when I'm interested in a woman." Though certainly he was on the hunt. Wrong breed, though. This one he'd have to toss back. Ah! *Poisson* meant fish. "I suspect I'm not your type anyway."

"What, or rather, who do you guess is my type, Monsieur Stryke?"

When she said his name like that Stryke wished they were the only two in the gallery, and that he had the courage to kiss her and steal away more of her elegant French words.

"Your type…" He stood and kept their close proximity by running his hand over her hip, and said, "…is rich."

She quirked a perfectly arched brow. The eyeliner circling her beautiful bright eyes had been drawn out at the corners in a catty tease. As he had with the marble statues, Stryke reminded himself not to touch. This wasn't the venue or crowd that appreciated his kind of sensual curiosity. He'd have to save the smoothing of his fingers over her skin for the bedroom. Which was never going to happen.

"So you do not qualify?" she asked. "Rich?"

"I do well enough."

In truth, he could probably beat most of the people here tonight in a show of financial statements, but he didn't like to brag. He was most comfortable living below his means. And if a woman judged a man by his checkbook? He wasn't interested.

She tapped his free wrist where the diamond cuff link glinted. "I suspect you do."

He wasn't about to correct her assumption. Why create another mark against him?

"I've been in Paris two days," he offered. "I have to say you've made the trip worthwhile."

"How is that?"

Leaning closer, just managing the skim of his coat front against her back, he spoke near her ear when a curl of her hair tickled his cheek.

"You've pulled me out of my world and into a fantasy. Not often that happens to a guy. Would it be crass to ask if you've a boyfriend?"

"It would."

He nodded. Yeah, he wasn't going to score interest from this glamour girl.

She tilted her gaze at him and he couldn't determine if she was disgusted or maybe intrigued. "Have you managed to detach yourself?"

He displayed the cuff link he'd freed from her dress

minutes earlier. But since she'd been engaged in talking, he'd not informed her of her freedom too quickly. And the stolen moments of standing in her air? Priceless.

She clasped the cuff link. And then he remembered it wasn't his. He shouldn't just hand it over like that.

"Blyss," he repeated, not addressing her, more feeling the taste of her on his tongue.

She dipped her lashes before looking directly at him and dragging the diamond cuff link across her kiss-me-now lips. *"Oui?"*

Oh, man, those lips said things he wanted to be true. He breathed her name again. It was so appropriate. Every pore on his body inhaled her perfume and imagined her sugar-flower taste as her silken skin glided against his body.

Before he could claim the cuff link, she strode off. Long legs moved her swiftly, high heels clicking the marble floor. The hand behind her back toggled the diamond cuff link, allowing it to catch the light teasingly. She didn't reenter the crowd, but instead veered toward the curved marble wall where he had earlier seen the waiters coming and going.

Before walking through an open doorway, she cast a look over her shoulder at him. The cuff link was in her mouth, glinting between those luscious lips.

Stryke's jaw dropped open. He didn't need an interpreter to guess what she was saying.

Come claim it. If you dare.

Chapter 2

Stryke Saint-Pierre was one gorgeous man. And polite. While he could have copped a feel when they'd been tangled out on the museum floor, he had remained the consummate gentleman. Too bad for her. Blyss wanted to feel his deft fingers smooth over her derriere. She wanted to lose herself in the rugged smell of him, the roughness of him.

And she wanted to feel that now.

She strode down the dimly lit hallway toward the back office. It was her office, but she shared it with Lorcan, her assistant, and used it principally for paperwork, business calls and the occasional make-out session with a sexy man. It was what she did. She saw an attractive man. She wanted him. She won him. The winning part gave her immense satisfaction. And sometimes a sparkler for her finger or ear. She was choosy, most certainly, and discreet. And never greedy.

Tonight the win was born of necessity.

"You live in Paris?" she called back.

"Staying for a week or so, then heading back home to Minnesota."

Perfect. He'd be gone and out of her hair as soon as she had accomplished her task.

Minnesota? Blyss vaguely imagined a tundra with blowing winds and snow and—not of interest to her.

As she unlocked and opened the door and strode into the office, she surreptitiously glanced over a shoulder to catch the strut of the man's long, confident strides. Following at a distance. Smart man. Well, she did have something of his that he wanted back. The cuff link was too small to sell for any worthwhile amount, so she would give it back.

But first, to enact part two of tonight's plan.

Stryke closed the door behind him.

"Lock it," Blyss cooed. She stood across the room and turned, back against the wall, one leg bent and a black patent leather shoe heeling the wall.

The man's long fingers flicked the steel door lock. Something about those sexy, strong fingers. She needed to feel them on her body. And she would. And the man's name was Stryke. So bold and macho. Everything about him screamed alpha—yet to think that term gave her a shudder.

She eyed the small drawer at the corner of her desk. Inside was the key to securing her future. She must concentrate on the task at hand. Not on his virile attraction or her increasing need to surrender to that virility.

"Where are you staying?" she asked, because it was important.

"On that little island behind the big church."

The man was quaintly rustic. But that smile of his was dangerous. It said to her, "I like to have fun, and if you're lucky, you can go along for the ride." Blyss couldn't remember when last she'd had fun with abandon. Had she ever?

"Île Saint-Louis?" she guessed, keeping her growing desire for his touch under control by pressing her palms against the wall behind her.

"That's the one. My grandfather owns one of the buildings and my entire family is staying there. We're in town for my aunt's wedding. The apartment I'm staying in is right above a candy shop. In the mornings I wake up to the smell of chocolate."

"Oh, I know that one. About center of the island."

"Yeah, exact center, I'd guess. It's a neat little neighborhood. I haven't done much exploring since arriving, but I hope to walk the city tomorrow. So..."

His eyes followed the lines of her body, up the slit that exposed her leg, which was darkened by a sheer black stocking. A red bow teased at the top of the stocking. All carefully planned, of course. Blyss thrived on male attention. It fed a part of her soul. If not her bank account.

He strode toward her and she smiled and placed the cuff link between her lips. He wanted her. She wanted him. Too bad this was to be a business engagement.

"Quickly," she said around the cuff link. "I can't be away from the event for too long."

"Is that so?" He stepped before her and plucked the cuff link from her mouth. They matched in height, but that was only because of her heels. She tapped his long blade of a nose, gliding her finger down it and to his lips, which were firm and, over the upper, topped with stubble. His tongue lashed her finger and she pushed it into his mouth for him to suck. "You want me?"

He pressed closer so she could feel the fabric of his suit brush against the lacy dress, yet he didn't push his body against hers. Teasing? Or not so daring as she had hoped?

"You are like those diamonds displayed out in the gallery," he said. "Pretty to look at, yet a man could never dream to possess them."

"Good boy. So you know you'll not be walking out of here tonight with me on your arm."

"I get your game. A quickie with a stranger?"

"*Quickie* is a vulgar term. I prefer *an amorous liaison.*"

"I like the sound of your French words, glamour girl. Then I guess I'd better get to it. Quickly," he whispered against her ear.

The brush of his mouth along her jaw made her sigh and tilt her head back, wanting him to paint his warm breath along her skin and to, for one moment, feed her the warmth she sought.

Stryke's hands glided up her thighs. One stopped at the ribbon that topped her stocking. The tickle of his finger shimmered a delicious hum through her mons and core.

"Mustn't tug," she admonished. Placing her hand over his, she again claimed the cuff link.

"Let me guess. You don't like to be mussed."

She slid her hands down to his fly and unzipped him.

"No mussing, it is," he groaned tightly.

He was hard and ready. Just the way she wanted him. But before they began, she lifted his wrist and stuck the cuff link through the buttonhole. "I'll let you keep this trinket."

And gliding her hands inside his coat, she slid them up his back between the crisp dress shirt and the silk coat lining. So many pockets lining the interior. Excellent. And then back around to unbutton his trousers and push them down.

"Take me," she insisted, defiantly holding his wondrous gaze. She did love it when they seemed shocked, the treat of a stolen liaison so unexpected to them. "Fast and hard."

His swallow was audible. But he didn't balk. Pushing up her dress, he lifted her against the wall at the same time. She wrapped her legs about his hips. His erection fit like a hot steel rod against her mons.

"You're soft and you smell great, and you're so hot," he babbled as he found his way inside her.

Blyss gasped as his thickness entered her in a smooth glide. She hadn't required lubrication because she'd been turned on since he'd gotten caught on her dress. Mmm, he felt like hot, hard steel. Every in-and-out motion teased at her apex, and she thought she might even climax, even though simple thrusting generally didn't do it for her.

She glided her fingers through his hair, seeking to grip hanks but it was so short, like uncut velvet. And then she did something she never did with her hookups. She didn't even think about it. Her head simply tilted and her mouth sought his. He tasted like champagne. His moan echoed inside her, stirring up her own moan. His powerful biceps flexed under her hands. His hips slammed her against the wall.

Gripping him at the back of his neck, she kissed him deeply, wanting to get lost in him, to find… *No. Mustn't be a fool.*

Stryke gasped harshly, yet quickly muffled the noise by pressing his mouth against her neck, his teeth pressing gently into her skin. "Shoot, I didn't use a condom…"

"I am on the pill," she whispered. "No worries."

"Whew." And as his body shook against hers, she reveled in his quick yet furious orgasm that shuddered his body against hers. Until she remembered…

The desk drawer beside her slid open with ease. She palmed the item she'd placed inside earlier and then slid her hand inside his suit coat. He was lost in the orgasm, oblivious to her actions.

"That was so—mmm, good." His eyes sought something in hers, so desperately, Blyss felt as if she'd done something wrong. "You're…" He sniffed, pushing his nose against her neck again and lingering at the base of her ear where her hair must tickle his face. "God, you smell good. But there's something…"

She dropped her legs and tugged down her skirt. "What is it?"

"I don't know. I just…" He pressed a hand over her breast, and it was only then that Blyss noticed how her heartbeats thundered. She'd love to do it again with this one—to actually take her time and find her own orgasm—but…

She would see him again. He just didn't know that yet.

"You're beautiful," he said. "But you don't belong here."

The hand at her chest suddenly felt like a two-ton weight. Blyss gaped. She shook her head. "Why do you say that?"

"I don't know why I feel that, but I do," he said. "Something about you. Are you...lost?"

A knock at the door sounded.

Stryke quickly zipped and Blyss tugged down her dress and adjusted the red ribbon at the top of her silk stocking. "Lorcan?" she called.

"You busy?" a British voice called from outside the door. They'd done this drill before. He knew never to simply open the door and walk right in.

"He's my assistant." And such perfect timing!

She pushed by Stryke and strode toward the door, hands smoothing over her hair. "I have to get back. They'll be looking for me. You should leave now. Please."

She unlocked the door and opened it, revealing Lorcan waiting outside. He knew better than to show a cheeky grin or even a raised brow. The man was ever discreet. She returned the same courtesy to him. Turning, Blyss gulped down the longing that had been planted there by Stryke's sensual prowess. She'd wanted to linger.

Really? Linger against his heat, his overwhelming essence of man, sex and muscle? Sounded delicious. But indulgence in what her heart desired was something she never allowed.

Stryke passed her and slowed, as if he wanted to say something to her, but with Lorcan standing in the doorway, his eyes respectfully gliding along the door frame, Stryke simply nodded and walked out.

"Don't go back into the gallery!" she called after him. "Please."

He nodded as his strides took him down the hallway and away from her.

And she turned and strode back to the desk, palm

pressed over her heart and biting her lip to prevent the tears.

Tears? What had he meant when he'd insinuated she was lost? Perhaps he hadn't been such a wise choice, after all. It was too late to alter her plan. She'd already completed the main step.

She would have to see Stryke again. And she looked forward to it. She dreaded it, as well.

"Everything all right, duck?" Lorcan asked.

She nodded. "I'm sorry. You know sometimes I just…"

"No need for an explanation. I'm headed out myself with a pretty young thing. Wanted to let you know I'm leaving. Unless you need me to stay and lock up?"

"No. Thank you, Lorcan. I've the security guard and the waitstaff will be around, as well. Go have some fun. I'll see you in a few days."

"Yes. We'll cement our plans for the showing then, eh?"

She nodded.

If all went well, that showing would never occur. And the only one aware it had failed would be her. She had a plan for keeping Lorcan in the dark about it.

He left the office door open, and Blyss bent and peered past her assistant to see if she could still see Stryke's back, but he was gone.

"The Île Saint-Louis," she whispered. "Now to step three in the plan. This will be the most difficult."

And if her heart got in the way again she truly would be lost, as he'd guessed.

Talk about the cold shoulder.

Stryke actually shivered as he strode down the darkened hallway, passed by the gallery and aimed straight for the exit.

Outside, he shrugged off the uncomfortable suit coat and tossed it over a shoulder. He should have hailed a cab, but he could see the river Seine from here. One thing he'd learned since arriving in Paris: if a man could locate the river, he'd never get lost. There was the left bank and the right bank, and the river. And he knew the island where he was staying was to his left.

It would be about a twenty-minute walk. He could use the fresh air. It was July and even nearing midnight the air was sultry. But not as sultry as the sexy handful he'd just held up against the wall.

"Blyss," he murmured.

And yet.

"What happened back there?"

Earlier this evening he'd donned a borrowed suit, met Blade on the street before the chocolate shop and entered the gallery with hopes to view some interesting artwork. A couple of rednecks mingling with the snooty set. It was supposed to be a kick. Stryke hadn't expected to pick up the hottest chick in the place.

And to have sex with her.

Blade and his miniskirted twins had nothing on what he'd scored.

But the craziest thing of all? There had been something about her. And it wasn't her beauty or her bold tease or the quick but satisfying liaison. He toggled the cuff link she'd returned to him. Her scent had been... Well hell, he didn't know how to categorize the uniqueness of her. Beyond the sweet flowery perfume, he had scented something deeper. Intriguing. Familiar?

"Crazy," he muttered as he strolled along the river.

Lights on the buildings cast a spectacular show across the Seine's darkened waters. He marveled that tourists were out in full force. The City of Light truly never slept.

"I was caught in the moment. And what a moment."

Would he ever see her again? If he returned to the gallery would she give him the time of day? Acknowledge they'd shared that moment?

Probably not. A woman like Blyss probably picked out a man to please her then tossed him aside without a glance over her sexy, bare shoulder.

Yet she hadn't gotten off. He'd come so quickly. Hadn't been able to stop himself. He felt bad about that. Normally he tended to a woman's pleasure before allowing his own. But the moment had jumped on him and he'd been swept away. He should have dropped to his knees and…

The assistant had banged on the door, ruining the whole thing.

Stryke paused at an intersection and glanced back the direction from which he'd come. A brightly lit Ferris wheel spun through the Paris sky to his left.

Why had he walked away? He should have waited around for the guy to leave and then got her phone number.

Was his hasty retreat because he'd felt as if she'd rejected him by pulling away from him so quickly? Probably. The woman defined classy. So out of Stryke's universe. Probably ate caviar and champagne for breakfast, then skirted around Paris in a Lamborghini painted pale pink, the color of her lips.

Rubbing his brow, Stryke shook his head and walked across the street on the green light. Smirking, he shook his head again. "It was a hookup," he muttered. "Let it go."

But with the lingering scent of flowers imbued on his skin, letting go was easier thought than done.

Chapter 3

Torsten Rindle was an interesting fellow. Stryke met him in a parking lot on the left bank down the street from a vast city park. The man drove an olive-green van, and he'd opened up the back doors to reveal some boxes sitting in the stripped-to-the-framework interior.

Tor was tall, slender and dressed in a tweed vest and pleated trousers. A polka-dot tie tightened about a crisp white dress shirt, of which, the sleeves were rolled to his elbows. A cicada was tattooed on the underside of one of his forearms, but otherwise, he appeared a dapper Englishman.

Stryke liked his accent. So *Downton Abbey*. Not that he'd ever watched the show. Okay, maybe once on a date a girl had suggested they cuddle on the couch and watch TV. The things a guy did for a little snuggling.

"So Hawkes Associates is strapped for help?" Tor

asked as he carefully peeled back the packing tape from the top of a cardboard box.

"Actually, Rhys Hawkes is busy with a family wedding. Which is why I'm in town. The bride is my aunt."

"Ah yes, Johnny Santiago and his girl are tying the knot. Good couple. Vampires."

"Yes, indeed." And this guy worked for a secret order that hunted vampires. "You, uh…ever try to stake them?"

"Me?" Tor grinned, exposing a boyish charm. "I don't do the stake. I'm spin. Someone has to make sure the mortals didn't see a vampire bite a person's neck, but instead, just happened upon a couple actors rehearsing for a show at the Moulin Rouge. You know? The Order of the Stake only pursues those vampires who are a danger to humans. Like me. I'm human." He turned and offered his hand to shake. "Sorry, didn't do this properly. Torsten Rindle. Human."

Stryke shook the man's firm grasp. "Stryke Saint-Pierre. Werewolf."

"I like werewolves," Tor offered, folding back the flap on the box. "But you guys can be a challenge when pissed off."

Stryke tilted his head in acknowledgment. "Nothing wrong with being a challenge."

"So." Tor gestured Stryke approach the back of the van to peer into the box. "This is what I've got."

"Rhys said your knights sometimes pick this stuff up from a slain vampire's lair?"

"This artifact came from a vamp who was trafficking in magical accoutrements. Most of the stuff—herbs, nostrums and small ritual objects—we toss. But there were some decidedly demonic artifacts mixed in with the more innocuous stuff. Didn't want to keep our hands on this, nor did we want it sitting around for any Tom, Dick or Edward to get his hands on."

"May I?"

Tor nodded. "You'll be taking it with you anyway."

Stryke peered into the box and spied what looked like a staff of sorts. About two feet long, it was sleek, re-sembled steel and the top portion jutted up into prongs, which looked as though they should be clasping some wizardly sort of crystal.

His fingers neared the staff and then he flinched. "Is this what I think it is?" he asked.

"Demonic scepter." Tor reached in and pulled out the item as if a child's toy and waved it before Stryke. "Demons can do very bad things with it."

Stryke took a step back and put up his hands. "That's silver, man."

Tor studied the length of the scepter, then nodded. "Yep, probably is. A good conductor of magic. I suspect a stone or some such fits in the prongs. Most likely the stone is required to activate the thing. Be thankful it's missing. Here you go."

"Dude, I am not touching that thing. Silver is—"

"Ah, right. Sorry. But the silver has to actually enter your bloodstream to do you werewolves harm, right?"

"In theory. But I had a bad experience with a silver-tipped arrow last winter." He clutched his left biceps. "Almost died. I'm not taking any chances."

"Yikes." Tor carefully set the scepter back in the box. "Take it in the box, then."

"So it's cool sitting in this plain old brown box?"

"Should be." Tor tugged out the box and handed it to Stryke. "But I'd get it back to Hawkes Associates and secure it with wards as quickly as possible. Just to be safe."

Stryke thought he felt a wave of heat emanate from within the box and glow in his biceps. He winced. His brow began to sweat. His mouth dried. Flashes of last winter when the silver had fought to take his life disoriented him. But a healthy dose of wolfsbane had defeated the poison.

"Stryke? You okay?"

"Huh? Uh, yes." Best to get the hell out of here fast. "Thanks, man. Do I need to pay you?"

"We've an account with Hawkes. It's all been taken care of. Nice to meet you, Saint-Pierre. Stay wary."

"Really?" Stryke asked, but Tor had already slipped around the side of the van and he heard the driver's door slam shut.

"Wary," he muttered as the van pulled away.

Again he felt the heat emanate from within the box. "You don't have to tell me that. Me and silver do not have a good history."

If he was going to run into more silver working for Rhys, he'd have to start carrying some wolfsbane with him.

Blyss touched up her eyeliner in the mirror, drawing it out in a cat's-eye tease. Her brows were tweezed and shaded to perfection. A hint of blush. And bright red lips. Her usual daytime look. She liked to look sexy, and yes, she knew she was pretty. Men told her as much all the time. But sometimes it was hard to justify the beauty when she knew a beast lurked within.

She shook her head at the mirror's reflection. *Do not fall into those dark thoughts.* She'd moved beyond such thinking and was managing her beast. Had been for years.

Only, now her life had started to unravel in incredible ways. Her supplier, Edamite Thrash, had always been kind and just with her, but even he could not put up with her missed payments. She was behind a year, and she needed to refill her supply soon. Only a few pills remained in the glass jar she kept on her vanity.

She must not allow the beast reign.

There was no questioning Edamite's generosity by letting her go a year without paying. She'd had no choice but to divert her funds. Her father, well... She hoped he had learned a lesson and would never gamble again. But Blyss knew better.

Her bank account was in the red, and her social life was faltering. While usually she relied upon extravagant gifts from her lovers to seed her finances, she had not received a gift in months.

And she'd been given a week to procure an item for Edamite. An item so valuable he would forgive her debt and cover her for the next year's supply. An item that she had obtained and then placed in another person's care to divert suspicion. An item she must claim today so she could clear up matters with Ed.

She exhaled heavily, watching her shoulders slump in the mirror. Quickly, she corrected, pushing her shoulders back and lifting her chin.

Never let them see you suffer.

She'd worked too hard to establish her position among the humans. Blyss Sauveterre, Parisian socialite and gallery owner. She'd even been photographed with celebrities and had once made the gossip page after a weekend fling with a Russian duke.

She adjusted the combs, brushes and makeup on the vanity table before her so they lay straight and evenly spaced. She liked neatness. She was so close to avoiding a complete life catastrophe and smoothing over that annoying bump in her road. Control was her only means to relax.

Yet now Stryke Saint-Pierre had strolled into her life.

Her reflection frowned. She had been attracted the moment she'd laid eyes on him walking the gallery floor. And the attraction had been like nothing she had ever felt for a man before. She'd wanted to feel his hands roaming her skin, his mouth tasting hers. And she'd gotten that.

She wanted it again.

No. He is just the diversion.

Right. *Stick to the plan.* She had to see him again today. In order to retrieve what she'd planted on him, she needed access to his personal things. She must get close to him without raising suspicion.

Seduction would be necessary. And while seduction should prove a simple task—a job, nothing more—Blyss knew once she again stood in Stryke's arms, all bets would be off. She'd fall into his beautiful brown eyes and sexy smile and wish only for his masterful kiss. A kiss that had left her breathless in the gallery office.

A kiss she wanted to taste again.

Shaking her head furiously, she battled with the devil and angel hovering above each shoulder. She would never be an angel. She tried not to be so devilish. But this afternoon she must tempt and seduce. And win back her standing with her supplier.

Because if she did not, she must then face her beast. And that was something she could not bear.

* * *

Outfitted in hazmat gloves and a face mask, Rhys Hawkes had been waiting for the delivery in his office. Stryke had chuckled, but then asked when he would be issued his own safety equipment.

"Sorry," Rhys said as he took the silver scepter from the cardboard box. "I knew it was silver, but the thought to warn you didn't occur at the time. I'll have the company car outfitted with some precautionary equipment."

"Precautionary," Stryke repeated as he followed Rhys into an open vault that stretched back about twenty feet and featured an aisle four feet wide. He strolled his gaze up and down the security boxes, each fronted by a digital entry pad. "What all is in these boxes?"

"Gold, silver, coins from ages past. Magical items. Demonic accoutrements. Personal possessions that hold such great power the owner fears keeping them too near. Everything you can imagine. This is the preliminary holding cell for items the owners intend to retrieve instead of having them stored long-term. As well, I keep items I've purchased in here—like this scepter—until a spot can be coded for them below. I've a marvelous warehouse underground this building. I'll show it to you sometime."

"Kind of Warehouse 13, eh?"

"Hmm?" Rhys punched in a code and pulled open a drawer. He hadn't gotten the reference to the sci-fi show Stryke caught on replay every so often that featured a massive storage shed for items and devices of supernatural origin.

"So that wasn't a very dangerous job," Stryke commented. "You know I am capable if you've a particularly harrowing task."

"Oh, indeed." Rhys closed the drawer and tugged off his gloves. "You looking for some danger, Saint-Pierre?"

"Always."

"Your father told me you're the wise one of his children. Sort of the calm center amid a storm of fur and trouble."

"*Trouble* being the key word in that statement. My brother definitely lives up to his name."

"Malakai also tells me he's encouraged you to start a pack?"

"Yes, Dad wants to retire. And we could use a more varied pack where I live. A mixture of families."

"Always wise to integrate the pack with new blood. So you are married?"

"No, but I'm looking."

"Heh. I'd introduce you to my granddaughters at the wedding—Trystan's girls—but no. I don't want you taking any from my family across the ocean."

"Thanks. I do have my eye out while I'm in town."

Rhys patted him on the back and led him back out to the office. "You enjoy the show last night?"

"It was interesting." If not curious. And a boost to his ego. Until Blyss had shoved him out the door, and then his ego had fallen onto the concrete. "Met a gorgeous woman."

"Ah? Werewolf?"

"No. Doubt I'll find such luck so quickly."

"You two have a date, then?"

"I think we've done the date, the first kiss, the— Let's say it was sweet while it lasted."

"Parisian women can be baffling. Such pretty baubles to admire, but try to nudge beneath the sparkle and learn them?" Rhys shook his head. "I am thankful for a long and loving relationship with my wife. Dating nowadays would stymie me. People don't even talk anymore. They text. What is that about?"

Stryke offered him a shrug. He wasn't much for texting. A long talk and hand-holding were more his style.

"But if you're looking for a hookup in town," Rhys continued, "talk to Johnny. He knows a lot of—"

"Vampires aren't really my style. But thanks, Rhys. I'm going to head out. Unless you've more work for me?"

"Not at the moment, but I'm sure I will in a day or two. Thanks for helping out, Stryke. See you at the wedding this weekend."

On the way home Stryke stopped for a crepe from a food stand across the cobbled street from Notre Dame. He'd been eyeing this stand every day since arrival. Worth the dive into unhealthy. Sickeningly sweet chocolate oozed out around thick slices of banana between the folded crepe.

Bananas were always healthy, right?

He consumed the crepe and wandered in through the lobby of the apartment building. Knocking on the door to the apartment his brother Blade was staying in, he waited, but no answer. Must still be out with the twins.

His parents were likely helping with the wedding stuff. And Kelyn had been serious about seeing the sights. The youngest Saint-Pierre brother had left the building this morning with a map in one hand and his iPod set to a city tour.

Shaking his head in admiration over Blade's roguish prowess, Stryke headed up to his place. He surfed the television but couldn't understand French or the

Indian-language stations, though the talk shows that emulated the confrontational style so popular in the US were a hoot.

After fifteen minutes all the hair-pulling and shoving annoyed him. Time to head out and explore the city. Maybe he could pick up Kelyn's scent and join him. He scanned out the window and eyed the row of shops across the river. He'd start there because he was pretty sure one of them was a bookshop.

A knock at the door must be a family member. Expecting a brother or even his mom or dad, Stryke answered the summons and chuffed out his breath at the sight of who it really was.

The sexy siren stood with one arm raised, her hand grasping high on the door frame, while her sinuous body slinked and seduced in red velvet. The dress hugged her from breasts to curvy hips. A party this early in the day? Stryke decided that every day—all day—was a party for this glamour girl.

"Blyss?"

She winked and strode across the threshold, handing him a filmy black scarf. He fumbled with it, not sure whether to scrunch it up and toss it aside or press it to his nose to inhale her scent. He compromised and brushed it over his face as he tossed it aside to land on the kitchen table littered with toast crumbs from a hasty breakfast.

Following the click of her high heels into the living room, which was bare of furnishings, save for a baroque couch and chair set that looked as if it hailed from the eighteenth century, Stryke waited for her to announce her reason for the visit.

Did he need a reason? Hell no.

The woman he'd thought to never see again stood not six feet away from him, looking like a sex goddess wrapped in red. Her dark hair was pinned up again, with a few wispy tendrils drawing his eye directly to her elegant neck. Right there. That was where he really wanted to kiss her.

She turned and crooked her finger at him and he almost lost it right there. But he was cool. Mostly. He got an instant hard-on, though. No fancy suit today, just a T-shirt and loose blue jeans that had gotten remarkably tighter.

"How'd you find where I'm staying?" he asked as he padded up to her and didn't dare touch her. Yet. She smelled like flowers. And again he got lost in a meadow of blossoms.

"You told me you live above the candy shop. Only one on the island."

"I didn't think I'd see you again after that hasty send-off last night."

"*Excuse moi.* I sometimes slip out of hostess mode, and then when I realize my guests are untended, I refocus with a vengeance. It's a thing with me."

"You often slip out of hostess mode at such gatherings?" Meaning, did she screw strange men in the office much?

Blyss tilted her head and fluttered her lashes.

Did he care what she did with other men? She was here now. She smelled like flowers. Looked like sin. And it was obvious she hadn't come for a chat.

Stryke pulled her to him in a swift move that married their bodies at hips and chest. He felt her nipples harden beneath the velvet and his hand glided to one breast to squeeze. There was something about a woman intent upon getting exactly what she wanted. And he sensed this flawless piece of female was here on a seek-and-have-sex mission.

He dipped his head to her breasts. The dress was cut low, and he dashed his tongue under the velvet. She gasped and leaned into him, asking for more with her body.

"I hope you're not busy," she whispered. "I don't normally stop by without first calling, but I didn't have your mobile number."

Mobile was what the French called the cell phone. He lashed his tongue over her firm breast. "Was only planning on sightseeing. Mmm, Blyss, you are incredible."

Her hand slid up under his T-shirt, fingernails gently clawing his abs. "And you are *très fantastique*, Stryke."

He slid the thin red strap off her shoulder and pulled down the dress to expose her breast. Kissing and suckling her erect nipple, he moaned at the pleasure of the surprise. And his inner wolf stirred, sensing the connection to—hmm…to what?

Something about her called to his feral instincts in ways that no woman ever had. It puzzled him, but then again, he couldn't question it too much. Maybe later.

Her leg hooked about his and she gripped him at the back of his neck, pulling him hard against her breast. When he nipped her skin she gasped. She liked that. A little rough? He'd always thought himself a gentle lover, but he could amp up the intensity if that was what she wanted.

Squeezing her other breast while he sucked in her nipple, he gripped her ass and lifted her so she wrapped her legs about his. The bedroom door was five steps away. Moving blindly, he managed to miss the door completely and crush her up against the wall. He knew she liked this position.

"Sorry, was aiming for the door."

"Your bedroom is through there? Yes, let's try it on a bed this time, *mon amour*."

My love? Oh yeah. She was here for more than a social call.

This time he made it through the doorway and they tumbled onto the king-size bed made with simple white linens and a scatter of fluffy pillows. He didn't let her go, though. Instead he pulled down the other dress strap and the dress fell to her waist. Burying his face against her breasts, he breathed in what was surely expensive perfume. He'd fallen into a rose garden.

She tugged at his shirt and he slipped it over his head. Cooing, Blyss ran her hands over his chest, setting his nerve endings ultrareceptive to all things good.

"So ripped," she murmured. "American men are so much more than the French man."

When he was about to foolishly say it was the wolf in him, she pressed a finger to his lips. "Let's not talk. Let's taste." She lashed her tongue under his jaw. "And touch." Her fingers slid over his crotch and curled about his erection. "And devour."

"Devouring sounds good to me."

Stryke made quick work of his fly, unzipping and shrugging out of his jeans. Boxer briefs hugged his erection, but they didn't stay up for long. Blyss shoved them down his hips and grasped his aching hard-on. The contact felt like fire singeing him in the sweetest way. He hissed.

She coiled her fingers about him and squeezed. Oh, yeah, that was twenty kinds of all right.

Stryke was about to kiss her mouth, but the red lipstick stayed him. She was so pretty, so perfect. She deserved mussing, but he'd do it in another way. Planting the kiss on her neck, he nuzzled there and gently bit down along her shoulder. Her hands busied themselves with his cock and he would come too fast if she kept it up.

He grabbed her wrists and pinned them up by her shoulders. This time, he intended to orchestrate their liaison. No coming for him until she did first. He owed her one. She cooed, her tongue dashing out to lick those teasing red lips. He'd caught her. Now what would he do with her?

Indeed, what to do with this gorgeous bit of glamour that surprised him at every turn and whom he wanted to figure out. And yet, he did not. The surprises were what made her so exciting.

Rocking his hips against hers, he teased at her hot, sticky wetness with his cock. She moaned and murmured, "Yes," but he was inclined to tease a bit longer.

The dress hugged around her waist. Her thigh-high stockings glided like silk against his legs. She still wore the shoes, and thinking about those spiked heels hardened his cock even more. He wanted to feel her softness and her dangerous sharpness all over his skin.

So when she struggled against his hold on her wrists, he relaxed his grip and allowed her to push at him. He rolled to his back, pulling her on top of him in a smooth movement. Straddling him, she pulled off the dress and tossed it to the floor.

Afternoon sunlight beamed across the bed and her body glowed as if she were a sun goddess. Stryke glided his hands up her stomach. When he cupped her breasts, she tilted her head back, offering her succulent fullness to him. She wiggled, her moistness heating his cock. And with a shift of her hips she managed to take him inside her.

"I don't have any—" Stryke never had unprotected sex. Werewolves could get mortal women pregnant.

She tutted him. "You didn't last night either, no?"

Right. She'd said she was on the pill.

"Lover, you are steel between my legs. Mmm…"

He closed his eyes and fell into the exquisite rhythm of her rocking above him, feeding off him, milking him, pairing with him. Bonding—no.

When two werewolves had sex together in werewolf form they bonded for life. It was a serious deal. And while he hoped to someday bond with a werewolf and make a family together, this woman was merely human and he just wanted to have fun with the glamour goddess.

Blyss cupped his hands, still wrapped about her breasts, and squeezed. Murmuring an approving sound, she quickened her pace, up and down, bringing him to climax with expert skill. Stryke's hips bucked up against her, and when she pressed her hands to his and watched him ride out the pleasure, he thought surely she was looking inside him for some secret.

The secret was that he was stymied by her interest in him. But then again, maybe he should stop thinking like a Northwoods hick and accept the Parisian ideal. Whatever that was.

Slipping his fingers between her legs, he found her swollen apex and stroked her until she gripped at his shoulders and tossed back her head. The scent of flowers and salty sweetness and…something so familiar filled his senses as she cried out in pleasure.

Stryke inhaled deeply, testing the scent she gave off and wondering… It was too familiar not to recognize. Was she really? There was no mistaking her feral scent. He knew it from long runs in the woods with his brothers while they were in wolf form and from the rush of adrenaline the wolves got when chasing prey.

As Blyss's body softened above him, Stryke gripped her by the shoulders. "You're a werewolf?"

Chapter 4

Blyss pushed out of Stryke's demanding grasp and shuffled off the bed. She clasped her hands across her breasts, the urge to protect herself heightened by his out-of-the-blue question. And his strangely accusatory tone. Inhaling, she fought to not mentally return to that moment in high school—the moment life had turned against her.

How could he have known?

In all the years she had been taking a pill to suppress her werewolf, never had anyone guessed her truth. Sure, she tended to live and socialize only with humans. Not too often a human was going to make the jump to ask "Could you be a werewolf?" But on occasion she sensed a vampire or other in the crowd—vamps could be so obvious at times. None had ever guessed at her beastly origins.

Yet Stryke knew. In the moment when she had cried

out as an orgasm had swept through her, and then he too had come—

Was it possible another werewolf could scent her during an aroused state?

Apparently it was. But not simple arousal, rather climax. It was the first time she had come when with him.

"Blyss? Are you...?"

A frightening truth assaulted Blyss like a blow to the gut. The only way Stryke could possibly guess such a thing about her was if he was also a wolf.

She had just slept with a werewolf.

Oh, mercy, what terrible thing had she done?

"It's okay." He moved to the edge of the bed, his hands up to placate. His eyes softened, as did his voice. "I didn't realize you were my breed. I'm werewolf," he offered, obviously sensing her distress. "I didn't realize what you were last night in your office. Usually I can scent another of my kind. Maybe your perfume overwhelmed my senses."

"I can't talk about this right now."

The innate instinct to flee when cornered moved Blyss's limbs. She excused herself to go to the bathroom and rushed across the hardwood floor. With the door closed behind her, and the cool bathroom tiles beneath her bare feet, she turned on the faucet and splashed her face with tepid water. Her reflection could not overlook that twitch at the corner of her heart that manifested in a frown. Her hair was tousled, her lipstick worn away. Her eye shadow still looked perfect, but...

Nothing was perfect. He knew.

And while she should have laughed off his guess and made a grand and confident exit as stunning as her entrance, she couldn't simply leave. She had come here for a reason. Her very life depended on securing the black diamond she had planted in Stryke's suit pocket.

Merde. Stryke Saint-Pierre was a werewolf.

Her heartbeats dropped to her stomach. Blyss pressed her palms to the cool vanity sink, bowing her head. He hadn't scented her because the pills she took to suppress her werewolf made her virtually human.

"How did he know?" she begged her reflection.

It had to have been the sex. When she had climaxed and her body had released…something had clued him to her heritage. Pheromones or something like that. No man had noticed before because she'd never had sex with a werewolf.

What luck—the one man she had picked out from the crowd to help her should be the very man she needed to stay away from. Wanted to stay away from. But now could not.

Not until she found what she'd come for.

She straightened and nodded firmly at the mirror. She would go out there, dress, and she had to check the closet for the suit he'd worn last night. How to do that without raising suspicion? And how to avoid the werewolf questions?

She wanted to run away from it all. As she had so many years ago when her fellow classmates had stared at her with horror.

"You can do this. You *have* to do this." She winced. Could Stryke possibly help her? No. She had a plan. She would stick to it. "He must never know what kind of trouble I'm in."

With a few adjustments to her hair and a pat of a towel to dry her face, Blyss wandered back into the bedroom. Her lover stood by the window, naked, with an erection. The sun beamed across his face and shadowed his body, silhouetting that proud jut of manhood before the glass. Gorgeous. Something she would miss. She already missed him. The whole man. His kisses. His firm yet loving touch. His sexy smile…

Hell, what was she thinking? *Get your head on course.*

Blyss sat on the end of the bed. She picked up the red velvet dress from the floor. Where was her purse? Must have left it in the kitchen when she'd entered. "Your water is nice and hot here."

"Is that a good thing? I mean, isn't it all over the city?" He strode over to her and stroked his fingers over her hair. A shiver trickled down her neck and tightened her nipples. He smelled like fire and strength and sex. It was annoyingly distracting.

"Usually takes mine five minutes to warm nicely in the winter," she provided in an attempt to stick to the plan. "I may live off the Champs-Élysées, but the plumbing doesn't care that it is the ritzy section of town."

"Is that the street with all the fancy shops on it? The one that leads up to Napoleon's statue?"

Blyss smiled and stood to face him. She trailed a finger down his chest that was dusted with brown hair. His muscles gleamed in the sunlight.

"It's not a statue. It's a monument. The Arc de Triomphe was erected by Napoleon to commemorate his military victories." She kissed his jaw. Avoided touching his hard-on. Not an easy task. "Wish I had a toothbrush."

"I might have seen an extra in the drawer. Give me a few minutes to brush my teeth. Then I'll set one out for you. Okay?"

"Perfect."

He kissed her on the mouth and she pushed away from him. "I just said—"

"Are we going to discuss the werewolf thing?"

Heartbeats rammed against her rib cage. "I don't want to. I... No. Please let it go, Stryke."

He sighed and nodded. But for a few seconds he studied her. Trying to look inside her? Figure how he had missed that she was a werewolf?

If only she had known the same about him.

Finally, Stryke strolled toward the bathroom.

Tearing her gaze from his sexy backside, Blyss sighed. The life she led was a difficult achievement. And she did strive for it. But it was to be her undoing.

When the bathroom door closed, she slipped the dress over her head as she made a beeline for the closet door. Inside, the walk-in closet was vast and empty. Only the first rack held a few items. Two pairs of men's shoes sat on the floor beside a large empty suitcase.

She touched the hung items. A few T-shirts. Some jeans and a pair of dressier slacks. One white dress shirt. Nothing designer. And one black tie that wasn't silk but rather something like polyester.

Blyss shuddered. The man's wardrobe was hideous. Not a natural fiber in the lot, and yet the suit last night had been Zegna, if she was not mistaken. And she rarely misjudged couture. Though it had been poorly tailored to fit him, it had been expensive. She was sure of it.

Where was the suit?

"Hey."

Blyss startled. She hadn't heard Stryke's return and now he stood in the doorway, filling the space with an easy confidence, shoulders set back and head tilted.

He'd put on a pair of jeans that hung low, revealing the hard cuts of muscle that veered toward his groin like some kind of traffic alert that screamed "Go this way!"

"What are you doing?" He held a boxed toothbrush in his hand.

"Uh, just…looking." She spread her palm down the front of one of the T-shirts. Shit. What to say? "I'm a bit of a snoop." Weren't all women? "A girl can learn a lot about a man by standing in his closet."

Oh, bad save, Blyss. Very bad save.

"Is that so? Tell me what you've learned about me?"

"That you're a terrible traveler. Didn't you say you were in town for a wedding? Where's the suit you wore last night?"

"It was a loaner. I dropped it off at Vail's earlier today. I've been doing a lot of running around for my family, picking up things they need for the wedding."

"Vail?"

"A vampire. He's the father of the groom. I borrowed the suit for the night. I've been informed by the female faction of all this wedding madness that I'll have a rental for the wedding. Although…I imagine Vail will probably wear the suit for the wedding."

"Vail," she muttered. "I don't think I've heard of him."

"You probably haven't. Vamps tend to stay off the radar."

"Yes, I suppose."

He discussed vampires with her so casually. As if it was something she was familiar with and engaged in discussion every day. The paranormal breeds were something she avoided with a passion. And talking about them made her uncomfortable.

"But since you don't want to discuss the werewolf thing, I'll assume vampires are off the table, too?"

She nodded and dropped her hand from the front of the dress shirt.

"So, do you want to go to a wedding?" Stryke offered as he waggled the toothbrush before her.

Blyss accepted the packaged offering and tapped it against her lower lip. A wedding with vampires? Oh, mercy no. But if the suit was going to be there? Had she any other choice?

The last thing she wanted to do was associate with werewolves and vampires.

"Weddings are always fun," she managed to say brightly. "When is it?"

"Saturday. It's an evening wedding. I'll pick you up around six?"

She nodded. "It's a date."

Step three of the plan had failed miserably. On to step four. Emergency procedures.

"I'll need your address."

Blyss strolled out into the bedroom, stepped into her heels and spied his mobile phone on the nightstand beside the bed.

"I'll enter it for you."

She typed in her address on the contacts app, but she didn't enter her number. She never gave any man her number.

When Stryke took the phone he leaned in to kiss her, but she performed a twist and managed to avoid the contact as his lips brushed her cheek. She clicked toward the bedroom door, abandoning the toothbrush with a toss toward the bed.

"I'm so sorry to rush off, but I have to get back to the gallery!"

She didn't listen for his reply, but suspected he was probably kicking himself for inviting her to the wedding after that cold brush-off. Of course, now the man would have another day to think and wonder over her. Not a good thing.

Grabbing her scarf and purse as she breezed through the kitchen, she hastened through the front door and skipped toward the elevator.

A vampire wedding would prove a challenge. But if she did not find the suit, she would not be able to pay off Edamite Thrash. And life as she knew it would never again be the same.

"It freaked me out," Stryke said to his brother Kelyn as they strolled down a narrow cobbled street somewhere in the 5th arrondissement. Trouble walked ahead of them. "I had no idea she was werewolf."

"Something must be wrong with her," Kelyn offered in his usual quiet tone.

Of the four Saint-Pierre boys, Kelyn had no wolf in him and was 100 percent faery, thanks to their mother's genes. Physically he looked like no one in the family—save their mother—and was tall, lithe and pale. He usually covered the faint white markings that traced his arms, chest and back of his neck. Faery markings even he wasn't sure about. His violet eyes had a tendency to make women swoon. And Stryke had heard more than a few whispers about Kelyn's prowess between the sheets that made the ladies collapse in delighted exhaustion.

His *sidhe* brother seemed to navigate Paris as if he knew the city, yet used the ley-line excuse when Stryke asked about it. Faeries were inexplicably connected to the ley lines that crissed and crossed across the planet.

Trouble, who strode in front of them, his shoulders swaying with each sure stride, eyed a pair of women in stilettos and brandishing patent leather purses as they sat sipping café au lait before a chic café. The dark-haired Trouble winked and nodded to them. The women ignored his blatant flirtations with a chill Stryke was all too recently familiar with. Blyss's quick escape earlier had made him want to check if icicles had formed on the doorknob.

There was something up with her. Beyond the weird aversion to discussing the fact they were both wolves. That was why he'd asked her to the wedding. He needed to know more. And—to have one huge question answered.

"The city girls are snobs," Trouble said as he slowed and parted Stryke and Kelyn to walk between them. "I can't get a rise out of any of them. I'm ready to go home."

"I like Paris," Kelyn commented. "It feels familiar. And Stryke found himself a werewolf without even trying."

"Dude, really? How'd you score that?" Trouble wrapped an arm about Stryke's neck and gave him a noogie. "Thought you were at some fancy-schmancy gallery last night with Blade? Did you hear about Blade?"

"What?" Kelyn asked.

"Scored twins," Stryke confirmed.

"That man is a master," Trouble said in awe. "But a werewolf, eh? 'Bout time my little bro hooked up with his own kind. Dad will be happy to hear you are serious about starting a pack. Where'd you find her? Vail hook you up?"

"I met her at the gallery. I think she's the owner, but we didn't talk about much. Mostly I pushed her up against the wall and had a quickie." Because brothers shared everything. And he had to tell someone about the insane but amazing encounter.

"Nice." Trouble wasn't the most discerning when it came to women. He liked them fast, sexy and amiable. And they couldn't be too fancy or prissy. Trouble was a man's man, and he liked a woman who did all the kinds of things he liked to do.

Same with Stryke. If she couldn't handle a fishing rod or ride behind him on the four-wheeler while careening through a muddy field, well then, that was it.

Blyss was none of the above. But hell, she was his Paris fling. And what happened in Paris stayed in Paris. Right?

"She stopped by my place earlier for more sex," Stryke explained, "and it was the first time I realized she was wolf. When she came, I scented her. How the hell could I have not known before then?"

"Weird." Trouble pounded his fists together, a sort of tic. "What did she say about it?"

"She didn't want to talk about it. I had sex with a werewolf. You know how rare that is? Back in Minnesota the packs guard their females so well, if you can manage a date it's like breaking into Fort Knox. I don't have a clue why she didn't want to talk about it when she learned I was wolf. But I'm seeing her again. Taking her with me to the wedding."

"I'll sniff her out," Trouble offered. "See what's up."

"Keep your nose away from my woman," Stryke said

with a less-than-gentle nudge to his brother's ribs. "I'll figure it out. She's...complicated."

"Ah, hell, complicated women are not for me." Trouble wandered ahead again at sight of a gaggle of tourist girls who couldn't be a day over the age of sixteen.

"This way," Kelyn called, and they veered to the right to distract their brother's wandering attention. "Let's get something to eat at that gyro place we ate at last night."

"I'm going to head across the river," Stryke said. "I want to walk through the Tuileries and check it out."

"The what?" Trouble asked.

"It used to be the royal gardens a few centuries ago."

"Dude, I don't care about flowers."

"I know. That's why I'll head there by myself." And he didn't need the harassment of his brothers should he manage to find Blyss's place while pretending to be interested in some stupid flowers. "I'll see you two later."

The brothers exchanged fist bumps, and Stryke headed across a bridge laden with padlocks and toward the garden. He'd eaten a sandwich after Blyss left and wasn't hungry yet, so he didn't miss the food break. Trouble could eat all the time. And Kelyn, well... That kid rarely ate. So he was odd. Stryke worried about him at times. This world was not the place for Kelyn, but he wasn't sure Faery would welcome him either.

The Tuileries was a disappointment. Where were the flowers? It was mostly espaliered trees and trimmed shrubs and some marble statues. The French had strange ideas about gardens, that was for sure.

Crossing a wildly busy roundabout intersection, Stryke then wandered down the Champs-Élysées, taking in the elegant storefronts and dodging tourists who wielded armloads of shopping bags. He pulled out his phone and clicked on Blyss's address. The GPS located her immediately. About two blocks from where he stood.

Spying a stand selling flowers, he detoured.

"Can't show up uninvited *and* empty-handed."

He purchased some flowers then wandered deeper down the narrow streets that hugged three- and four-story buildings that he guessed must be centuries old. He knew Paris had been drastically redesigned sometime in the nineteenth century by Haussmann, and Napoleon had also torn down many structures, but the ancient history remained. Everything was elaborate, the building fronts featuring carved stone edifices and mascarons and even gilding on some of the stone and ironwork. Locked gates and digital entry systems clued him he had entered a ritzy neighborhood.

Stryke suddenly felt very underdressed in his Boundary Waters T-shirt and jeans with the worn hems dusting his scuffed Doc Martens. Maybe this was a bad idea? Showing up at a socialite's pied-à-terre looking like a tourist? He wasn't even sure what pied-à-terre meant, but it sounded cool.

He paused on a street corner paved in cobblestones. A red Vespa scooted by, and an elderly woman with gray hair bound behind her head and a pair of leather chaps nodded at him. The image made Stryke smile and he decided to go for it.

But as he stepped off the curb he heard the click of high heels.

"Are you stalking me, Monsieur Saint-Pierre?"

He turned to find Blyss looking like some kind of magazine model in a tailored pink dress and matching high heels. One hand clutched a slim purse and in the other dangled a dainty bag sporting the store name Pierre Hermé. She'd changed since seeing him only a few hours earlier.

"Uh, I was in the neighborhood and I thought I'd see if I could find your place." He held out the red roses, bound with twine. "These made me think of your lips."

She strolled slowly across the street, her eyes never leaving his, and the sexy tilt of her head pretty much went straight for his loins. She traced a delicate fingernail along a rose petal. Stryke could smell her perfume and the sweetness inside the bag she carried. Must be pastries. Yet he couldn't scent her wolf now.

"So you've found me." She walked across the street, away from him.

That was it? She hadn't taken the roses. "Uh, maybe you want to invite me up?"

She paused before a steel door, her fingers perched upon the digital entry pad. Did she have to think about it? Yep, he should have tried more for suave instead of tourist with his look today.

She punched in the code, pushed the door open and strode inside. She didn't close the door, so Stryke took that as an invite to follow. The woman had a way with leading him places. And he liked what happened once he arrived.

Closing the door behind him, he saw she walked through a small open courtyard lined with militantly trimmed green shrubs and simple flowers. It was amazing how Paris had all these hidden gems of greenery tucked in private courtyards. Reminded him of being home in the country.

Well, not really, but he'd use his imagination. It was

necessity when surrounded by tarmac, buildings, and nothing but humans for miles and miles.

Blyss veered right and disappeared into the cool shadows.

He hastened his steps to keep up with her. Normally, Stryke could follow another werewolf by scent alone. Why was it that he had only sensed her innate wolf when they were having sex? It was as if the adrenaline had to be rushing through her system to stir whatever pheromones his wolf could react to.

And he understood the subject of their breed was off-limits. It shouldn't bother him, but he couldn't help being curious. How often did Blyss happen upon another werewolf? Was it so common to her that she'd grown bored of the discussion? Couldn't be.

He'd lucked out. And as little as he knew about her, he did like her. Could something come of this? He daren't hope, but at the same time, his inner wolf howled with joy.

Blyss opened her front door. Stryke looked so innocently hungry staring at her with that adoring expression and underlined by the gorgeous bouquet of roses. The wedding wasn't until tomorrow but she believed his excuse that he had been walking in the area.

She never invited men into her home. It wasn't wise. Once invited in, it was often difficult to make them leave after she tired of them. And they sometimes returned. It was a sticky business to have to deal with.

And this particular man was more than man. He was werewolf. The last creature in this world with whom she wished to be intimate.

Alas, she had ignored any intuition that would have

kept her safe from that emotional danger. And even as she vacillated with grabbing the roses and slamming the door in his face, the compulsion to pull him in by that awful T-shirt and let him have his way with her was even stronger.

She couldn't resist his wild allure. It was an accidental allure, she felt sure. The man wasn't a master seducer. Though he was an amazing lover. And he wasn't suave or polished, as she preferred her men. He was a rough and awkward man from the United States, of all places, who had happened to fall into her scheme, and now he was milking it for all he could. Because he knew something about her that others did not.

Would he use that information to blackmail her such as Edamite Thrash had?

He thrust the roses forward. Sweet blackmail, if there was such a thing. And that smile. She wanted him to teach her all the things that smile promised.

Blyss took the bouquet by the ribbon-wrapped stems, and then she grabbed her suitor by the shirtfront and pulled him inside. Turning, she walked down the long hallway, roses dangling at one side, man clutched at her other side.

If she was going down the wrong path, she might as well do it big. At least, until the wedding was over and she held the key to her future safe in hand.

Chapter 5

Stryke followed Blyss down a long white hallway and into a kitchen that gleamed white and silver. It looked like something out of a minimalist designer's dream. White marble countertops, not an appliance on the counter, no signs it was a kitchen if not for the sink and sleek, glass-fronted fridge that sported wine bottles down one side.

Placing the roses on the counter, Blyss veered left into a living area that featured a white furniture set beneath a ceiling that was entirely glass. It was like standing in a conservatory without the plants. Everything was white. He didn't dare sit down because he'd been walking through Paris. His shoes must be dirty.

How could a person relax in a place so white?

The gorgeous contrast of pink silk and blackest hair and eyebrows turned and tilted a brilliant red smile at him. "I didn't think I'd see you until Saturday. But now that you're here…"

She pushed her hand up under his T-shirt, her glossy nails gliding over his abs. At the erotic touch Stryke sucked in a breath. The intention in her eyes was apparent. This woman went from cool to boiling faster than a rocket ship.

He abandoned his need to ask about her werewolf and instead slid a hand about her hip and pulled her to him. Her fingernails dug in at his chest, and one of them tweaked his nipple. Yep, that gave him a hard-on.

"You are so hard to resist," he growled.

"Then why must you? I certainly have no intention of denying myself what I want."

"I'm guessing you are a woman who likes to be spoiled."

"Very much so."

"Then why me?" He caught her hand against his chest, the shirt between his hand and hers. Leaning closer to her face, he tried to scent her innate wolf but could not. "Am I just a fling?"

"Of course you are." She kissed his mouth without making a connection—more like breath against breath—just enough of a tease to keep him close to her. "I never get attached to a man. It's a rule. Can you deal with that, Stryke?"

It sounded fifty ways wrong. But he needed only one reason to stay. And that reason had grown hard as steel, standing at attention, ready for some action.

"Works for me," he said and lifted her up against him.

As her thin pink skirt slid up high, she wrapped her legs about his hips and Stryke set her on the back of the white sofa. He bent to kiss along her neck, smelling only the sweet flowers that blossomed on her skin. The heat of her combined with the sweetness melded into an intoxicating perfume that he inhaled deeply. Still no wolf. He'd ask her about it later.

He slid down the zipper at the back of her dress, his fingertips strolling slowly over her skin, the straightness of her spine, until he felt the sexy divots that topped her derriere. There he rocked his thumbs against the concave curves.

"I gotta taste you." He pulled her from the couch, turning her, so her gorgeous ass faced him. Bending to lick the Venus dimples above her hips, he curled his hands around in front of her mons. One glided up toward her breasts; the other sought the moist warmth between her legs.

"Blyss," he muttered against her sweet skin. It wasn't so much her name as an experience, and he intended to take it to the maximum. "So good."

She turned and put up a foot on one of his shoulders, forcing him to kneel. So that was the way of it?

"S'il vous plaît," she asked sweetly.

He didn't know what that meant but that wasn't going to stop him from taking and giving what he desired. Stryke kissed her mons and glided his hand up her thigh until her wetness enticed him to dash his tongue down her hot seam. Mmm…he was hungry now.

He lashed at her sensitive apex and her body shuddered in response. Fingers clasping his hair, she balanced there on the back of the couch, one leg sliding over his shoulder, the other, toes barely touching the floor.

Reaching up, he was rewarded with her hand clasping his. She squeezed tightly every time his tongue hit the spot. She moaned appreciatively.

The best feeling a guy could have? Kissing a woman between her legs as she came, her thighs squeezing his face and her hands tugging him in desperate release. That he could make her ride a high like this gave him immense satisfaction. He felt pride and also needed to feel her heat wrapping about his cock.

Before he could stand, Blyss sank to the floor and straddled him, taking his erection inside her. She was so wet and still spasming from the orgasm. The tug and tease on his cock lured him to a speedy orgasm.

Werewolf or not, this woman was something else.

Blyss woke to the sun beaming across her face. Half of the apartment was capped by windowed, cathedral-style ceilings. She thrived on the sunshine, and this bedroom with the slanted ceiling and the windows that faced the eastern sky fed her very soul.

She yawned and then realized there was a tremendous body heat lying next to her. He mastered the bed, as if staking a claim.

She silently swore, clutching the bedsheets up over her breasts. And yet, she could only blame herself for this mistake called Stryke Saint-Pierre. When she'd spied him on the street yesterday afternoon, she should have stepped around the side of a building and pressed her back to the wall as if a thief fearing capture, and waited for him to leave. But something about him had inexplicably compelled her. Drew her to him as if starved for the lust and sensual cravings he seemed to fulfill every time he touched her.

She turned onto her side, and the movement startled him awake. He reached over and pulled her against his chest, sliding his hand up her stomach to cup her breast. He whispered sleepily, "Come here, glamour girl."

Mercy. If this was a mistake then why did lying next to Stryke feel so right?

Stryke dressed as the shower clattered in the next room. Blyss had woken, slipped out from under his arm and padded toward the bathroom. "See you tonight," she had called. "You can let yourself out."

A cold send-off.

He considered pulling his clothes off and lying back on the bed in wait. They could make love again. He could lose himself in her. Fall into her strange world of glamour, perfection and sensory disguise. Because he forgot everything when wrapped in Blyss's arms.

But he knew she wanted him gone by the time the shower stopped. Call it instinct. She was a hard one to figure. She was hot and wild in bed, but out of it she was like porcelain. Smooth and cool to the touch. And not at all wolflike.

He glanced about the bedroom, seeking something, anything, that would clue him to her breed. Not sure what he was looking for exactly. Wasn't as if wolves kept totems around signifying their packs, or—

He wondered what the name of her pack was. Obviously, she didn't live within the pack, as most tended to gather in large compounds. Of course, many had a central gathering place while the members had their own homes and lived away from the pack.

That was how he planned to form his pack. A central compound for gatherings while the individual families lived in their own homes. It was a good way to build a strong yet diverse community.

Tilting his glance upward, he squinted at the bright sunlight beaming through the overhead windows. He hadn't taken the time to look up last night to sight in the moon. He bet lying here beneath the full moon was awesome.

That was, if the full moon didn't tug at his need to shift to werewolf. The last thing he'd do in this city was shift and risk being seen in werewolf shape. He wondered where Blyss went to shift.

So many things he wanted to ask her, and yet there was no way to bring up questions without causing her affront. He was damn sure she'd slap him or storm out again should he even whisper the word *werewolf.*

His shoes were out in the living room somewhere. Stryke wandered down the hallway. He was afraid to touch anything for fear of leaving a stain. Near the couch he shoved his feet into the Doc Martens, and as he was walking down the hall to the front door, his phone rang.

He closed the front door behind him and answered.

"Stryke, where are you? I thought you were going to help with errands today?"

His mother, Rissa. Indeed, he had offered to ferry her about Paris as they collected whatever was needed for tonight's ceremony. His mother was at the Santiago mansion today. They lived in the 7th, which if he knew the city—and he did not—might be across the river from where he currently was. It was near the Eiffel Tower; he did know that much.

"I think it'll take half an hour to find the place," he said to his mother. "Then you've got me for most of the day."

"Most?"

"Are you going to release me from servitude to get ready for the wedding?"

His mother laughed. "Of course. Could you pick up some *pains au chocolat* on your way here?"

"I have no idea what that is, but I'll try my best to sniff some out."

"Chocolate pastries, son. Point your nose toward chocolate. You know how much I love my sweets."

"Will do. See you in a bit, Mom."

The phone rang again before he even stuffed it back in a pocket. This time it was a brother asking for directions home from someplace beyond the ring road that circled the city proper.

"Don't you have GPS, Trouble?"

"I did, until I lost my phone. Dude, it's like country out here. But the countrywomen sure are fun. Kelyn and I met a bunch of faeries last night. They are hot. Where are you, anyway?"

"I'm finding much better luck in the city," Stryke offered as he exited the courtyard and strode over the cobblestones. "Listen, I have no idea where you are. I'm headed to the Santiagos' right now to drive a carload of wedding-crazed women all over."

"Ah hell, sounds like you got the shit job today."

"It'll make looking forward to this evening and my date with Blyss all the sweeter."

"She's the wolf who's weird about it, right?"

"Right. I think I see a place selling those chocolate things Mom wanted. I gotta go. Why don't you have Kelyn fly up above the trees and locate your position?"

"Good call. See you later, bro."

Blyss sat before the vanity in a lace pink La Perla bra-and-panty set. Pink marabou fluffed on the toes of her kitten-heeled slippers. Carefully, she drew eyeliner beneath her lower lid. Her hair was still up in a towel, but she liked to do her eyes before drying it. Rest of the makeup was done after her hair. It was a two-hour morning ritual.

And it was nearly noon.

She could have lingered in bed with Stryke well into the afternoon. His skin against hers had been insanely exquisite. His hands gliding across her limbs, caressing a breast, even tracing her lips, was a feeling she didn't ever want to forget. His mouth at hers. His moans harmonizing with hers. His hard, hot cock buried within her.

Blyss sighed, and her reflection blinked, messing up the eyeliner.

"What the hell am I doing?" she muttered as she swiped a tissue over the mess. "I don't turn into a swooning schoolgirl when a man knows how to make love to me. I remain calm and distant, and thank him for whatever sparkling gift he wishes to give me."

Stryke had gifted her gorgeous red roses. Nothing that could be resold, such as diamonds or platinum, or even a new car. She'd collected hundreds of thousands of dollars in gifts over the years. All of which were now gone. Ransomed to pay for her addiction.

"It's not an addiction," she whispered. "It is necessity."

Because she couldn't live as a werewolf. It was unthinkable.

And she did still own one gift—the gallery. Would she have to sell it to pay for her habit?

It wasn't a habit; it was her lifestyle.

The mobile phone sitting on a silver tray played the opening organ notes from Schnorr's Toccata and Fugue in D Minor. The caller ID was blocked. Blyss knew exactly who it was from the ringtone. She drummed her fingers on the vanity.

The phone rang insistently.

She finally picked it up. *"Oui?"*

"Mademoiselle Sauveterre."

Even knowing who it was, her heart dropped to her gut. And it pulsed so erratically she clutched at her stomach, feeling as though she would be sick.

"You have *Le Diabolique*?" the deeply calm yet sinister voice asked.

It was Edamite Thrash. A demon. Her supplier.

"It is in transit. I'm to collect it tonight."

The diamond had been their deal. If she obtained the *Diabolique* diamond, he would forget that she owed him five hundred thousand euros and also front her for another year's supply. Those pills were what suppressed her werewolf.

"I don't understand, Mademoiselle Sauveterre. I know the diamond has been taken from the gallery."

How he knew about that secret operation, a crime she intended to keep out of the media by replacing the original stone with a fake, was beyond her. She hadn't been in to check on the fake today. There was no reason to. And if Lorcan should see it he wouldn't be able to tell it was a fake.

"I had to divert suspicion from me in order to get it out of the gallery," she said. Any chance of Lorcan finding the diamond on her had to be reduced. The handoff to Stryke had been the only plan she could live with. She hadn't expected the suit loan, though. "I will have it in hand tonight and can bring it to you tomorrow."

"I'll send a car for you in the morning." The phone clicked off.

Blyss dropped the phone on the marble vanity. Her makeup supplies scattered, spilling across her lap, and she caught her face in her palms. Tears slid down her wrists.

There were six pills left in the jar she kept on the vanity. And she must take one today.

She sat up abruptly. "No."

Racing down the hallway and into the kitchen, she clicked on the iPad and selected the calendar app. Counting out the days, she tapped her finger on the end date. And there, at the bottom of the day square, was a tiny circle.

"Full moon," she gasped. "Oh, mercy, this can't happen."

Chapter 6

After he'd parked in front of Blyss's building, Stryke adjusted his tie in the rearview mirror. He was oddly ambivalent about this evening. He had an unnerving suspicion about Blyss, and it hadn't anything to do with the fact she wouldn't admit to being werewolf to him. It had everything to do with what he'd found in the pocket of Vail's suit. He didn't know Vail well, and the guy did like his sparkly gemstones, but really?

He struggled with giving Blyss the benefit of the doubt or straight-out questioning her before they got to the wedding. And then he decided to play it by ear. If his suspicions were correct, she would reveal herself. And he wouldn't like that.

He didn't want her to be anything but the glamour girl he loved to make love to. And hell, he knew this was a fantasy. There wasn't a woman in the world like her. It was foolish to entertain the idea that she could be a part of his future, the werewolf wife he wanted and needed to start his own pack.

Even if she never wanted to see him again, he would always have memories of her.

Plucking the white flower from the cup holder, he held it by the tiny plastic vial that held a few drops of water to preserve its freshness. Daisy Blu, his sister, had told him this was freesia. The bride, Kambriel, had them stuck all over in the wedding bouquets. It smelled like the best kind of perfume. Yet it was a simple flower, so opposite Blyss.

He slid out of the steel-gray Audi Rhys Hawkes had loaned him and strode across the cobblestoned street. He'd been borrowing a lot from his aunt's new in-laws, but Rhys had insisted, and besides, he'd use it if Hawkes had any more jobs for him while in town. It was a lot nicer than the twenty-year-old Ford he drove back home.

Blyss buzzed him in at the entry and Stryke strode through the courtyard and to her door, where she met him with a kiss to both his cheeks. The French called the double-cheek kiss *bises*. He'd learned that from the groom's mom, Lyric, this afternoon. But he wouldn't let Blyss get by with that noncommittal greeting. Before she could pull away, he pulled her to him and kissed her long and deep. He felt her soften in his arms, and then her fingers clutched at his biceps and she pulled him over the threshold.

She wanted him. And he wanted her.

His hand roamed up her leg, noting a slit in the long skirt that allowed him free rein across her skin. His fingers danced over the lacy tops of her thigh-high stockings. He hadn't intended to push her against the wall and have sex with her—the wedding began in less than an hour—but...

"No," she gasped as she pulled away from the kiss, but then kissed his eyelids and the tip of his nose. "You'll muss me."

"I like you mussed, glamour girl."

"Control yourself. *S'il vous plaît.*"

Stryke pressed his forehead to her shoulder. Yeah, she was right. Though he had the sinking feeling this would be his last opportunity at ever having sex with Blyss again. Tonight truths would be revealed. He just hoped they weren't more startling than discovering he'd had sex with a werewolf unawares.

He displayed the tiny flower for her and she tilted her head in wonder. "What is it?"

"Freesia. Smell it."

She sniffed, her eyelids closing to reveal dramatic dark and sexy eye shadow. Her red lips parted and a tendril of dark curl fell across her forehead. Diamonds hung at her ears and a single diamond glinted at her neck.

Stryke wanted to devour her. But she was right. He mustn't muss this jewel before the big soiree.

"Smells like candy," she offered. *Très jolie.*

"It's from the bride's wedding flowers." He pulled the tiny flower out from the vial and flicked off the water droplets. "May I?"

She nodded.

He tucked the flower into her thick black curls, then sniffed it. "No match for you."

"You are a sweet man, Stryke Saint-Pierre. I..." She suddenly looked aside.

Yeah, she was riding the same vibe as he. They both knew this night was going to end with a big kiss-off.

"Are you ready?"

She picked up a sheer black shawl from the floor, and smoothed a hand over her violet skirt that fell to the floor in a filmy swoosh. She looked garden-party ready, save for that sexy slit up to the thigh.

"Let's do this," she said, locking the door behind her, then heading out to the street. "You've a car. Delightful."

Stryke was sure she'd expected a cab and was thankful for the loaner. The wedding was in an old rented mansion in the 8th arrondissement. He had already entered the directions into the GPS, though he'd been to the place a few times already so he could look around while Blyss pointed out the landmarks along the way.

The Champs-Élysées was a big long stretch of elite shops and tourist traps. The street was double-wide and filled with cars, tourist buses, sports cars and the occasional bike weaving in and out of traffic as if it owned the road.

Blyss pointed to her favorite haunt: Louis Vuitton. "I love their purses." She clutched hers, a little pink number that had some weird finger holes along one side in the shape of skulls. "This one is Alexander McQueen."

"Uh-huh," Stryke said. Best thing to do when a woman dropped into shopping mode was just nod his head and agree. "So if all the shops along this road are spendy then why do I see a McDonald's over there?"

"They are not all so expensive. There are the DVD rental stores, as well. So gauche."

He could only smirk at her obvious disdain for those lesser shops. Taking the roundabout by the Arc de Triomphe, he marveled that the setting sun beamed under the arch. Paris was a beautiful city, but it would take him a lifetime to see everything and to begin to feel comfortable in this land of the tourists and foreign babble.

When they were but a few blocks away from the wedding site, he took her hand and squeezed it. "I just have to warn you…"

He stopped the car at a stop sign, and she turned a wondering gaze on him.

"My whole family is here for this event. So there's going to be lots of questions and stares, and you can expect downright ogling from my brothers."

"How many brothers do you have?"

"Three. Be cautious of Trouble. He's a flirt. So is Kelyn. And, hell, Blade has this sort of silent seduction thing going on that seems to render women into puddles of mush. He was at the gallery with me, but left fifteen minutes later. With twins."

"I know those twins." She chuckled. "I'm sure I'll be fine. Social events are my thing. I can mingle with the best of them."

"Right, but I'm sure you haven't had to dodge questions like 'How long have you been dating?' and 'When are you getting married?' Expect that stuff from my family. And my dad, well, he expects me to start a pack and if he sees me with a werewolf—I want to warn you in advance."

"I see. No problem, Stryke. I can do this. Are we dating or just friends?"

"I, uh…" He'd love to answer that they were dating, but he wasn't stupid. This felt more like an extended hookup than anything.

"We are lovers," she decided. "That should give them something to whisper about behind our backs. Yet your father won't have reason to believe we are committed to one another."

Her wink twirled Stryke's world out of orbit. He almost gushed out that he loved her, but he knew that would be a stupid reaction to a beautiful woman calling him her lover. He wasn't some idiot who fell head over heels before the first gorgeous woman who gave him the time of day.

"Lovers." He kissed her hand. "I like that. And, uh… they'll also want to know that you're wolf. My father again."

"Ah." She stared straight ahead. Stryke noted the delicate muscle in her jaw pulse once. "Well, you know the answer to that, don't you?"

"I do, but— Why do I sense it's not something you want to talk about?"

"Because it isn't. And can we leave it at that?"

"The place is going to be swarming with werewolves. And vampires. And witches. And probably a few faeries."

"I can deal."

But why she had to "deal" bothered him. What was wrong with hanging with her own kind? Had to be better than some boring gallery showing among vapid humans. Now was not the time to get into an intense conversation. He'd save it for later.

If later didn't blow up in his face.

Stryke drove onward and spied the building. "There's parking around back. Do you want me to let you off at the front?"

"No, I'd like to walk in on your arm."

If she kept saying things like that he may turn into that gushing idiot before the night was over.

Social events were Blyss's air. She lived for the champagne and small talk. Mingling was her language. Air-kisses and light bon mots were her toys.

But as she stood in the reception hall draped with crimson chiffon and twists of black roses amid dozens of people, she realized this event would try her. It was a wedding between two vampires. She doubted there was even a human in the crowd.

Humans were the species she most related to. She strived to be human.

A mix of paranormals buzzed about the dance floor and chattered over the bubbly. But she couldn't determine who was what. Her heightened werewolf senses were suppressed. As she preferred. Yet she felt the lone man on the raft right now. Unsure if she would sink or swim.

And the trouble with paranormals was that most lived for hundreds of years and yet aged slowly. A person could never tell if they were talking to someone their own age, or in fact, a five-hundred-year-old vampire who may have a witchy wife who had passed the millennial mark. It was enough to make Blyss nervous.

"You cool?" Stryke asked.

He hadn't let go of her hand since they'd walked in, and while normally she would untether herself from her date and float among the masses, at the moment Blyss preferred the leash.

She nodded. "I need some champagne. Could you grab me some from that oncoming tray?"

Stryke scored two goblets, pressing one into her shaky

grasp with a sweet kiss to the base of her ear. "Don't worry. There may be vamps and witches running amok, but there are lots of wolves here tonight, as well. You're in good company, glamour girl."

That was the least comforting reassurance.

"They are dancing already?" she asked. "Did we miss the ceremony?"

"No. According to what I've gleaned from the female faction, tonight is all backward. Johnny's band is playing for the dance right now. Later, when the clock strikes midnight, they'll get hitched."

"Interesting. Johnny is the groom?"

"Yep." Stryke pointed over the dance floor toward the stage. A decidedly goth band sang a catchy tune that had all the guests dancing amid a flicker of strobe lights.

Hooking her arm in Stryke's, she followed as he pushed through the crowd. The male eyes tilted toward her as they passed. Blyss couldn't manage to lift her chin and beam as usual. This night couldn't end quickly enough.

"Hey, man!"

Blyss turned to find Stryke hugging a burly man with wide shoulders and dark hair, and his eyes immediately went to her. A quick assessment found he wore a leather kilt and combat boots beneath the crisp white dress shirt and black suit coat. Even more interesting.

"This your girl?"

"This is Blyss Sauveterre. Blyss, my oldest brother, Trouble."

Trouble took her hand and kissed the back of it, but Blyss noticed he sniffed at her skin for a few seconds before tugging her into his embrace and hugging her.

He was strong, and he smelled great, but she wasn't accustomed to such gregarious greetings.

Stepping back on wobbly heels, she managed a smile at the unrefined behemoth. "You're quite the friendly one."

"And you smell great. Flowers and sex. Gotta love that."

"Chill, Trouble," Stryke warned. He slipped his hand into Blyss's and she was grateful for the grounding connection. "He's the rowdy one in the family, in case his name didn't clue you in."

"She's a looker, bro. Good catch," Trouble said while tilting a wink at his brother.

"I think I saw faery triplets back that way."

Trouble bounced on his toes to see over the crowd. "Where?"

Stryke pointed again. "We're going to say hello to Kelyn. See you around, Trouble."

Blyss hugged up close as he led her away from Trouble's smirking summation of her. "I think I prefer the cool calm brother."

"That would be me," he confirmed. "Don't let Trouble scare you. His bark is worse than his bite. He's all show. Except when he picks a fight. Then you'd better run. Hey, Kelyn."

A man Blyss would never have guessed was related to the well-muscled Stryke and Trouble turned and greeted them with a nod. He was tall, blond and slender, and his violet eyes smiled before his mouth met the emotion. A faery?

"Kelyn, this is Blyss. Kelyn's the youngest Saint-Pierre brother," Stryke offered. "Not sure where Blade is tonight."

"Ah, Blyss," Kelyn said. "The woman from the gallery." He eyed Stryke, and Blyss sensed they were communicating silently. Had he told his brothers about his wild discovery that she was werewolf? Likely.

"How are you finding Paris?" Blyss asked, if only to break the brothers' communication.

"It's to my liking. But I don't sense Faery here."

Good, she hadn't had to ask after his breed. Interesting mix in the family, to be sure. "I'm sure you know Faery does not survive over the well-populated areas. But there is FaeryTown. Rather a dodgy area, though, if I must say."

She'd only been told what it was like by her brother, Kir. Blyss had as little interest in faeries as she did werewolves.

"I've heard about FaeryTown and may check it out," Kelyn offered. "Interesting wedding, eh? Dancing and eating first, and saving the ceremony for the end?"

"Thought it was a vamp thing," Stryke said and his hand glided up Blyss's back. "Speaking of eating… Want to find something to munch on?"

"Sure."

The food table was covered in red linen and sparkled with silver candelabras laden with more of the black roses. Stryke popped various hors d'oeuvres into his mouth, while Blyss managed a crunchy bit of toast with caviar. She wasn't hungry. In fact, her stomach was churning. When would Stryke introduce her to Vail? Only then could she leave this crowd of misfits behind.

"Rhys!" Stryke chewed the last of a cherry tart, then introduced Blyss to a handsome Frenchman with salt-and-pepper hair and a generous smile. "Rhys Hawkes is the groom's grandfather," Stryke explained, "and he's been giving me some work to do while I'm in town."

"Hawkes Associates," Rhys said as he shook Blyss's hand. Of all the people she had met tonight, he felt the most grounded and sincere. Truth in his eyes. But what was his truth? Werewolf? Vampire? "And you are?"

"I'm sorry," Stryke said. "This is Blyss Sauveterre."

"Is that so?" Rhys's smile was warmly reassuring. "Isn't your family with the Valoir pack?"

Blyss tightened her jaw, but quickly softened it. "Yes, of course."

"Excellent. That pack is well regarded in my book. Listen, I hate to be quick, but I'm getting the wink from my wife across the room. Viviane adores this song. Johnny wrote it for her. Time to dance."

"So you do have a pack," Stryke commented as they again wove through the crowd of black ties and silk-and-satin gowns. "Valoir, eh? You've been hush-hush about, er, things, so I didn't want to press."

"I'm no longer with the pack," she commented and set her empty goblet on a passing tray. "I'm going to look for the ladies' room, if you don't mind?"

"Sure. But you look perfect."

"Just a little touch-up. You know we girls can't make it through any event without primping," she said and walked away as quickly as she could.

If she had been forced to converse further about her pack, Blyss would have had to confess more than just her absence from Valoir. She wasn't prepared to do that. And she wouldn't need to, if she could find the vampire Vail, who had loaned Stryke the suit. Pray, the vampire was wearing that very suit this evening.

Weaving through the crowd, using her clutch purse

as a shield she held in front of her chest, she almost walked right into a tall, broad red-haired man who turned and caught his hands against her shoulders. "Sorry, lady. Wow."

He stepped back to look her over, running a hand over his tousle of hair. "You here all alone, pretty lady?"

"I'm with Stryke Saint-Pierre," she said, with the intention of swiftly bypassing him and avoiding conversation, but he caught her about the waist and spun her around.

"So you're the glamour girl Stryke caught? My father mentioned he was looking to hook up with a wolf. You are so pretty." He blatantly sniffed the air between them. "Would have never guessed you for wolf, though."

She managed a smile and shrugged out of his grasp.

"Sorry." He offered his hand to shake. "Trystan Hawkes. Father of two eligible werewolf daughters and trying to protect the hell out of them tonight with all the single young wolves stalking the crowd."

"A doting father. Always refreshing. I was heading that way. If you'll excuse me."

She made a dash and almost cleared the ballroom with the hallway in sight when a gaggle of giggling bridesmaids scurried up behind her. Red skirts swishing, they rushed on their stilettos toward the same door she had spied.

"Sorry!" a woman with braided pink hair called back. "Emergency pee break!"

Blyss paused and pressed a shoulder against a cool marble column. A tuft of red chiffon dusted her head. The black roses had no scent. She didn't need the facilities, and the privacy she had been seeking would not be found in the ladies' room.

Sighing heavily, she turned to face a man who gave new meaning to *sexy*. He was tall, dark and dressed in black velvet, and silver rings glinted on his fingers as well as diamonds in both his ears. His eyes were black and his smile was slightly crooked. He'd flipped his hair back in a rock-star swoop and his smile made her want to fall to her knees and sigh in adoration.

Had to be vampire. He wore the dark, fanged vibe so well.

"Vaillant," he said, offering his hand to shake.

Blyss shook and told him her name. "I'm here with Stryke Saint-Pierre," she provided weakly. "Wait. Vaillant? Are you Vail? The father of the groom?"

"Ch-yeah. So you've heard about me? Makes sense. Why is such a gorgeous catch as you hanging out all by yourself? Isn't Stryke taking care of you?"

"I needed to catch a breath of air away from the crowd," she offered. Assuming a modicum of cool, Blyss set back her shoulders and traced a finger down the front of Vail's suit. "This is nice." Yet the lapels were velvet.

Not the suit she needed.

"Thanks. Black's my color."

"The suit you loaned Stryke the other evening was classy, as well."

"Yep. Zegna all the way."

"I had thought you'd wear it tonight."

"No, I gotta bring out the romantic stuff for the big event." He tilted a shoulder forward and Blyss then noticed the silver studs spiking up as if a warrior's armor. "My wife loves it when I work the rock-star vibe."

Blyss pulled her hand away from the velvet. Wife. Of course. She didn't want to start any rumors. Or fights, if indeed Stryke's father had an eye to her as a potential wife for his son. She was glad she hadn't been introduced to her lover's father yet. But it didn't matter anymore. Her mission had hit a brick wall. No suit. No diamond.

"I think the ceremony is starting soon," Vail said, checking his wristwatch. "I have to go and make the announcement for everyone to file in to the next ballroom. Nice meeting you, Blyss."

She mumbled a *bonsoir* and turned to search for Stryke, but her eyes unfocused and she again felt as if she balanced upon a raft amid treacherous waves. Edamite Thrash was sending a courier in the morning to pick up *Le Diabolique*. What would she do now?

Was there a way she could possibly get into Vail's closet tonight? Had she any other option? Where could he live? And did vampires sleep through the mornings, as she'd heard rumors, so she could sneak in without detection?

What was she thinking? She was no cat burglar. The snag from her own gallery had been possible because she had received the diamond and had processed it herself. She'd been vague with Lorcan about plans to exhibit it, which was why he hadn't questioned its absence yet.

Come to think of it, she hadn't heard from Lorcan since the Marie Antoinette showing. Generally they checked in with one another every day.

A warm hand slid around her waist. Blyss stiffened, until she realized who it was. Stryke kissed her at the base of her ear. Briefly she relaxed, sinking into his presence, until she remembered that now was no time to relax.

"Flirting with Vail?" he asked.

"Hmm? No. It's not called flirting if you don't get

their number." She tossed out the tired old line because right now her brain wasn't functioning properly. "He wasn't wearing the suit."

"Nope. Let's go find a seat, shall we?"

Stryke nodded to Kelyn, who sat across the red-carpeted aisle from him. He caught his little brother's wink. Trouble kept giving him the head nod, as well. Yeah, he was sitting with the most gorgeous woman in the entire room. Hands down, he had won the Paris woman search among his brothers.

But when he'd seen Blyss talking to Vail, and running her fingers along his suit pocket, his heart had fallen. She had to have known it was a different suit, right?

While the officiate read through the vows, and Kambriel and Johnny stood facing one another, Stryke couldn't help but be distracted by the woman sitting next to him. He could smell the freesia and beyond that the traces of her floral perfume. But he couldn't sense her innate werewolf. Hell, he could pick out every werewolf in the room by scent alone. It wasn't an odor they put off, but something internal, a knowing they shared among their breed. He could even scent a few vamps because some carried an iron-tainted tinge of blood about them.

He tried to pay attention to the ceremony. The bride wore black latex, and the groom, clad in black velvet, wore a caterpillar of silver rings along one ear and his boots were studded and wrapped with silver chains. Johnny Santiago sang goth rock with a local band who had entertained friends and family tonight. Kambriel had lived in Minnesota all her life until running away to Paris to "find herself" a few years ago. It looked as though she'd found happiness.

Could he ever be so lucky?

Stryke threaded his fingers through Blyss's. What a woman to spend the rest of his life with. Yet it was an irrational thought. He knew nothing about her. Sure, they had some amazing chemistry between them. But what kind of distortion made her werewolf so imperceptible to him?

And would he really have to ask her the big question? The one that had troubled him since the night he'd returned home after the gallery showing and had shoved his hand into the inner pocket of the suit coat. He'd found something odd, interesting and couldn't believe it had belonged to Vail.

He had to do it. He would do it. Now, while it was relatively quiet and they sat toward the back. The bride and groom had recited their vows, and the officiate was babbling on about loving one another until death parted them. Long wait, if they could avoid the stake.

"So were you disappointed Vail wasn't wearing the suit?" he whispered close to Blyss's ear.

"Uh…" Startled, she flashed her bright greens at him.

Right. He'd caught her out.

"Were you looking for this?" He reached into his pocket and pulled out the incredible black diamond that seemed to glow red from within and which was the size of a small plum.

Up front, the officiate pronounced the couple happily married and called for, instead of applause, a blessed moment of silence.

Blyss gasped and reached for the stone. "How did you—?"

Amid the silence a surprisingly loud sneeze echoed out.

Johnny, the groom, glanced over the crowd, his eyes landing on his little sister, Summer. "Ah hell," the vampire muttered.

Chapter 7

"**D**emons!" someone shouted. The entire audience jumped to their feet. Shouts to protect the women were answered by demonic growls.

Blyss grasped for Stryke's hand, but he snatched the diamond away. "I need that!"

"No time for this argument." Stryke's eyes scanned the crowd and focused on the back door, where the bride had walked in and down the red-carpeted aisle. His jaw tensed.

Blyss grabbed him by the suit lapels. "Just hand it to me."

"We'll discuss this later. You have things to tell me." He gripped her by the shoulders. "Yes?"

"I'll tell you everything if you'll give me the diamond."

"I'm going to hang on to it until after your confession. Now stay behind me. There's a lot of them. Hell, what are demons doing here?"

Screams and shouts erupted. Demonic growls curdled over the gaiety. The brother Blyss knew as Trouble charged for the dark-skinned red-eyed demon in the lead of what looked like a cavalcade of demons. All around her Blyss saw people spring into action, and it wasn't just the men. Witches attempted to repel the demonic approach with chants and gestures, and the witch with the dark purple hair even threw fire—of which, a demon caught in his mouth and gobbled up as if candy.

The bride was swept off the dais in a swish of black latex by her groom, but neither left the fray as demons poured down the aisle, slapping at vampires and werewolves to clear their way. The bride slid up her skirt to reveal a dagger strapped to her thigh. The groom smirked and pulled out knives from the holsters beneath his velvet suit coat.

Stryke punched a slender demon with long, disjointed arms and wicked talons. The demon growled, infusing the air with a foul miasma.

Stryke reached back to shove Blyss away. "Stay close."

She appreciated his need to protect her, but all she wanted was to grab the diamond and get out of there. She hadn't seen him put *Le Diabolique* back in his pocket. Right now he lifted and swung a demon over the buffet table, bringing it down on the chocolate fountain in a spectacular crash.

A demon leaped from the aisle and landed before Blyss. The creature inhaled through long slit nostrils—all the demons wore their true forms—the gills on his cheeks fluttering. "You are the one."

Blyss choked down a scream. Grasping at her throat, she stumbled and went down, landing on her butt and up against a marble column. Stryke was nowhere to be seen. The wedding guests engaged in a wild tangle with an assortment of demons. She smelled blood and sulfur. And she tasted her own fear.

The demon looming over her opened his mouth to reveal chunky, dull teeth. A scream rattled at the back of her throat.

"D-did Edamite send you?" she asked.

"Thrash?" The demon chuckled. "Heh. If that's how you want to play it? Sure, Thrash sent me."

He hadn't. This demon was working for someone else. She knew it from his dismissive attitude.

"Hand over *Le Diabolique*," the demon demanded, thrusting its blocky hand out for something.

"I don't know what you want!" She tried to scramble away, but a meaty hand slapped onto her ankle.

Overhead flew a tatter-winged demon, screeching wildly. Somewhere, an infant sneezed repeatedly.

Blyss heard someone shout congrats for defeating a demon. A death cry preceded the spill of sticky black blood that spattered her cheek. Struggling against the hand that gripped her ankle, she looked up to spy one of the Saint-Pierre brothers, the dark one with the long hair she'd seen at the gallery. He held a long, curved blade that dripped with black blood.

The demon managed to drag her body across the marble floor. Blyss grasped for chair legs, but they were metal foldables and clattered off balance with every one she grasped.

"Got him!"

Her ankle was suddenly free. Stryke stood over her, repeatedly punching the demon in the face, and finally picked him up and shoved him toward the brother with the blade, who caught the creature on his steel. The demon shattered into black bits that scattered and settled like dust.

And suddenly Blyss stood in Stryke's arms. "You okay? Blyss?"

She nodded, tilted her head against his chest. Demon blood stained his shirt and he smelled of sulfur. Yet when he bracketed her face and kissed her, she returned the seeking touch. Safe. She'd initially sought safety in his embrace that night in the gallery office, but had brushed it off as stupid. But right now, she fell into the feeling.

"I'm so sorry," she muttered. Guilt struck as if a demon's tongue spearing directly into her heart. "This was all my fault."

"What are you talking about? It was a random wedding-crasher incident. Bunch of demons heard about two vampires getting married. That's it. We're all safe."

"No, Stryke, the demon after me wanted it. The diamond. Do you still have it? Where is it?"

He patted his coat pocket, then shoved his fingers in, but they came out with nothing in hand. "Must have dropped it."

"What? No!"

"Listen, Blyss, I don't know what's up with that funky black diamond, or why you slipped it into my coat pocket the night at the gallery, but if there's something deeper going on here, you'd better tell me."

"I...I can't." She tried to stand by herself but it felt as if her knees would give out. "It's too personal. I have to find that diamond." She began searching the floor, strewn with chairs and bridesmaids' bouquets and ripped lace and demon blood. "Please help me find it!"

"Hey, Stryke, you and your date okay?" Vail asked.

"Yeah, we're good. How's everyone?"

"Head count shows only demon casualties. But a few got away. We're sending out a hunting party to track them. You in?"

Stryke nodded. "I'll put Blyss in a cab and then join you."

"Excellent. I've troops to gather." Vail wiped black blood from his face and winced. "That stuff tastes nasty."

Blyss shook her head when Stryke offered his hand. "I can't leave until I've found it."

"It's not here! I must have dropped it, and someone, likely a demon, grabbed it."

"But you don't understand."

Stryke knelt before her. With a stern twist of his finger, he tilted her chin up to look at him. "Enlighten me."

She sighed, weighing the consequences of a confession. She looked around. Everyone was in tatters. A few women were sobbing, but most were celebrating the win, including the bride, who wiped a black smudge from her groom's cheek before kissing him. What a way to start a marriage.

Had this been her fault? Who could know that the diamond would be here? Even she had thought it would be found in Vail's closet.

This didn't make sense.

"I think they came looking specifically for *Le Diabolique*," she said quietly.

"What?"

"I don't know how they knew the diamond was going to be here. But the one that was after me asked for it by name."

Stryke hissed. "What the hell is it?"

"It's just a diamond. I don't know what it means to the demons." Edamite had told her about it. And she had chosen to look the other way and let him have it, no matter the consequences. Because at the time what mattered was securing her future. "I...I have to leave."

He gripped her upper arm tightly. "But you stole it from the gallery. You must know what it means to the demons. Were they the ones you were to hand it off to?"

"No. I don't believe the ones here tonight were working for Ed—"

Blyss pulled away from Stryke and ran for the exit doors. She couldn't do this now. Not this confession. Much as the whole family deserved it. The best thing she could do for them was to get the hell away and never show her face to any of them again.

Stryke followed on her heels, gripping her by the arm again. She could sense his anger and smell his wolf. Whenever her emotions were stirred she could sense her breed. It was disturbing, yet she couldn't deal with that at the moment.

Stryke hailed a cab, which pulled over immediately. He opened the back door, but held her firmly when she tried to enter. "You brought this upon my family?"

"I'm sorry. I didn't know this would happen."

"You admit it?"

She nodded.

"It's over between the two of us."

He shoved her inside the back of the cab, more gently than she'd expected. When she pulled in her feet, he leaned in, looking to say something more. He couldn't meet her eyes. His jaw was so tense. But then he shook his head and closed the door.

Stryke's brothers joined him at the curb, and she saw them talking to him, but Stryke's gaze remained on hers as the cab rolled away.

If they intended on tracking the demons perhaps they would find the diamond.

She'd lost this one. She'd lost…

…everything.

"I can't believe that bitch," Trouble said as the cab drove away. "You're going to let her get away, Stryke? She was the one who brought those assholes on us!"

"Give it a rest, Trouble," Kelyn said. The tall, cool faery bumped his fist gently against Trouble's shoulder. "Stryke never has been lucky at love. The day he finds a good woman…"

Stryke closed his eyes and inside he felt the wince. So he'd had a tough couple of years with women. Blyss had been different. Perfect. A glamour girl so out of his league he'd have to climb a staircase just to touch her feet. And he had known they had an expiration date. He'd even suspected that date was tonight.

Well hell, wasn't as if he'd actually given the relationship any hope. The last woman he could imagine standing at his side while he led a pack was Blyss Sauveterre.

"She screwed you," Trouble said as he wandered down the sidewalk. "This way, guys. The demon scent goes north."

Stryke clenched his fists and turned to follow the half dozen men who intended to track down the demons.

For as perfect as Blyss was, she had cleverly hidden a nasty dark side. How could she have done that to him? To his entire family?

Though really, she hadn't been the one to bring the diamond into the wedding. He had. Blyss had only thought she might find it in the coat pocket where she'd left it. But he had found it that night and had waited for her to ask about it yesterday. When he'd caught her in his closet he'd known what she was looking for, but still, she hadn't said a thing.

If she had been using him, would she really have had sex with him that much? They'd done it more than a few times. And this morning he'd woken in her bed. No means for her to search for the diamond then. It was as if she'd actually wanted to have sex with him for no reason other than that she'd been attracted to him.

He wanted to believe that.

Right now, Stryke didn't know what to believe.

What was important about the diamond? It was black. Yet he'd almost thought to see a glint of red in the center when he'd held it up to the bathroom light. Was it demonic?

Then why was Blyss after it? Had she stolen it from the gallery? Her own gallery? So many questions, and... he shouldn't be asking them. He'd put her in a cab and sent her off. End of story. He did not need her kind of trouble.

Her soft, sexy, seductive kind of trouble.

"You all right, man?" Blade brushed his shoulder as they strode into a dark alley. His older brother didn't talk much, but when he did, he meant it.

"Not sure. I think there's more to this, and part of me thinks Blyss could be in trouble."

"You should follow your instincts."

Wise words from the one brother who had experienced more than his share of pain in his short lifetime. "First let's go kick some demon ass."

"Try to keep up, brother." Blade strode onward, a curved blade clenched in his fist.

As far as a demon slaughter, the results of tracking the demon scent led the crew of wolves and vampires to an empty warehouse. The sulfur trail ended abruptly, and someone conjectured a witch's hex might have facilitated that under-the-radar sneak.

Vail, the vampire leading them, talked to Trouble and Stryke.

"It was probably a wedding crash," Vail decided.

Trouble eyed Stryke hard. Like, why didn't he speak up about his nasty girlfriend? It wouldn't matter if Stryke did reveal Blyss's involvement; they'd come to a dead end.

"Sorry for the disastrous wedding, guys," Vail offered.

"Are you kidding?" Trouble pounded a fist through the air. "Dancing, food and ass-kicking? That was awesome!"

"I'll keep my ears open," Stryke said to Vail as they headed back. "And my nose to the air. I'll let you know if anything turns up."

"Cool. I think it was a spectacular end to a great party myself. And Summer is safe, so it's all good."

Stryke refused Kelyn's offer of a ride home. They were on the right bank close to the huge forest that edged the city. He was pretty sure if he walked east he'd wind up on the Champs-Élysées. That fancy street where she liked to shop.

He didn't want to see her again.

And he did.

He needed answers. And he would get them.

* * *

Blyss rang him in immediately. Stryke wandered through the courtyard. The scents of yew and flowers seemed too fresh and out of place after the night he'd had. He wondered now how Johnny and Kambriel were handling the destruction of their wedding ceremony. Though he distinctly recalled seeing Johnny hugging Kambriel and kissing her amid the melee, while both had brandished blades dripping with black demon blood. And Vail had agreed it had been a hit.

Vampires. Go figure.

The door to Blyss's apartment was open. Stryke walked in, closing it behind him. He wandered down the long hallway to the kitchen. It was well after midnight, but moonlight beamed through the skylight in the adjacent living room, casting a pale glow across Blyss's shoulders. Standing beside the marble counter, with her head bowed, she didn't face him. She sniffled.

"I didn't think I would see you again," she whispered.

"You and me both, sweetie."

"Désolé," she said softly and turned to him. "It means I am sorry."

Stryke rubbed his scalp, winced, then splayed out his hand before him. "I know it's late, but I think you owe me some answers."

She nodded. Shivered.

He couldn't stand there and look at her, fallen and so small. He crossed the floor and wrapped his arms about her, and she stood and pressed her breasts against his chest.

"You mean something to me, Blyss," he confessed. "And if something bad is going on in your life right now

I want to help. And that means you need to come clean about it all. You've got to trust me."

Her fingers clung to his shirt, tugging, tears spilling hotly through the fabric. "Oh, Stryke, it's become so terrible and big. I can't do this alone anymore."

He bowed his head and kissed her temple. "You don't have to. I'm here."

"Were you able to track the demons and…?"

He knew she wanted to ask about the diamond. All he wanted to know was what it meant to her. "Dead end. We gave up. No sign of the diamond."

Blyss's body went weak against his. She pulled him down with her as she collapsed. He lifted her in his arms and carried her into the bedroom. There, he sat on the bed and held her, sobbing gently, until they both fell asleep.

Chapter 8

Stryke woke on Blyss's bed. They'd fallen asleep in each other's arms still dressed. His shoes were on. And everything he touched, lay on or could see was white. Oops. He carefully extricated his hand from under her shoulder but managed to wake her.

"Sorry," he said.

She blinked lush lashes and yawned. "Morning?"

"Yeah, I fell asleep with you. Sorry, I should have kicked my shoes off. Just a little smudge on your bed-sheets."

"Doesn't matter. Oh. I must look a terrible mess. I'm still in my gown." She sat up and caught her fingers in her tangled hair. "Oh, *mon Dieu.*"

"You look gorgeous, as always."

"Please don't lie to me, Stryke. You don't owe me any kindnesses."

He touched her cheek below a faint smudge of black

makeup. "Your eye stuff is a little smeared, but it works for me."

She touched her cheek and looked aside. "I'm so sorry. I promised I would tell you everything last night. I want to. I need to, but..." Her sigh rifled down his spine.

"Why don't I run out for some *pains au chocolat* and orange juice? That'll give you some time to freshen up, and then we can have a chat."

"Thank you. Take the key lying on my vanity with you. You can let yourself back in. That'll give me a chance to take a shower."

He kissed her at the temple, but she flinched. Probably because she suspected she looked a mess. There was nothing about Blyss that could offend him physically. But he was leery about what she would tell him, so he'd not overthink this.

Leaving her in the bedroom, he collected his suit coat and the key. Demon blood stained his white dress shirt, so he buttoned up the coat and strolled outside, through the courtyard and...

What was that scent? Smelled familiar—

Stryke felt an excruciating pain fire at the back of his neck. He immediately knew he'd been clubbed by something more than a fist—and then he blacked out.

Stryke came to and realized he was stumbling down a long steel-walled hallway toward a glass door. Not voluntarily, either. He struggled, but determined the men on either side of him were both taller, bulkier and stronger. The instinctive urge to shift to werewolf tingled at his bones, but he wasn't sure where he was and didn't want to risk wolfing out if there were humans near.

But if these guys were stronger than him he guessed they were not human. When he inhaled, the distinctive scent of sulfur coiled in his nostrils.

What was up with the demons lately? Since arriving in Paris, they had been pointed out to him by Vail and Rhys. They'd crashed the wedding last night. Blyss was somehow inextricably involved with demons.

And now he was being escorted by a pair of demons to the devil knew where.

A glass door opened automatically as they approached, and the demons shoved him through the doorway to stumble forward across a gleaming black marble floor. It was some kind of office. Two walls were all glass, probably many stories up. Rain sheeted the windows. At the opposite side of the room loomed a black desk with a silver lamp upon it and a sleek silver computer. Behind it sat a man with his back turned to them.

"What the hell?" Stryke asked.

The man behind the desk spun around swiftly and snarled. "You brought me *this*?"

Stryke tried not to take offense from the remark, but really? The man's coal hair was slicked back to expose small hematite horns at his temples. And on the knuckles he flexed were also small, gleaming growths that looked like hematite thorns and which Stryke sensed could serve a stinging punch.

"Uh, boss, you said to take him when he leaves the building."

"I did not say *him*," the demon said icily. Below the thorny growths on his fists were dark markings that looked like tattoos, but Stryke suspected they were much more evil in nature. Generally tats on a paranormal were magically enhanced. Bad mojo. "I told you to grab her when she leaves the building. Her!"

"Uh…"

Stryke cast a smirk over his shoulder at the idiot henchman who struggled for an answer to his idiocy.

"Who are you?" Stryke and the man behind the desk asked each other simultaneously.

"I…" The man stood, tugged at his neat black tie and said, "…am Edamite Thrash. Businessman. Collector. Purveyor of Essentials. And you…" The demon's left nostril nudged up. "…smell like a werewolf."

"Stryke Saint-Pierre," he offered, now unwilling to take offense from a demon's snide assessment of him. "Why the nab? Were you going after Blyss? Are you the one she was supposed to get the diamond for?"

Edamite's expression softened from tight disapproval to a surprising smile. "Ah. So you are colluding with her?"

"Colluding? I barely know her. Well—" No need to explain how well he knew her. And no matter how conflicted about the socialite he was at the moment, that was no reason to throw her under the bus to save his ass. "What's going on?"

"Where is *Le Diabolique*?"

"Is that the name of the black stone? I don't know. It was lost last night. A gang of your thugs came after it. Crashed a private wedding."

"My thugs? I do not have thugs, Monsieur Saint-Pierre. They are minions. Tell me exactly who you believe was after the diamond."

"If you don't know your own people, I certainly can't help you there."

"Make him remember, Inego," Edamite said curtly.

Stryke took a punch to the middle of his back, directly on his spine. The pain was beyond belief and he couldn't stand for the sudden loss of muscle control. He dropped to his knees as another thick demon fist swung up into his jaw. Blood trickled down his throat.

He caught the next punch with his palm. The demon sneered at him and narrowed its red gaze—and Stryke forgot about the other henchman, whose claws tore the side of his neck.

He dropped to his palms and spat blood onto the marble floor. These two did not fight fair.

"I don't know anything," he managed to say, wincing at the stinging pain seeping from the cuts. His blood dripped onto the black floor. Assholes.

Swinging back his arm, he called up his claws and delivered triple slices across the face of one of the demons. The henchman stumbled backward, hand gripping the black spurts of blood.

"Cease!" Edamite called as the other demon growled and swung toward Stryke.

Stryke didn't take orders from a demon, so he gripped the henchman's wrist and snapped it back so quickly the bone broke and splintered out from the flesh. Shoving him off to lick his wounds by the other, Stryke turned toward Edamite.

"You next?" he challenged.

"Blyss," Edamite insisted. "How are the two of you involved?"

Retracting his claws, Stryke growled deeply as he stood at full height and stretched back his shoulders imposingly. "I met her a few days ago. The diamond was a surprise."

"So you're telling me Mademoiselle Sauveterre doesn't have the stone?"

Stryke shook his head. Though he knew little about this situation, the feeling that he needed to protect Blyss was strong. Had to be why she had been so frantic about obtaining the diamond. And he could only be thankful they had nabbed him by mistake.

"Are you threatening her?" He punched a fist into his palm. Thrash may look imposing but he wasn't half as built as he was, and Stryke was always willing to jump into the fray.

Laughing, Edamite gestured subtly with a forefinger.

Stryke was suddenly lifted by both minions and pummeled in the face, chest and gut. The punches came so rapidly, he couldn't return with defensive punches. It was all he could do to keep his wits about him.

"Hold him!" Edamite charged.

The horned demon leaned over Stryke and blew a gust of black smoke into his face. Sulfur entered his senses and clutched his brain, causing him to black out.

He came to outside. Sitting against a brick wall. In an alley, he guessed, for both directions to either side led down a narrow path and out to streets where cars passed by. The tarmac was wet and his pants leg and dress shirt were also wet.

Unsure what had gone down, Stryke suddenly had the thought that he'd left Blyss waiting for orange juice and pastries. How long had he been gone? Where had they taken him? He didn't know the city. And he'd blacked out twice, so he had no clue to his whereabouts.

And he hurt. Everywhere. "Damned demons."

He pushed up to a stand and spat blood to the side.

Rubbing his neck, he felt the scabs from the talon cuts. Yeah, this was going to take a good day to heal and feel up to par. But at least he'd gotten in some good punches himself.

Edamite Thrash. Businessman and collector? Purveyor of Essentials? What the heck did that nonsensical bullshit mean?

Didn't matter. "If he's threatening Blyss, he'll have to go through me to even breathe her air."

Stryke winced as he wandered down the alley. Right. The demon *had* gone through him and look who was bleeding now.

He should have wolfed out while in the marble office. Could have taken out those demons, no problem. But he still didn't have all the pieces to a strange and aggravating puzzle.

Blyss could provide some of those pieces.

Turning onto a main street, he caught his reflection in a storefront window. His face was mottled with bruises and his lips swollen. No black eyes, though. Score! Not. And blood drops dotted the front of his white shirt, some red, but more than most black.

"I need a shower."

He tried to button up the suit coat but only one button remained. Wandering down the street, he tucked his head. Thankful his cell phone was still in a pocket, Stryke brought up the GPS app and within a few minutes pinpointed his location. A couple miles walk to Blyss's place. He'd stop at a McDonald's on the way and eat breakfast, then pick up the pastries and orange juice for her. It was already past noon.

He always kept his word. Even if it was a little late.

Chapter 9

Three hours after he'd left, Stryke arrived at Blyss's front door. She'd had more than enough time to shower, put on some makeup, get up her courage to reveal the big secret—and then lose that courage when she'd decided after hour two that he wasn't planning to return. That he'd given up on her. That he never wanted to see her again.

Smart choices.

So when her handsome werewolf lover stood in the doorway holding a bakery bag, a carton of orange juice and smiled through a pair of bruised lips, tears spilled down Blyss's cheek. She hugged him, crushing the bag against his chest, and held on longer and tighter than she probably should have. But it didn't matter. He was here. He hadn't given up on her. And she needed someone on her side right now.

"I didn't think you'd come back." She sniffed away tears.

"Took a long detour."

"I can see that." She stepped back and studied his bruised face and then noted the bloodstains on his shirt. There were more than from last night. "What kind of a detour?"

He handed her the bag and orange juice. "It's an interesting story. I think it'll mesh with what you have to tell me. Or I suspect so. What's with the tears? You didn't miss me that much, did you, glamour girl?"

She nodded and sniffed away yet another tear.

He gestured beyond her. "Let's go sit down and talk."

Blyss hurried down the hallway and put the juice in the fridge, leaving the pastry bag on the counter. She wasn't hungry. And if Stryke was, he could help himself. Taking him by the hand, she led him into the living room, capped by the skylights, which beamed in gorgeous bright daylight. It was too bright for her, and she had probably smeared her makeup when crying, but she resisted the urge to go check it.

It was now or never. She'd never gain his trust if she didn't lay it all out in the open.

"Were you really crying because you thought I wouldn't return?" He brushed his finger under her eye to wipe away a tear.

She nodded. "Men don't usually come back to me. Not unless they want something."

"I do want something. The truth. Because these bruises? Got them from some demon thugs."

"I don't understand." She gently touched his cheek where the bruise was already green and fading. Werewolves healed quickly. "Why are demons after you?"

"They're not after me." He sat on the sofa and patted the seat beside him. "They wanted you. But when idiots are sent to do a job…"

Blyss sat on her knees beside him, tucking her skirt along her legs. Stryke reached for the simple diamond suspended from a platinum chain about her neck and tapped it. It was the only valuable piece of jewelry she still owned. Her father had given it to her after a winning streak so many years ago.

"It's all about the black diamond, isn't it?" he asked. "And Edamite Thrash."

At the mention of that name, Blyss gasped. She bowed her head, catching her breath. It felt as if her heart had leaped into her throat and swallowing it back down was awkward. "Is that who gave you those bruises?"

"I was knocked out in your courtyard as I left earlier. I woke up in a fancy office building and was escorted into the demon's lair. Thrash's idiot henchmen had been charged to bring you to him. And the diamond."

She nodded and drew in a breath of courage. "I was supposed to bring him *Le Diabolique*—that's what the diamond is called—and my debts, both past and future, would be wiped clean. And since our gallery was exhibiting it, it was easy enough to steal. But getting it out of the building without causing suspicion was something else. Lorcan—you met my assistant—he doesn't know, and I didn't want him involved."

"You needed to hand it off to an unsuspecting party for a clean getaway."

She nodded.

"So our little tryst in the gallery office was a ploy to sneak the diamond into my pocket?"

"It started that way."

It was never going to sound good, no matter how she put it. But truly? Something about Stryke Saint-Pierre begged her to let him know her truths. All of them, even the dark, ugly ones.

"You were a dupe I picked out from the crowd. And yet, I keep returning to you for a reason."

"Because you were looking to reclaim the diamond."

"That's one reason."

He crossed his arms over his chest and huffed. "Seems like the only reason to me."

"I could have broken into your apartment and searched your closet. I didn't need to spend more time with you. I certainly didn't need to have sex with you again. And again. I—I wanted to."

He chuckled softly, shaking his head. "Do not tell me you actually feel something for me. I won't buy it."

"I do."

"Please. Miss Precise and Always In Control? Your whole life is planned down to the last detail like your perfect hair and impeccable makeup. I'm one of those details."

"I know it won't hold weight against my confession of using you, but, Stryke, there is something about you. I admire you. And I, well… Let's say when I take a lover it's for one purpose."

"Which is?"

"Because I want something. Material items. Valuable jewels and gifts. I like to be spoiled. I've established a particular lifestyle that enjoys fine things. Sex is a means to getting what I want. But with you…" She dared to meet his brown eyes. "I don't want anything."

He met her gaze with a challenging glare that cut through her heart as if with a silver blade. "Except a large black diamond that glints red and which all the demons in Paris are hungry to get their hands on. Blyss, this is wild. I want to believe you, but this is really..." He sighed. "...fucked."

"I used you to get the diamond out of the gallery. I'm not proud of that, but it was a necessary evil. But believe me, every time we've been together, I was using you for my heart."

He scoffed.

"I like you, Stryke," she rushed out. "Every chance I've been with you was a selfish grasp at something good."

He rubbed his palms over his face. "I like you, too. Despite getting a feeling, that first night, that something weird was up after finding a big black diamond in my pocket."

That he had kept that knowledge a secret when he'd found her snooping in the closet made him as devious as her. Almost. All right, not at all. He was trying to figure things out and had every right to do so.

"I told myself it was probably something Vail left in his pocket," he continued. "But when I found you in the closet looking for the suit, I knew it had been you. That's why I invited you to the wedding and put out the idea that Vail might be wearing the suit. And when I saw you with Vail..."

"I'm sorry. I was desperate. I need that stone."

Stryke sighed and shook his head. "I don't know what it is, but there's something about you that keeps me coming back."

"I feel the same way."

"Then be honest with me, Blyss, and tell me what I

really want to know. Avoiding talk about werewolves bothers me."

"Stryke, I...can't. Not right now."

"Uh-huh. You're asking a lot of me. But if I can shove that elephant in the room aside—which is going to be tough—right now, you need to tell me how you got involved with Edamite Thrash. And what, exactly, this diamond means to him and all the rest of the demons. When I told him demons crashed the wedding, and that I suspected it was over the diamond, he got real nervous. I don't think the demons who showed at the wedding were his thugs."

"You think demons that *don't* work for Ed are the ones who crashed your aunt's wedding?"

Blyss turned on the couch and tapped her lip with her finger as she thought about it. She'd only ever seen one or two henchmen, as Stryke named them, when she had to go to Edamite's office for business. And none had ever come to her home.

They'd taken Stryke from the courtyard? Why hadn't Ed waited for her to bring the diamond to him as they had agreed?

"Ed told me it holds a demon within," she murmured.

"The diamond?"

"Yes. Some evil, powerful demon. I assumed he was going to release it. But that didn't concern me. I just wanted to hand it over to him and..."

Stryke's phone rang but he ignored it. "So if there's some demon trapped inside the diamond, that might be reason for other demons to want it, as well. And maybe they wanted to get to it before Thrash could?"

"It's possible. It's a guess. I don't know much about demons and what they do. Ed is like this kingpin sort of demon. He's got a firm grasp on most of the demon activity in Paris. He also collects all sorts of paranormal ephemera. Dangerous stuff. He buys and sells it like a drug dealer."

And she knew all too well how desperate a person could get for the drugs Edamite sold.

Again Stryke's phone rang, and he checked the screen, but then directed his attention back at her. "How did you get involved with Thrash?"

A fourth and fifth ring sounded. "Would you please get that?"

Reluctantly, he answered. "Hello? It's Rhys Hawkes," he said to her.

She could hear the other side of the conversation because the volume was turned up high.

"Hi, Rhys. Wild wedding last night, eh?"

"Indeed."

"I hope Johnny and Kam are okay?"

"They're fine. Everyone is fine. Just a few scratches and a lost deposit on the building. I understand the woman you invited to the wedding may have had something to do with the demon attack?"

Stryke met her gaze. "I don't know, man." He ran a palm over his short-cropped hair. "Whatever was up last night, she's an innocent. I know it."

Blyss clasped his hand and he squeezed, then winked at her.

"As I've said, there was no harm done," Rhys's voice echoed out. "Normally, I would let it go. Keep a vigilant eye for demons in the future because you know, things happen. But not after what happened early this morning."

"What's that?" Stryke stood, wandering to the window that looked out over the vast sea of Haussmann rooftops.

"Hawkes Associates was robbed," Rhys offered. Blyss had to tilt her head to hear it all. "I found the safe in my office open. The safe I use to store items until they can be placed in a permanent position in the warehouse."

"What was taken?"

"Only one thing. Which is odd, considering the valuable jewels and coins I store for my clients. The silver scepter was stolen."

"Wait. Didn't I just accept a scepter from Tor for you?"

"The exact one. The one missing some stone or jewel in the top."

Stryke turned to Blyss, raising an eyebrow. She shook her head, silently conveying her confusion. She was hearing only about half the conversation now.

"It's a demon scepter," Rhys offered. "So it makes me wonder if that's what the demons were after last night at the wedding. But then I tell myself, no, they must believe I wouldn't walk around with a scepter in hand. So are the two incidents related? I don't know."

"I'm talking to Blyss right now. Can I call you in a bit, Rhys?"

"Sure. I wanted to let you know what was stolen, see if you had any thoughts. It could be entirely random. I'll have to mark it as a loss."

"Right."

"Though, if you had the time, it might not be a bad idea to try to track the scent trail. I can pick it up, but since you handled the scepter most..."

"That's a good idea. I can come over right away.

I'll see you soon, Rhys. Thanks for letting me know about this."

"Sure thing."

"A scepter?" Blyss asked after Stryke had hung up. "I don't understand."

"It was a fancy silver thing. Like something a king holds when he sits on his throne. But it was missing the main piece. You know the top of the scepter is usually clasping a big jewel or probably—"

"Le Diabolique?"

Stryke nodded. "Did Edamite mention anything about a scepter?"

"No, but again, it wasn't important to me to ask questions."

His discerning look said so much, but Blyss wasn't ready to tell him all. "Rhys wants me to come over and try to track it."

"I'll come along."

Stryke lifted a hand, as if to stop her. He gazed into her eyes for so long, she felt his touch, and it was more gentle than she'd expected. Finally, he nodded. "Yeah. You know more than I do. I think it would be a good idea for you to come along. Two noses will serve better than one."

Stryke picked up the trail from the massive safe where Rhys had temporarily stored the scepter. With Blyss at his side, they tracked outside, around the building and down a street for half a mile before he paused and had to focus on the scent of sulfur in order to determine if the trail turned left or right.

"What do you think?" he asked Blyss as he clasped her hand. Focus was required not to get lost in her gorgeous scent. "Left or right?"

"Don't ask me."

He turned to look into her eyes, seeing the glamorous socialite and not the werewolf he expected. She was decked out in a classy black dress and perfect makeup. The shoes were killer, but she'd said she could run faster than he could when he'd questioned whether she could keep up.

"Don't you have the scent?" he asked. "I saw you lean over the storage box in the safe. It's a distinct odor."

She shook her head and brushed a curl of hair from her long lashes. "I'm just following you."

"But I thought you were helping? Blyss, didn't you pick up the scent in the office?"

She shook her head again.

Hadn't she tried to focus on the scent? Or was she so distracted by the crazy goings-on lately that she couldn't find that focus? So much about her baffled him. And there was yet much to learn. They hadn't finished their conversation. She still held secrets. And he guessed those unspoken words were about her werewolf.

But right now, he wanted to stay on the scent. He had an opportunity to prove himself to Rhys Hawkes, and he wouldn't let that go. Because he liked working for the man, and even if he did plan to leave Paris soon, he always did a job 100 percent. He had been the one to bring in the scepter; he felt responsible for its loss.

"Left," he decided, picking up the scent.

Blyss's heels clicked quickly behind him.

"We're nearing the Pigalle," she commented.

"Pig alley?"

"It's the red-light district. At night it attracts tourists and prostitutes. The streets are lined with sex shops and assorted dives."

"Sounds like my brother Trouble's kind of place." He

clasped her hand and they crossed a double-wide street, pausing on the middle intersection to wait for the light. The air was scented with motor oil, some kind of summery flower that blossomed on the nearby trees, and human musk and salt. The faintest tendril of sulfur wavered in and out of his senses. "This way."

"Oh my goddess."

"What?" he asked. The scent lured him toward the black metal doors of a nightclub.

"This is Club l'Enfer. Are you sure you've been on the scent? This place is always occupied by demons. You could have picked up anything."

"Let's go inside and find out." He pushed the door open to expose a black maw and the distant sound of drumbeats. "Ladies first."

Blyss remained on the sidewalk. This was not her scene. She avoided contact with paranormals, and this club was all about the paranormals. Had she never gone to the wedding last night, would she have protected Stryke and his family from this problem? Probably.

"Too scary for you?" he asked with a challenge to his voice.

"This club is generally filled with demons and vampires. I'm not sure werewolves go in there. At least, not often. Maybe I should wait outside?"

He pulled her to him and held her against his body. It was the first time today that he'd taken a moment to hold her. And it felt wonderful. As if only they two existed in the world. And all the bad stuff that had crashed around her shoulders did not exist. He was still wearing last night's shirt spattered with blood and his face was bruised. Yet when he kissed her, she sighed. It was a sweet, quick kiss, but it stole something from her.

And she wasn't sure she wanted that something back.

"I'll hold your hand. It's day. I'm sure it's not rowdy until later, eh?"

She nodded. He clasped her hand. "I won't let anything hurt you."

She wasn't afraid of getting hurt. She'd already been hurt. What Blyss was afraid of was facing the truth that lurked within the darkness.

They strolled inside. Immediately a broad-shouldered bouncer stepped before them. Red eyes glowed as he looked over Stryke, sniffing and then nodding as if he approved. "But what is she?" The bouncer thumbed a thick digit at her.

"Werewolf," Stryke said. "Promise."

Casting a wary summation over her, the demon finally stepped aside and muttered, "Not much going on right now."

They wandered into the din, which was no brighter than the insides of a coffin, Blyss decided. The walls, floor and ceilings were black. The dance floor flashed like red flames set on a low burner. A few people swayed to some recorded heavy-metal music. A few of the dozens of tables held lonely souls before them. Caught in a daze as they stared into their drinks.

It could be any bar that catered to humans. Her kind. But Blyss didn't do bars. Period. She hated the feeling of utter desolation that enveloped when wandering among the drunk and weary-eyed patrons.

A shiver traced her system. She clutched Stryke's hand.

"You still have the scent?" she asked as he scanned across the balcony and over the empty stage.

"No, I've lost it. But whoever stole from the safe at

Hawkes Associates came here. I can feel it. I wonder if we can get through that door over there. Might lead backstage."

He walked around the dance floor and she dutifully followed. Every so often her shoes stuck to the sticky floor, and she winced. This was abhorrent, and it smelled awful. Not so much like demons but like smoke and sex and all the nasty body odors of creatures she'd rather not consider.

If she never recouped her losses, would she someday find herself in such a low and desolate place?

Before Stryke got to the back door, the bouncer once again stood before them. "What are you looking for, buddy?"

"Uh, was tracking a friend. I have his scent." He tapped his nose. "I'm worried about him. Didn't come home last night."

"There's no one back there. I think it's time for you and your pet to leave."

Blyss bristled at the term. The demon did not believe she was wolf and probably assumed she was Stryke's human pet. Ugh. Well, that was as it should be if her world was moving along the trajectory she had planned for it. Not the pet part. Normally she wouldn't be caught dead hanging around a werewolf.

But oh, she couldn't step away from Stryke. Not now. He'd gotten under her carefully applied veneer. And she liked the feeling of him so close to her. Everything about the feeling was wrong. Unless she could make it right. And the only way to do that was to come completely clean to him.

"Let's go." She grabbed Stryke's hand. "I need to tell you everything."

He turned a surprised look on her.

"The scepter can wait," she whispered. "Will you help me?"

"Help you?" His surprise turned to worry, and then he nodded and quickly escorted her outside.

"Let's take the Métro," she suggested because there was a station right across the street. While she avoided the Métro more than she avoided paranormals, she just wanted to be home, where she felt safe, and with Stryke.

Chapter 10

They entered the apartment in a tangle of kisses and groping hands and stumbling feet. Blyss wanted to be a part of Stryke, to feel him all over her. She couldn't deny the combustible attraction she felt when near him. Werewolf or not, she needed to know every part of this man.

"Thought we were going to talk?" he mumbled between kisses to her neck, the rise of her breasts, her collarbone. He slipped off her dress sleeve, his fingers tracing shiver-tickles down her arm.

"I need to know you first," she said on a gasp. "A man. A wolf. I want to feel your strength, Stryke."

"I don't know how this will change things," he said as they stumbled into the bedroom and landed on the bed. "But you won't hear me protesting. Blyss, you're so hot and wanting. My greedy glamour girl. I like that."

"Then give me everything you can," she whispered

as she unzipped and shrugged down her dress. He pulled it off her and tossed it to the floor. The silk would wrinkle; she didn't care. "Get undressed. Quickly!"

He still wore the bloodstained shirt, which was quickly relegated to the floor, followed by his dress trousers, shoes and boxers. That was one rental suit that would not receive a return on the deposit.

She gripped his erection and pulled him onto the bed. She wanted him inside her. She wrapped her body against his and he glided between her legs, entering her, thrusting briskly at first and then slower until they barely moved yet the world swirled around them.

His tongue teased at her nipple. A finger slicked her clit. They maintained the slow rhythm, but it was too much to contain. Release overwhelmed them both and Stryke's body stiffened above hers, his muscles tensing and then relaxing as she shivered into a delicious orgasm. She thought he growled—it was some kind of wolfish sound. And then he collapsed to her side, yet rolled over to kiss her on the shoulder.

"The only time I really know you are werewolf is when we have sex." he said. "You get all hot and bothered and your true nature is revealed."

"It's the only time I can recognize your wolf, as well."

Blyss stared up through the overhead windows. The sky was bright. She felt terrific. Depleted and exhausted, yet also somehow...different. Complete? That a man could complete her was not a belief she subscribed to. Yet she felt somehow *right* lying beside Stryke. Even knowing he could sense her true nature.

And he smelled homey and warm, like sex and salt and everything she wanted to immerse herself in. The glide of their moistened skin against skin allowed her to gauge his strength. And the skim of the stubble on his jaw as he kissed down from her shoulder sent new shivers through her body that felt like joy.

For as little as she knew this man, she felt as if she could trust him. That, of all the people walking this world, this one would accept her.

The time had come to reveal all. Pray, he could accept her awful truth.

"All right." She blew out a breath and brushed aside a curl of hair from her lashes. "This is my story. You may hate me after I've told you, so I am thankful that we've had one last moment together. It means a lot to me, this being comfortable with you. I've never felt like this with any other man. It's so special."

He rolled to his side and propped up on an elbow, catching the side of his face against a palm. "I'm sure there's nothing you can say that will scare me out of your bed. Even demons haven't scared me away from you."

She stroked his neck where the talon cuts had healed yet faint dark lines remained. He nuzzled his face against her hand. It would be so easy to curl up against him and make slow love right now. But she couldn't conceal anything from him anymore.

"You wanted to know how I got involved with Edamite Thrash. I sought him out after learning he might have the fix I needed for my life. It was about six years ago, right after I'd left Valoir."

"You purposely left your pack? Banished?"

"No, I wasn't banished. My brother stood up for me, asking for a lesser punishment. I was expelled with the condition that I could return if I wished. And then, only if I accepted my wolf. I was honored they chose not to banish me."

Banishment was forever and left the werewolf permanently scarred as a sign to others that he or she had been extricated from the pack, usually for a crime against their own or for committing a deed so foul none in the pack could condone it.

Blyss hadn't harmed anyone. Yet her deed could be considered foul by some. Who was she kidding? All in the pack had voted to expel her. Including her mother.

She inhaled a breath of bravery.

"Stryke, my deep, dark secret is that I hate being werewolf. It's nasty, messy and horrible. Ever since the shift came upon me at puberty I've felt wrong. As if I was born into the wrong body. Shifting is not easy for me, and coming back from a shift into this human body is terrible. I feel ugly and— Oh, you're making a face."

His wince smoothed away and he shook his head. "I'm… I don't know what to say."

Who could know how to react? Blyss was aware she was one among millions who felt as she did. She'd never in her lifetime met or heard about other werewolves who denied their very heritage.

"This life I have now?" she said. "The diamonds and glamour and socializing? It is the life I've created that suits me best. No shifting. No fur or claws, or nasty running through the woods on all fours. No feeding on small animals or living among—well, wolves."

She shuddered. Memories of living in the pack were ugly. She had only ever been close to her father and brother, Kir. She rarely saw Kir nowadays. And her father had abandoned his family for another woman when Blyss was younger. Pack Valoir had banished Colin

Sauveterre for his propensity to engage in illicit love affairs with demons and vampires. Now she saw her father a few times a year, and not on her terms, but because he showed up at her door groveling. Sometimes she wished he could get his act together so she didn't feel as if she had to keep an eye on him.

Stryke sat up and brushed his hands over his face. "Blyss, what you're saying… It's like… I don't know. It's like denying your heritage. How can you not be what you were born to be? My mind goes to people who are gay and try to deny it, or even—hell, a person of color who denies their race. It's wrong. I couldn't imagine being anything but wolf."

"Then you should understand that I am not denying what I am but am trying to be what I know I should be."

"That doesn't make sense." He stood and paced beside the bed, the glow from a streetlight worshipping his naked form. His skin gleamed. The tight muscles strapping his thighs and buttocks a lure to her sensual lusts. "You were born a werewolf, yes?"

"Of course. Our breed can only be born."

"Was one of your parents something else? A faery?"

"No, both my parents are wolves. As is my brother, Kirnan."

"You've a brother? What does your family think of you trying to be something you're not?"

"Stryke, I am trying to be the thing I feel I was born to be. And my family…"

Blyss sighed and sat up against the pillow. She couldn't look at him, couldn't face his accusing stare. Yet she felt his concern in her heart. He feared for her even while not completely comprehending her situation.

"My mother thinks I'm insane. My father tolerates

me only because he was banished from the pack a decade ago after he'd had an affair with a demon. And there's the money. I've bailed him out more times than a child should have to. Mom and Kir remain in the pack. Dad lives on his own with his demon girlfriend. And I am where I need to be."

"But you weren't banished from the pack?"

"I can return if I accept my werewolf."

"Will that ever happen? How?" He sat on the bed, leaning in to seek her truths. "How can you not be werewolf?"

"Right before leaving the pack, I heard there was a means to suppress my werewolf. Pills."

"Pills?" He shook his head and exhaled. Again he stood and paced. "You take pills to not be wolf? That sounds impossible."

"I take a pill to prevent my werewolf from demanding release every full moon. I get them from Ed."

"The demon?" Stryke blew out a breath. Hands to his hips, his back to her, he bowed his head, eyes closed. "So that's why you owe him money? Why you needed to get the diamond?"

"A year's supply of pills costs five hundred thousand euros. I take them daily. I do need to shift only one full moon every year. Sort of a means to let out everything I've suppressed. It's awful."

She sensed his utter horror at her confession. His back muscles were tense, as was his neck. He couldn't look directly at her. She had lost him. But there was no turning back now. She had to put it all out there.

"I've but a few pills remaining. And the full moon is closing in. I owe Ed for this year's supply still because I needed to divert the money elsewhere."

"Elsewhere?" he muttered. Sitting on the bed, his back to her, he caught his palms on his knees. "Continue."

"My father has a gambling problem. He was in debt. A nasty bunch of vampires were after him, a tribe who is known to hunt wolves. I paid off his debt thinking I could easily get the money to replace it. I...have a tendency to collect expensive gifts from my lovers. It's how I've survived."

Stryke's body bent forward, his head shaking as he exhaled.

"Not lately, though," she continued. Her heart pounded. Her soul ached for exposing her terrible truths. And she couldn't stop, although she knew every word was only driving a wedge deeper between the two of them.

"When Ed heard that our gallery was exhibiting *Le Diabolique*, he called me in and offered the deal. I had no idea the diamond was anything more than a stone. A demon trapped within? The legend of it is that whoever has held it through history has suffered a terrible fate. It's been in the hands of royalty, thieves, murderers and more royalty. But it's never been in demon hands."

"So you were going to hand over this nasty diamond to a demon, who had plans to do God knows what with it?"

"And in turn Ed would forgive my debt and cover me for the next year's pills. I need those pills, Stryke. Without them..."

"You're just a werewolf." He turned to pin her with an accusing gaze. It felt like silver cutting into her veins and sizzling directly to her heart. "A werewolf like me. Now I understand why I couldn't scent you in the gallery. And why you were so upset when I pinned you for werewolf. You must have been disgusted to know you'd just had sex with a werewolf."

He grabbed his pants and shuffled them up, swinging an arm through his bloodied shirt as rapidly.

"I can't listen to this," he said. "All I've ever wanted my whole life is to fall in love with a beautiful werewolf and make a family. I'm looking for a wife, Blyss. I'm to start a pack so my father can retire. And what happens when I begin to think I may have found that woman? She is the one wolf in the world who doesn't want to be a wolf."

He charged out of the bedroom, shoes in hand.

Blyss didn't call for him to stay. He had every right to be angry. To be disgusted by her. She knew the feeling. She'd been disgusted by wolves all her life.

Until she'd met Stryke Saint-Pierre.

Chapter 11

Stryke kicked off his shoes inside his apartment's kitchen. He tore off his shirt and tossed it across the back of a chair. He strode into the living room, smacking a fist in palm. The intense need to punch something tightened his muscles. He usually matched Trouble while sparring. He could use a punching bag right now.

Blyss didn't want to be a wolf.

What. The. Hell?

He couldn't conceive of such a notion. How could a person not want to be something they had been born to?

Blowing out a breath, he paced before the windows that overlooked the Seine. The view was gorgeous. He should be out touring the city, taking in the summer air, holding hands with a sexy werewolf…

Okay. Stop.

He was a rational man. He was able to look at things from more than his perspective. All his life he'd been a pseudo counselor to his brothers and their troubles, especially regarding women. He could do this.

If he considered what Blyss had revealed to him, he could understand that there were people in this world who wanted to change their circumstances. That no matter how others looked at them, and assumed them to be happy, they might never be happy with their life. So, sure, he could grant that Blyss wasn't happy. Hadn't been happy. And she'd taken measures to find a certain happiness that better suited her.

He shrugged his fingers over his scalp. "But not a wolf?"

Here he'd thought he'd happened upon a good thing. A gorgeous woman, who was also a werewolf, who seemed to like him and definitely seemed to enjoy having sex with him. He'd thought they'd hit it off. Had even allowed himself to take a step toward thinking she could be *the one*.

Yet the truth was, she had been using him. Mostly. He could believe her when she'd explained that initially she'd been looking for a dupe to carry the diamond out of the gallery, and then she'd warmed to him as a lover.

He wanted to believe that. He wanted to believe in something.

But it was too late. Tomorrow his family boarded a plane for the States. So long, Paris, romance and Blyss. Sure, he'd intended to stay a few days longer, but he would eventually leave.

Could he leave her?

"I need a shower." He'd been wearing the same clothes for two days. And he needed a good night's sleep. With hope, the morning would bring a new perspective.

* * *

The morning brought Stryke upright in bed with a name on his lips. "Blyss."

And all the angst he'd been feeling returned. Jumping out of bed and pulling on his jeans and a shirt, he wandered into the kitchen but wasn't hungry, so he swung back into the living room.

A knock on the door jerked him around from his fervent pacing. He marched to the door and pulled it open, cautioning himself from growling. Kelyn and Trouble barged in.

"We're heading to the airport this afternoon," Trouble said. "You packed and ready?"

"No."

"What?" Kelyn asked.

"I…" And he made a knee-jerk decision. "I'm going to stay on for a while longer."

"What the hell for?" Trouble asked. "I mean, the city is cool. It's got sexy chicks walking around, if you can sift through the crazy tourists and find a real Parisian femme, but seriously? I'm so ready to head back home."

"Rhys Hawkes has more work for me." Stryke summoned a simple excuse. "It's interesting work. And I like the city, so yeah, as long as I've a place to stay, I think I'll hang out for a while."

And there was one other, bigger reason.

"What about that chick you brought to the wedding?" Kelyn guessed correctly. "Is it true what I heard that it might have been her fault the demons attacked?"

"That's probably not true." He didn't want his brothers going after Blyss because of something she may or may not have been involved in. Because if Trouble smelled trouble then he'd stick around for the dangerous fun. "It's a complicated deal."

And Stryke didn't want to discuss it with his brothers. They would form an opinion of Blyss, and he'd rather they not think of her negatively. She was a complicated woman. And he decided right then and there that he wasn't going to walk away from her just like that. He couldn't. If there were demons looking for the diamond, Blyss could be in danger.

"Demons or not, she was one hot chick," Trouble said. "Isn't that the kicker? The dangerous ones are always the most exciting."

"Yeah? Then your ultimate match will probably knock you into tomorrow," Stryke offered.

"Hey, I'd like that." Trouble rubbed his jaw and bounced a couple of times on his feet. Boxer's moves. Their eldest brother was a frenetic bundle of energy. "So you want to head out to that street where they sell those chicken sandwiches with all the fries?"

"The Greek restaurant," Kelyn provided.

Dozens of restaurants tucked within the 5th arrondissement served up shredded chicken gyros on soft pita bread, slathered with tzatziki sauce, and piled with veggies and mountains of crispy fries. Heaven.

"Sounds like a plan," Stryke offered. "Is Blade around?"

"Yeah, we'll grab him on the way out the building. We'll get Dad, too. He's been complaining that Mom made him take her to all the froufrou restaurants that serve a carrot stick and a blop of mush."

Stryke grabbed his shirt and shoved his feet into his shoes. He needed a hearty meal and some time hanging with the guys. He could worry about the crazy werewolf glamour girl later.

* * *

Blyss pulled a bottle from the wine cooler, turned around—and dropped the bottle on the marble floor. The glass shattered. Cool liquid splashed her ankles, and shards of glass cut across her bare feet.

Edamite Thrash stood in the kitchen. His pale gray eyes narrowed on her, his mouth equally as narrow. The horns at his temples caught the sunlight with a glint. She hadn't heard him enter, but she knew he was powerful. He must have the ability to transport himself wherever he wished. She wasn't up on demon abilities. Didn't want to be up on them either.

"Cabernet 1945?" he asked. "Pity."

With a sweep of his hand, the black glass pieces re-formed into the bottle, and the wine puddles refilled it. The undamaged bottle found its place onto the kitchen counter.

Blyss was no longer in the mood for a glass of wine. She'd been anxious and had sought something to calm her nerves. Yes, at eleven in the morning.

"What are you doing here?" she had the audacity to ask.

"Talked to your lover yesterday. He's a werewolf," Ed said with unexpected surprise. "What's up with that? I thought you were anti-werewolf?"

"It's complicated" was all she could answer. Because it was. And she didn't want to chat with Ed. "I'll get the diamond. I promise."

"My confidence in you actually accomplishing that task has waned." Another gesture of his fingers glided her across the floor to stop abruptly before him.

Blyss stepped back but her thighs met the countertop, keeping her an arm's reach from the demon. "I'll find it. I need to."

"Right. Because you're almost out of pills. Full moon on the horizon. Without those pills you'll be getting your wolf on. That is, if you live that long."

Blyss held her breath. The threat was nothing new.

"Are you aware a demonic scepter has also been stolen?" he queried. He pressed his fingertips together before his chest. The deadly thorns on his knuckles glinted menacingly. They looked as if carved from obsidian, and Blyss knew one slice from them could render most dead from the poison contained within.

"No. A scepter? What does that have to do with the diamond?"

"Everything. The diamond fits into the head of the scepter. Once *Le Diabolique* is placed in its rightful position, the scepter is capable of releasing the demon contained within. Xyloda is what it is called."

Her jaw dropped open. "But I thought that's what *you* wanted to do with it?"

He did want to release the demon. Or so she had assumed. He hadn't actually told her what his plans for *Le Diabolique* were.

"You think to know so much?" he asked in a measured tone.

Did she? Or did she only assume she knew his plans for the diamond? What else could he possibly have wanted it for?

Ed tilted his head to study her, his eyes glowing red. She noted a surprising change in his expression. The icy hardness melted at the corner of his tight mouth. And the red glow receded.

"A ritual is required," Ed continued. "The blood of

twelve demons is required to release Xyloda from *Le Diabolique*. Twelve rare demons."

"Well, if they're rare—"

"Silence."

She did not tolerate a man speaking so rudely to her, but she knew better than to stand up to Edamite Thrash.

"All that means is you've yet time to obtain that which I've tasked you to get for me. And I have no choice but to let you seek it because you have a connection to the one man who may be able to sniff it out."

"Stryke? But—"

Ed flicked his fingers toward her. Blyss's feet left the ground, and her chin tilted up as if he was lifting her. "Bring me *Le Diabolique* before the moon is full. If you do not, I will kill your father. And then I will kill your mother and your brother. Then I will take off the Saint-Pierre werewolf's head while you watch. But I won't kill you, because to watch you shift to the one thing that appalls you most will give me great pleasure."

Blyss dropped to her feet and Ed disappeared from the kitchen. She caught herself from falling to her knees by grasping the counter behind her and leaning across it. Teardrops splashed the marble surface. Her heartbeats clambered against her rib cage.

How was she going to find *Le Diabolique*?

She needed Stryke's help. And he had walked away from her, disgusted by the choice she had made with her life.

Chapter 12

Blyss watched from a distance as the Saint-Pierre family piled into a stretch limo and rolled away from the island. En route to the airport, no doubt. Stryke had mentioned they were here for only the week.

Too late. She'd missed him! Now what to do?

She should have never agreed to get the diamond for Thrash. Yet Ed had always treated her well in the years she had been buying the pills from him. Today had been the first time she had felt genuine fear being near him. What evil would he unleash on the world when he finally got the diamond and scepter? What was the demon Xyloda? She shivered to consider the menace of which it could be capable.

A walk had felt necessary to rid herself of the anxiety, and she'd needed to get out of her home and away from the spot where Ed had stood and threatened her.

The Île Saint-Louis had been a long stroll in her heeled Louis Vuitton suede boots. Good thing they were comfortable. And now her only hope had left. He'd washed his hands of her. Yet she had been compelled here, to where he had stayed. Because she hadn't known where else to go. And she thought that maybe, if she offered to pay Stryke, he would stay and help.

Of course, she hadn't any money. The only thing of value she hadn't hocked yet was the diamond she wore around her neck. It wasn't worth more than five thousand. A pittance to what she owed Thrash. Could it have been enough to interest Stryke in tracking demons for the one woman he must hate more than demons?

Didn't matter anymore. She was alone with no one to turn to.

A hand glided up Blyss's back, and she spun about, prepared to slap whoever touched her— "Stryke?"

"Sorry to scare you. I saw you standing here and couldn't figure out why."

Lowering her hand, she offered a shrug. "I was… I thought you had gone. I saw your family drive away."

"Headed home to Minnesota. They've had enough tourism for a while. I, on the other hand, am looking forward to a trip to the Eiffel Tower today. Might even take the stairs to the top. I hear that line is shorter."

"Infinitely shorter. I imagine a man like you could run up the stairs and not feel winded when you reach the top."

He shrugged. "I need to let off some steam. The workout will do me good."

He probably needed that workout because of her. Blyss looked aside, not wanting to look into his bright brown eyes because she knew she'd see the hurt there. Hurt caused by her.

"So, you're staying?" Her voice cracked slightly. "Just to do the tourist thing?"

"Yep. There are a lot of sights I'd like to see."

She nodded and looked aside. Dare she ask him for help? No, she couldn't. He owed her nothing. And she had already taken too much from him.

"I'm sorry I left the way I did last night," he offered.

"No. You had every right. I'm not the most upstanding person."

"Don't say that, Blyss. You were doing what felt right to you."

"Thank you. You are quite the man."

"Yeah, well, I was too hasty. Judging you. I shouldn't do that. I don't want to do that. You have every right to feel the way you do about your...werewolf thing."

"It's what I'm comfortable with."

He touched her chin, forcing her to look at him. "I think I could be comfortable with you."

"You're lying to yourself. You want a werewolf, Stryke. You want the picket fence and the pack. I can't give you that happily-ever-after." And her heart cringed because it was a truth she despised.

"All I want from you right now is trust," he said.

"I do trust you."

"And maybe companionship?" His eyes gleamed with sunlight. "I do have another reason for staying. You. We've started something. It's a weird something, to be honest with you. But it's a something that I don't want to end so abruptly. If that makes any sense."

"You really mean that?"

He kissed her. Hand gliding along her neck and up

the back of her head, he held her there as the kiss mastered her, filled her. Spoke to her all the things he probably couldn't put into words. It said: *let's try this*. At least, that was what she hoped it said.

"I'm going to keep my options open," he said as he pulled away. "But you know, I'm not rich. I suspect I'm not exactly tops on your wish list either."

"I think it's high time I focus on something beyond the material."

"Really? Because if you owe some asshole demon half a million dollars, I'd think right now would be an excellent time to focus on laying your hands on some cash."

Blyss smiled. "You'd think. But I don't want that from you." Then she sighed, because she did want something from him. And it wasn't an easy friendship or a sexy kiss. "Time for total honesty and the reason I'm here. I need to track *Le Diabolique*. You know why?"

"I suspect Thrash has threatened you."

"He's now threatened to kill my entire family if I don't bring him the diamond by the full moon. He told me there's a ritual required to call the demon out from the stone and it requires the blood of twelve demons. It'll take a while for whoever has the stone to collect all those demons because they are rare. I hate telling you this, because once again, I need something from you."

"Just ask, Blyss. I stayed in Paris because I want to help you."

"You—you did?"

He nodded.

She swallowed down the lump in her throat. His generosity was immense and so selfless. And she deserved none of it. He was truly one in a million. She couldn't afford his kindness.

"Blyss, talk to me. Tell me what you need."

"I, uh…" She exhaled. For all he knew about her, he was still standing before her. And that meant a lot. "I need your expertise in tracking. I need your help locating the diamond. I need so much from you and I've done nothing to deserve it."

"You need help. That's all that matters."

"It shouldn't be. I should have, at the very least, done something to deserve your help."

He leaned in and kissed her again before whispering, "You've touched my heart. That's reason enough."

She didn't want to cry. She didn't deserve his kindness or his sweet words. He was being too nice. And she didn't know why. But right now, she didn't have time to question that kindness.

"How will we find the diamond?" she asked softly.

"We need to go back to Club l'Enfer. I think Johnny, the groom, knows the place. I'll give him a call and see if he's got a suggestion how to get into the back rooms. Come on."

He grabbed her hand while he pulled out his phone with the other. Walking her up to his apartment, Stryke talked to Johnny while they did so. By the time he opened his front door, he closed the phone and gestured to walk inside.

"Johnny said the place is owned by Himself. It's a demon and vamp hot spot."

The devil Himself owned the place? Blyss shivered.

Stryke embraced her from behind, nuzzling his face aside her neck. "You're not coming along with me this time. L'Enfer is no place for a woman like you."

"You mean a silly girl who walks around in diamonds and high heels?"

"I mean, a woman who will most likely be construed as only human. You don't give off the werewolf vibes, Blyss. The bouncer thought you were my human pet before. It's best you stay behind."

"But I don't want you to go there alone. It's dangerous. Can Johnny go with you?"

"He's on his honeymoon. He suggested I check with Vail. It would be better to go in with numbers than alone. Why don't I walk you home? Then after dark I'll go check out the club. It'll be wiser to go there when the place is full. Best chance to find whoever might have taken the diamond."

"I'd like to stay here until you go. If you don't mind? I won't bother you. I'll just curl up on the couch with a book or something."

Stryke chuffed. "No books in the place. Much to my annoyance. Though there is a travel guide on the coffee table. Let's do this. We'll head out for a nice meal, an afternoon of chatting, getting to know one another beyond what we've done in bed."

"Sounds lovely, and I don't deserve—"

Stryke kissed her quickly, then said, "Stop telling me what you don't deserve. You deserve whatever I'm willing to give you. And what I want to give you is another kiss."

And that kiss was the best kiss Blyss had ever received. Because it was a promise. The man wore integrity like a brightly gleaming badge. And with his kiss he gave her hope and the desire to make his dreams come true.

Happily-ever-after? Blyss didn't believe in the fantasy. But maybe it was worth a try?

Blyss handed Stryke her mobile after they'd been seated in The Lounge Club in the Hotel Regina. She loved this cozy restaurant and had eaten here a few times.

"Put your number in there," she said. "And…you can copy mine, if you like."

He took out his phone and did so, with a wink to her. "Why do I sense I've just crashed some golden gate that would normally be bolted and barred with digital codes that not even a seasoned thief could crack?"

She took her phone back and tucked it in her purse. "I never give my number to a man. You have cracked my code, Stryke. And I'm not saying that because I need help from you."

"I can tell when you're being genuine. You look me directly in the eye and it's as though I can see clear into the next life in those gorgeous greens of yours."

"That's quite a distance. What's going on in the next life? And where are you?"

"I'm right here, sitting next to you," he said and moved around the curved bench so their shoulders hugged. "Is it cool if I sit so close?" He stretched his gaze about the room. "Kind of a fancy place. I don't want you worrying about whispers."

"Let them whisper," she said and tilted her head to kiss his cheek. "Mmm, you always smell good. But you don't wear cologne."

"It's all me, glamour girl. Plain, showered and just your average wolf."

She tilted her head with a smile. "You're not an average anything. Most especially not a, er…"

"You don't like the topic of wolves much, do you?"

"I strive to walk a life parallel to all things wolf. I respect the breed. I just don't relate to it. As for you, I imagine your perfect life would involve living in some country cabin surrounded by miles of forest. Having a werewolf wife who is barefoot and pregnant, busy creating the pack you so desire."

"You hit it on the head. But she doesn't have to be barefoot if she doesn't want to be."

"So Louboutins would be all right?"

"I don't even know what that means."

"Louboutins are a brand of shoe. I own many pairs."

"Ah. Those sexy pumps you're always wearing? Not sure how they'd go over out in the country. Kind of *Green Acres*. But I could get into that fantasy."

"Green Acres?"

"Yeah, it's a TV show from decades ago that featured a New York millionaire and his wife who packed up and moved to the country. He embraced the farmer's lifestyle while she wandered about in her pretty clothes and shoes and dreamed of moving back to the big city."

"So they eventually divorced?"

Stryke smirked and sipped from the water goblet. "Nope. They were in love. Love conquers all challenges."

"Getting the heel of my Louboutin stuck in the mud is not a challenge I ever want to face."

"I know that about you. Don't worry, glamour girl. I won't toss you over my shoulder and haul you out to the country. Unless you ask me to." His wink softened the tension in her neck and melted the bars about her heart.

If he kept saying the right words she might follow him anywhere.

The waiter arrived and Blyss could but sigh. Having Stryke toss her over his shoulder and take her anywhere he pleased sounded like a delicious adventure. And if she had to, she'd even trip across the forest floor in her Louboutins if she knew he waited for her with his arms held open.

"Uh, Blyss?"

She waded out of her thoughts and back to reality. The waiter frowned at Stryke.

"You'll have to handle this one for me," he muttered conspiratorially. "This guy isn't much for my English."

"Of course." In French, she ordered him filet mignon and a nicoise salad for herself. A bottle of Krug sounded lovely, but she declined. She hadn't the finances to cover the cost, and she didn't want to put Stryke out.

Wow, this roughing it was really quite a change from the usual tossing aside all caution and ordering anything she might care for, along with the wine. But as well, it felt strangely freeing. Blyss the socialite would frown upon the man sitting next to her in jeans and a T-shirt.

Who was she now that the very sight of Stryke's easy confidence and devil-may-care smile tapped into all her desires and made her lean in toward him for any contact she could manage?

"So what am I eating tonight?" he asked.

"It'll be a surprise."

"If it's frog legs…"

"Don't worry." She kissed him on the cheek. "I may not know how to cook, but I do know how to take care of my man."

"So no cooking? Ever?"

She shook her head. "I was never taught. I have standing meal orders from the area restaurants. Cooking is not something that interests me." She smiled again. "Yet another mark against me on your list, I suppose?"

"I don't have a list."

"Really? Your *Green Acres* fantasy doesn't appeal to me," she offered. "And you really do need a wolf. Someone who can race through the woods with you."

He did. And yet. "You say that with a certain reverence. Memories from childhood of doing just that? Racing through the woods?"

She shook her head. "I doubt it. I've forgotten a lot of my childhood. I don't think of it. It's not important to me."

"Or maybe the mask you wear won't allow you to think about all those things you left behind?"

She clasped both palms about the wine goblet, but didn't drink. "I do wear a mask. It's the woman I let the world see."

"The woman running away from the wolf?"

Her fingers curled more tightly about the goblet. Stryke wasn't about to retract that question. She was hiding from things she didn't understand. "When you came into your wolf, didn't anyone show you the ropes? Guide you along?"

"I don't want to talk about this."

He touched her wrist. "It's important to me. I want to learn about you, Blyss."

"Why? We don't have a future together. Haven't you figured that out yet?" Why had she said that? Her cruelties would push him away. And yet, cruelties were a part of the mask that protected her from heartbreak.

"I know our future isn't bright," he offered. "But I

like you. And I'm here right now, for good or for ill, trying to help you out. Will you at least talk to me?"

She nodded. Because moments ago she had been grasping for the fantasy at Stryke's side. Could she risk the heartbreak? It could be worth it, if only to have these few wondrous days with the most amazing man she had ever known.

"I used to go to a public school," she said softly. Fine. The final bits of her truth must be revealed. Her mask cracked and fell away.

"Ah." Stryke nodded knowingly.

"It was during my sophomore year. That awkward time for teenagers."

It was difficult enough to go through puberty and gain the need to shift and heightened senses, and hell, the desire to howl at odd moments. But to do it in a public school, surrounded by humans who sought any little oddity to tease? Why hadn't her mother warned her? Or even allowed her to complete her schooling at home?

"Did you ever see that movie *Carrie*?" Blyss asked. "It was sort of like that. Only my first shift came on me during an outdoor track event. I began to shift and raced into the nearby woods. The wolf came upon me so fast, my clothes tearing and falling away. And, as you know, you shift right back from *were* form and are left there naked and stunned by what just happened. I was found by a group of mean girls. They hadn't seen the shift, but finding me naked without an explanation? I can't even talk about it."

He clasped her hand, and she melted against his shoulder, sniffling back tears. To show such emotion in a public restaurant was unthinkable, but she couldn't stop the tears that needed release. And, thankfully, she felt safe with Stryke holding her hand.

"I know it's stupid," she started.

"It's not stupid. Your pack should have prepared you for the first shift. Your…mother?"

"She's always been self-possessed. And my brother was much older than me. He'd been out of school for years. He's an Enforcer."

"What's that?"

"Sort of a werewolf cop. We police our own here in Europe. Kirnan is one of the highest-ranked wolves in pack Valoir under the principal and the scion."

"You're proud of him."

"I am. I wish we could be closer. But I struggled with my wolf so much after that first shift. I wanted out of it all as soon as I could make it happen."

"When did you leave your pack?"

"When I was seventeen. A vampire in school be-friended me. We weren't like besties, but he was kind and told me about some girls who went clubbing at the elite clubs and were able to…" She sighed.

There was a limit to removing the mask. She didn't want to tell Stryke all the things she had done in order to survive on her own. All that mattered to her now was what happened to her moving from this day forward. Desperation had gotten her to this point. She didn't want it to continue.

"Are you happy?" he asked.

She tilted a look up at him. His deep brown eyes gentled her anxiety. And yet… "I'm not sure what happiness feels like."

The confession gripped at her heart. No one should

ever have to confess such a thing. And yet it was her truth. Her deepest, darkest truth.

"Being with you makes me happier than I've been in a long time," she whispered. "But I've already gone and spoiled my chances of us ever having a trusting relationship."

"And I am a wolf. Not your favorite kind of guy."

She smiled through tears. "I've never actually given a wolf a chance. You seem pretty cool to me. Not half as hairy as I'd expect."

"Wait until you see me wolfed out. Which probably won't happen. Because the glamour girl keeps away from all that mess. The full moon is in a few days. Don't you need your pills? What will happen if you don't get them?"

"I'll shift. I do it once a year, as I've explained. I hate it. It's so messy."

"If messy is the worst complaint you've got about the shift then maybe you just need to learn to let your hair down and…"

Stryke's phone rang. He didn't want to take the call—it would be rude, he gestured—but Blyss encouraged him to dismiss himself to the lobby. It could be important. Promising he'd be right back, he headed out of the restaurant.

"Vail? Sorry, I'm out with Blyss at some fancy restaurant. What's up?"

"I found a witch who might have some information on the demonic ritual that's required to release *Le Diabolique*. I figured if you knew what you were dealing with you might be able to stop it before it happens."

"Works for me."

Vail gave him the witch's address and said she expected him tonight. She said he'd know the house when he arrived; it was the only octagon-shaped house in the city.

When he returned, he discovered the food had arrived at their table. Maybe. Was that tiny medallion of dark stuff on his plate the food? And there were three peas artfully arranged around it in a dash of red stuff.

"Filet mignon," Blyss offered. Her salad looked much more filling, but Stryke nodded politely and sat.

He wasn't sure if he should cut the thing or swallow it whole, but to be polite, he made nice by cutting it in six small pieces. The peas barely topped off the meat in his stomach.

By the time the bill arrived and he handed the waiter his credit card, he was praying she wouldn't hear his stomach growl.

Blyss leaned over and kissed him. "Not full?"

"Well, uh…"

"Please. That wouldn't have filled a baby, let alone a strapping man like you."

"I'm good." For about five minutes, he figured. "That was Vail on the phone. Want to visit a witch?"

"I wouldn't place it on my top-ten list of fun things to do, but sure. Why not?"

Chapter 13

The witch's house was indeed an octagon. Eight white walls, capped by a turret-like roof and red slate tiles. The yard was larger than most in the neighborhood and was filled to the edges with lush green plants, trees and shrubs so abundant they looked as if they belonged in a tropical climate.

Stryke pushed open the creaky iron gate and someone popped up from behind a shrub. A tall, broad-shouldered man with dark hair and a keen stare. He wore a leather apron filled with gardening tools wrapped round his hips, and chain-mail gloves clasped a particularly nasty strand of thorned vine.

"Who are you?" the man insisted, eyeing both Stryke and Blyss with a pit-bull sneer.

"We're here to see Libertie St. Charles."

"It's rather late for a social call."

"I called earlier," Stryke offered.

"Ah yes. You the werewolf with the demon problem?"

Stryke nodded. He didn't sense the man was anything but mortal, but he could feel strength resonate from his body. He decided then and there that he'd be an equal match to him should the need to go head-to-head arise.

He was thinking like Trouble. Always assessing the possible competition. *Just be cool,* he coached inwardly.

"Go ahead, then." The gardener stepped forward happily. "I'm Reichardt, Libby's boyfriend. She's inside making cookies. Be sure you do not leave without sampling a cookie."

"Thank you," Blyss said as they wandered down a mossy stone path to the front door.

Twilight painted a beam of setting sunlight across the path. Stryke wasn't a fanciful sort, but he thought he saw a twinkle skitter amid the tall blades of emerald grass. Nah. Couldn't be. Maybe?

The red front door magically opened inward when they'd breached the top step. Stryke and Blyss exchanged glances.

From within the house, a woman called out, "Come in! I'm in the kitchen."

Blyss clasped his hand and they wandered beneath a massive crystal chandelier in the center of the living room. He bent to kiss her and whispered, "It's going to be okay."

"Thank you," she whispered, but he sensed a catch to her voice.

She was nervous. And he was, too. Not about talking to a witch, but rather, *could* he actually help Blyss? Was he promising her something he couldn't deliver?

He wasn't sure how to track *Le Diabolique* now that the trail had gone cold. He hoped the witch had an idea.

Through swinging white doors, they entered a cheery, vast kitchen that smelled of melted chocolate and brown sugar. A woman wearing a curve-hugging purple dress and a white-and-pink polka-dot apron stood up from closing the stove and turned with a wide smile on her face, which was framed by red hair.

"You must be Stryke Saint-Pierre," she said, offering her hand to shake. "Mmm, firm grip. Definitely werewolf."

"And this is Blyss Sauveterre," he introduced his anxious partner.

The women shook hands. "Your hair is gorgeous," Blyss offered. "So vibrant."

"Thanks. It's natural. As is everything else," she said with a slide of hand over her ample hip. "I'm not getting a read on you, though, sweetie. Werewolf?"

Blyss nodded.

Libby leaned closer to Blyss as if to peer into a child's eyes. "You sure, sweetie?"

"I, uh, take pills to suppress my wolf."

"Ah." Libby righted. "That explains it. No judgments here."

Yet she did slide her eyes down Blyss's figure in an assessment that Stryke felt was more judging than she would admit.

"So, you two are wondering about the *Diabolique* diamond and the spell to remove the demon from within? Who would want to release that nasty demon? I mean, seriously? You know the demon's name? Xyloda. Sounds like some kind of prescription drug that'll screw you up big-time. Ha!"

"We would like to keep the demon inside the stone," Stryke said. "But most important, we need to find the stolen diamond and…" Then he'd hand it over to Blyss and let her do as she wished with it.

But would that make him responsible for unleashing untold evil if Blyss handed the stone to Edamite Thrash and he then released the demon within? Stryke could not live with that.

Now was no time to state his doubts. First, they had to actually find the missing diamond.

"Come with me," Libby directed, taking off the apron and hanging it on a hook near the door. "I've found the spell already."

She led them into another clean, bright white room. It was some sort of study or lab, and the table stretching in the middle was glossy and high-tech. It was lit by halogen lights from beneath the glass surface of the table. As well, the cupboards hugging the room were glass and lit with bright white light.

"The spell room," Libby offered. "My sister Vika designed it. She's into ultraclean high-tech stuff. I prefer a little less order to my things, but I haven't gotten around to making it less sterile, if you will. Been spending most of my time with Reichardt. He used to be a soul bringer, but now he's completely mortal and learning all about the world. He loves to garden."

"Isn't a soul bringer an angel?" Stryke asked.

"Yep. Used to be, anyway, until he took his earthbound soul. I gave it to him. Held his halo above his head and—bam! Mortal. So. You two a couple?"

"Yes," Blyss offered, while at the same time Stryke wasn't sure how to answer.

He glanced at Blyss. She smiled up at him. He took her hand and kissed it. "Yes," he said. "We are."

At least until she got what she wanted.

Which he was oddly okay with. He wanted her to be safe and to have the life she desired. And if that meant not being a werewolf? He'd hand over the diamond and kiss her goodbye. Remember his adventure in Paris forever. And lament a lover lost. On to the next story.

Right?

He met Libby's green gaze and sensed she understood what he was thinking. Could she read his doubt?

"So the weird thing is…" Libby pulled a white linen cloth away from a large, ancient book that sat on the center of the white table. "…we happened to have a demonic grimoire in the library. Not sure how or why. My sisters and I only practice light magic. Demonic magic is very dark. Malefic, even. We leave that stuff for Vika's man, Certainly Jones. He's a dark witch, but the world needs dark magic to balance the light, you know?"

Stryke had no clue about magic and how it worked or what the various forms were. He did know Desiderial Merovech, who lived back home, an ancient witch who was the keeper of the Book of All Spells, an actual grimoire that contained all magic spells ever written or cast. It was constantly, and magically, updating itself. Creepy, but kind of cool. And she had saved his life when he'd been nicked by a hunter's silver-tipped arrow. As well, she had helped Blade recover from a torture so heinous his brother had been forever scarred by it.

So magic was cool, in his opinion.

"This is it." Libby pushed the book forward. Stryke and Blyss stood on the opposite side of the table. Both leaned forward to look over the old paper with dark writing scribbled across the page. "Don't get too close," she warned. "The magic will sense your innocence."

"I don't think I have to worry about that," Stryke joked.

"There are degrees of innocence," the witch stated seriously. "You are innocent of all malefic magic. At least, I hope you are."

"Right." Stryke stepped back a pace along with Blyss. "What does it say?"

"Is it written in Latin?" Blyss asked.

"Yes. It details the spell, and how when all the blood sacrifices have been made, then they must be added to the stone to release the demon."

"Blood sacrifices?" Blyss said on a gasping tone.

"Twelve demons must be sacrificed simultaneously," Libby explained. "They are each a different breed of demon and some quite rare. It may take a while to gather them all. Which could buy you two some time."

"Does this spell list the twelve demons?" Stryke asked.

"It does. Why don't I copy it out in English so you can understand it? It won't take but ten minutes. While waiting, the two of you go help yourself to some cookies."

Reichardt waited with the plate of cookies in hand. Stryke politely took one, but after the first bite, he nabbed two more. The former soul bringer nodded in agreement as the threesome enjoyed the most delicious cookies Stryke had ever tasted.

The conversation was stilted, but he did manage to seem enthusiastic over the clump of silvery-green herbs

Reichardt showed them and asked them to smell. Very pungent and not like any kind of cooking spice he'd ever encountered.

"For death spells," Reichardt said with a wink. "I harvest it for Certainly Jones, Libby's brother-in-law."

"The dark witch," Blyss confirmed at Stryke's lifted brow.

"Right. Witches are an interesting bunch," Stryke said.

"Indeed."

Libby spilled into the room on an air of hyperenthusiasm and before handing Stryke the list apologized for the hearts dotting the *I*s. "Reichardt thinks it's funny I do that. I just like to spread the love," she said. "The world is desperately short on love, isn't it? Well, save for Reichardt and me. He's my sweetie."

"And she's changed my air."

"Aww, I adore you, lover." The witch kissed her cookie-eating former soul-bringer gardener of a boyfriend.

Hugging both of them, and sending them off with a spoken spell for their best future, Libby and Reichardt watched them leave down the path before closing the red door.

"Now what?" Stryke asked as he handed Blyss the spell.

"I don't know. I thought you might take the lead."

He wrapped her into his embrace. "I can do that. I need some time to think about it. I have no idea where to start hunting for demons. Want me to take you home?"

"Sounds good."

"How about we head to my place and muddle over what we've got?"

She nodded and turned against his body, allowing him to lead her. She was lost and fragile, and he didn't want to hurt her or break her.

But was it even possible to protect her from the ultimate harm? If they couldn't find the diamond, she'd never get more pills. And without that Blyss would have to face the one thing she had kept out of her life so well.

Blyss had not balked when Stryke had suggested they pick up chicken gyros on the way. Food was a necessity after that pitiful afternoon snack he'd had at the fancy hotel. He suspected fast food was the last thing she would ever eat, but as she settled before the white marble counter in her kitchen and forked in her first taste, he noticed her shoulders relax and she even smiled as she sipped wine.

"Not bad," she said. "This came from that sorry little restaurant? I'm impressed, even. I've never walked in the 5th where all the tourists go."

"That is not a surprise." He swallowed a few bites, eating the sandwich as it was meant, with both hands instead of a fork. This was heaven. He should have ordered a couple for himself. "You like neat and orderly. I think it's time…" Stryke dipped his finger in her wineglass then snapped it toward her chest, dispersing red droplets across her skin and blouse. "…you get messy."

"Stryke, don't. This is silk—I wish you wouldn't."

"Wishes don't always come true, glamour girl."

He bent to lave the wine off her skin with a lash of his tongue. Blyss's protest ceased with a pleasurable moan. He'd never thought to pair wine with chicken gyros, choosing water to go with his, but this vintage was delicious. Or probably it was because he now followed a droplet down between her cleavage and caught it as it curved along the side of her breast.

Blyss stroked his hair. She slid a leg along his thigh and cooed. She was in the mood. And so was he. But first, he had a point to make.

He picked up the goblet, and before she realized what he would do, he poured the remaining wine down the front of her chest, soaking into her silk shirt and down her belly. She jumped, but he caught her by the wrists, drawing her close and pressing his tongue against her slick skin.

"But my blouse—"

"Fuck the silk," he growled. "I'm going to mess you up, glamour girl."

Stryke pulled her blouse off and Blyss let it fall to the floor where the wine had puddled. The shirt was a loss. And the man remained determined as he lapped his tongue up her stomach to her breasts, where he circled around one nipple and then the other. She almost wished there had been more wine. She would have poured it over her skin.

But what he did next made her shriek and struggle to get away from him. He reached for her plate, slapping his fingers on the food. White cucumber sauce coated his fingers. He then smeared the cool goop over her stomach.

Blyss backed up against the fridge, moaning at the ickiness of it—until his tongue lashed over her hip and up along her side where the sauce had been painted.

She couldn't prevent a satisfied moan. Even as she gripped his head, wishing his hair was longer for a good hold, and tried to pull him away, with her other hand, she pulled his shoulder closer, wanting him there, everywhere on her skin. Tasting, licking, teasing.

"I like the red sauce, too," he murmured.

When he reached for the plate again, she grabbed a handful of the finely shaved chicken and fries and tossed it at him.

Stryke gave her an incredulous gape. "Really?"

"You want to get messy?" she challenged.

Her clothes were ruined. And she didn't see a way out of this mess unless she fought. So fight she would. She grabbed another handful of lettuce and sauce, and lobbed it against his neck and shoulder. She dashed away from him before he could grab her.

Pulling off his shirt, Stryke licked his fingers. "Now you're in trouble."

"*Oui?* A little food never scared me."

She was bare-breasted and smelled like Greek food, and something had dripped down behind her skirt, but she kept an eye on Stryke's hands. She grabbed the wine bottle, which had about a goblet remaining in it and, holding the base, flung the neck outward, catching Stryke across his chest with the wine.

"Mmm," Blyss cooed. "I could take care of that for you."

"Then come here." He gestured with his fingers. A teasing grin enticed her around the counter to drag her fingers through the sauce and wine on his chest. He grabbed her by the wrist and spun her around.

She didn't hear him open the fridge until it was too late.

"Oh no." She struggled, but slipped on something.

He hugged her against his chest with one arm, while he drew something out of the fridge with the other hand.

The cream was cold as it hit her skin, tightening her nipples to hard buds. His tongue followed closely, warming them and sucking at the cream. He hummed and dropped the cream carton on the floor, pulling her to him and sliding his hands down to grab her derriere.

"This needs to come off." He tugged at her skirt and found the zipper at the side.

While he slid down her skirt, Blyss managed to wrangle the can of whipped cream she'd bought to top some petit fours she'd ordered last week. A bend of the nozzle delivered a froth of white whipping down the side of his face, and when he realized what she was doing, he pulled back. She blasted his chest with it and drew lower.

"You're going to need to strip too, *mon amour*," she said. "I know where I want to taste this."

He didn't argue. He zippered down, his pants dropped and he kicked them aside. Splaying his hands to display ripped abs, defined hips and an upright erection, he said, "Bring it."

"Ooo la la!"

Blyss squirted whipped cream down his stomach and drew a line along the length of his hard shaft. Dropping to her knees, she lashed her tongue down his stomach. Tasted amazing and she didn't even think about calories. This was crazy. But it was kind of fun not caring what anyone else would think of her.

Pulling him toward her by his cock, she licked the head of him, tasting the whipped cream and sucking until his moans deepened and his sticky fingers threaded into her hair.

"Blyss, that's... You are one hungry woman."

It didn't take long to bring him to a shuddering climax. Stryke cried out in pleasure, his hips bucking. The sound of his pleasure was a wicked delight in and of itself.

Blyss sat back against the open fridge, her hand landing in a puddle of cream and her head tilting against the stainless steel.

Her lover was covered with smeared whipped cream, wine and cucumber sauce. As was she. And he looked amazing, his muscles tight and flexing as his body shook with the tremendous force of climax. A beautiful man.

That had messed her up. And she had enjoyed the messing. She couldn't remember a time when she'd forgotten to be perfect, to not worry about her hair, and certainly not about getting food on her clothes. Or face. Or… Oh, that couldn't be good to get between her legs.

Standing, she slid her fingers up her lover's abs, greasing the wine and whipped cream in a finger-painted design. "Shower," she said and pulled him down the hallway.

They lingered under the hot shower. Stryke soaped up Blyss from head to toes. He even sucked her toes into his mouth and tickled between them with his tongue. She hadn't expected such an erotic thrill from that touch. And he licked between her fingers, kissing them from tip to hand. Another delicious sensation that skittered throughout her system. She came three times in the shower. She never wanted to leave.

Why did the man have to be a werewolf? He was the perfect lover, even the perfect partner—except for that one small detail.

A huge detail.

The water shut off and Stryke wandered out onto the tiled floor to claim a fluffy white towel from the warming rack. But instead of handing it to her, he teased her with a matador's flick of cape. "Come here, glamour girl."

Normally the moniker would annoy her, but coming from him, in his teasing tone, Blyss loved the way he claimed her. She stepped into his arms and he wrapped her up in the warm towel and hugged her.

"Sorry to have messed you up," he said.

"I'm not sorry at all. I needed that."

"I'll clean up the kitchen for you."

She'd forgotten about that mess. Now would have been a terrific time for the maid to stop by. But she'd had to fire her three weeks ago when her savings had dried up.

"We'll do it together," she said. "It'll make faster work."

The doorbell rang, and Stryke's head went up. He sniffed the air instinctually. Something she had never seen previous lovers do. The move was so alpha, so commanding. It excited her all over again. "You expecting someone?"

"No." She grabbed the silk robe from the hook on the bathroom wall and wrapped it around her body. Hair still wet and dripping, she squeezed it over the towel she'd dropped. "I'll see who it is. You..."

His clothes were a mess. She intended to put them in the wash before sending him away today.

The doorbell buzzed again. "Just stay here," she said and headed to answer the door.

She hadn't a peephole to look through, and at times like this Blyss really missed the werewolf's heightened ability to scent others. Clenching a hand in a nervous fist, she opened the door. "Oh. Hey. I haven't seen you for a while."

"Blyss. Sorry to stop by like this, but I've been thinking about you. Just catch you in the shower?"

"Yes—"

"Who the hell is this?" Stryke strode up behind her, his hips wrapped with a towel and his chest puffing up as he eyed the tall man in the doorway.

"Who the hell am I?" her visitor asked. "Who is this, Blyss? And why...?" He sniffed and tilted his head curiously. "Is he a wolf?"

Chapter 14

"Kir, this is Stryke Saint-Pierre." Blyss could feel Stryke's posture stiffen in defense behind her. "Stryke, this is Kirnan Sauveterre. My brother."

"*Brother*. Nice to meet you." Stryke offered his hand and Kir shook it. "Uh, sorry." He wore nothing but the white terry-cloth towel around his waist. "We were just, uh…"

"I don't want to know." Kir stepped inside, his long casual strides moving him down the hallway. "Didn't mean to interrupt, but— What the hell?"

The kitchen looked as though the fridge had exploded.

"You don't want to know," Blyss singsonged as she gestured her brother to head toward the living room. "Give us five minutes to put some clothes on. If you're hungry…" She glanced over the mess on the floor.

"I'm not," Kir said. "You two do what you gotta do. I can entertain myself."

The wolf chuckled as Stryke and Blyss headed into her bedroom. His clothes were wet and covered in food, but that was the only option for now. He snapped his jeans out over the shower and scraped away the cucumber sauce. A sniff took in only faint scents. "Not too bad," he decided.

"I may have a men's T-shirt that will fit you," Blyss called from the depths of her closet. "Ah, here!" A blue shirt flew out from the closet and landed on Stryke's head as he returned to the bedroom.

He didn't want to know who this had once belonged to. He sniffed it. Smelled like fabric softener and not another man. Whew. He pulled it on and the cotton fabric stretched over his biceps and pecs. Tight, but he'd survive.

Blyss appeared in a soft red jersey dress that hugged her curves and looked like something he'd like to snuggle up against and never let go.

"You're gorgeous, as usual," he said. "And your brother is going to wonder if I peed my pants." He looked over his soaked jeans. "I remember you mentioning you had a brother, but I didn't think you and your pack…?"

"He stops by a few times a year. We still love one another, but he had a hard time accepting my choice to leave the pack. And, well, I'm glad when he visits. He reminds me of things and makes me question myself. But you do that, too."

"I make you question yourself?"

She nodded, but didn't elaborate. Stryke decided if she questioned her decision to not be wolf then he was damned glad to stir that up in her.

"He'll stay and chat for a bit."

"Do you want me to leave?"

"No." She tucked a few pins in her hair, making it look as if she'd styled it up just so. "I wish you'd stay. Please?"

"Good, 'cause I really don't want to go outside looking like this. And I'm going to need another shower after he leaves. I smell like a chicken gyro."

"And wine," she said, then kissed him. "Kir may have some info on the demons in the area. He once mentioned to me that the Enforcers run into them at times."

"Then I'm all for a chat." He followed her to the kitchen, where they veered around the food puddles, and into the living room, where Kir stood looking up through the skylights.

Blyss's brother was tall, had light, curly brown hair and wore a leather vest over a long-sleeved shirt. A gun holster was strapped across his chest, but there was no weapon in it. Not that Stryke could see. The wolf stood with hips squared and hands akimbo. Imposing. And rightfully so, because surely the brother would be suspicious of any half-dressed man he found in his sister's house. And smelling like cucumber sauce didn't help either.

"Food fight, eh?" Kir asked. His grin was easy and not at all accusatory, even when he slid his gaze down Stryke's attire.

"A little fun," Stryke offered. "You ever eat at the Greek places in the 5th arrondissement?"

"Love those chicken gyros. I thought that's what I smelled. Good choice. Stryke, was it?"

"Yes. I'm from Minnesota. My family is—or rather

was—in town for a wedding. I'm sticking around awhile longer. Rhys Hawkes has some work for me."

"I'm aware of Hawkes Associates. The pack keeps some valuables with them. Hawkes is half werewolf, half vampire?"

"Yeah, but it's weird because when he's vamp his werewolf brain is in control, and when wolf, his vamp brain wants him to drink blood. That would be a hell of a condition to keep in check."

"No doubt." Kir glanced to Blyss. "So how are you, sis?"

"*Très bien*. As usual. What about you? How is *ma mere*?"

"Do you really want to know?"

Stryke sat on the couch while the siblings remained standing. He wanted to learn more about Blyss but he didn't want to intrude on anything private. 'Course, he was stuck here until his pants dried out.

"She's still harsh and judgmental," Kir offered with a chuckle. "Good ole *ma mere*. I wanted to stop by and see if you needed anything. But it looks like all is well. Okay, I'll just ask." Kir turned to Stryke, but addressed his sister. "You've hooked up with a wolf. Does that mean…?"

"Non," Blyss said quickly.

Stryke looked aside. Yeah, he was the mistake. Much as he liked to believe they were growing closer, he knew it was all an illusion. Wishful thinking on his part.

"I didn't know she was wolf," Stryke offered, "until… well."

"My senses are as a human's," Blyss offered to her brother. "I've explained this to you before. Stryke is, well, he's a good man. But I didn't know he was were-wolf when we first met."

The brother was understandably confused, but to his credit he didn't push the issue. Probably he'd been dealing with his sister's refusal of their breed for a long time.

"So Blyss tells me you're with some kind of enforcing team?" Stryke tossed out in hopes of warming the chill that iced the air. "What's that about?"

Kir sat on the chair opposite Stryke. Blyss lingered by the wall, arms crossed, yet her gaze lingered on her brother.

Kir said, "The European wolves police their own. Various enforcements teams are spread throughout the countries. My pack, Valoir, is responsible for policing Paris. We keep an eye on those packs that may be gaming, victimizing vamps. Lately there's been a weird uptick in demonic activity in the city. We don't police demons, but we like to keep an eye on everything."

Stryke stabbed a look at Blyss. She shrugged and nodded. An approval to ask what he really wanted to ask.

"Did you hear about Hawkes Associates getting robbed a few days ago? We think it was demons because all that was taken was a demon scepter."

"No, but I did hear something about a demon attack at a vampire wedding?"

"That was the wedding we were at." Stryke again exchanged looks with Blyss but she flickered her gaze aside. Apparently whatever she was involved in she'd not revealed to her brother. "They were after a demonic diamond."

"Like Kir said," Blyss broke in, "he doesn't police demons, just werewolves."

"It's all right." Kir leaned forward, interested. "I had no idea it was a demonic artifact that was the lure to the wedding incident. A diamond? Do you know anything about that, Blyss?"

She sighed and her shoulders dropped. Stryke sensed she didn't want to discuss this with her brother, but if the guy could help, wouldn't she welcome his knowledge on the local demons? Time was ticking away. The full moon was fast approaching.

"It is called *Le Diabolique*," she offered. "It is a rare black diamond that contains an all-powerful demon. Edamite wanted me to obtain it for him."

"Thrash?" Kir turned to face his sister. "He's the one, isn't he? The demon's a good guy, but—is he your supplier?"

Blyss nodded and bowed her head. Apparently her brother had not known that information. And it was difficult for Blyss to reveal that part of herself to him.

"Come here," Stryke said gently, and she sat down beside him. He wrapped an arm about her shoulder and nuzzled her against his chest. She relaxed against him. Felt good to know he could be the soft place she needed to land.

To Kir, he said, "Thrash has threatened her because she owes him money. She was trying to hand over the diamond to him and everything went wonky. And now we know the diamond fits into the stolen scepter. The demons who have both pieces can release the demon within once they collect twelve rare demons and make a blood sacrifice."

Kir whistled and shook his head. "Blyss, why didn't you come to me?"

"Because this isn't your problem. I know what you

think of me. I try not to bother you or *ma mere*. I made a choice when I walked away from Valoir. I'm a big girl. I can take care of myself."

"I don't want you to have to take care of yourself," Kir said tightly. He shoved his hands over his scalp and shook his head. "You helping her, Stryke?"

"I am. Or I'm trying to. I'd like to track down the demons and return the diamond so Blyss can get Thrash off her back. And there's always the bonus of preventing demons from releasing some insane evil on the world. What did the witch call it?"

"Xyloda," Blyss provided.

"If you have any information about the local demons," Stryke said to Kir, "I'd appreciate your help, man."

"There is a group that has been particularly rampant lately. I don't know locations or even names, or if there's a specific leader. Like I said, the Enforcement team keeps tabs, but it's not high on our priority list. But I can certainly look into this further."

"I can tell you everything I've learned so far," Stryke offered. "I tracked the scent the night of the wedding to Club l'Enfer."

"Yeesh." Kir stood and began to pace. "That's Himself's territory. I can't imagine The Old Lad would have an interest in something like unleashing a demon. Sounds like competition to me. You want to head over to the club and have a look right now?"

"Great idea." Stryke stood. The tight shirt stretched across his chest. "I think I need to stop and get some clean clothes along the way. I'm staying over on the island behind Notre Dame. Blyss, do you mind if I go with your brother? I promised I'd help you clean up."

"I've got it. But, Kir, I don't want you getting involved. You've enough to do with the Enforcers."

"Blyss, you're in trouble. This involves me. Don't ever think otherwise."

She nodded.

Stryke bent to kiss her. "You going to be all right alone?"

"Of course."

"You've got my cell number. I'll call and check in with you on the hour."

"Why?" Her eyes frantically searched his. "Do you think I'm in danger?"

"Thrash has been here once."

Kir lifted his head at that statement.

"He's kidnapped me and threatened you, Blyss. Yeah, I think I need to keep a close eye on you now. Let me do this. Let me protect you."

She kissed him and whispered so Kir couldn't hear. "Thank you."

Kir and Stryke stopped quickly at his apartment on the Île Saint-Louis, where he changed into fresh jeans, a T-shirt and leather jacket. Blyss's brother didn't ask for clarification on the food debacle. He wasn't stupid. And Stryke appreciated the man's discretion, even though he was bursting with questions.

Such questions being: What were the packs like in Europe? Were they big, small, located in the cities or country? Was pack structure the same as in the US with the principal leading the pack followed by his scion as second-in-command? Did they have as big a tiff with the vampires as the wolves back in the States? Granted, the werewolves and vampires were supposed to be peaceable, but that was more PR than actually put into practice.

And were the pack females as prized here in Europe as in the United States? So much so that only a rare few male wolves actually married their own breed because of the shortage of females.

And while he'd picked up that Kir was none too pleased with his sister's lifestyle choice, he wanted to ask why Kir hadn't tried to keep her in the pack, maybe to teach her more about the life. Had anyone taught her how to actually be a wolf? Because while it was mostly instinctual, there was a lot to deal with if the wolf had grown up in human society and had to learn to hide their true nature. Which apparently Blyss had not been taught.

Hadn't her mother talked to her about coming into her shift? It was a basic fact-of-life talk. They must not be close. He'd not forgotten the gibe the siblings had made about their mother not caring. Stryke was thankful his family was so close. And even though his mother was faery, the mixed blood that ran within his siblings' veins had only fortified their understanding and acceptance of other breeds. There weren't a hell of a lot of breeds the Saint-Pierres didn't associate with.

Except demons. That breed was nasty.

Kir drove a small but sturdy black SUV toward the 9th arrondissement, where the nightclub was located. It was eleven in the evening and he'd warned that the club would be crowded and loud. A good time to sneak around.

"I care about your sister," Stryke felt the urge to say over the low background noise of the talk radio. "We came together in a weird way, but trust me, I only want what's best for her. And I want to do what I can to keep her safe and protect her."

"I get that about you," Kir said, one wrist resting on the steering wheel as he navigated the Parisian traffic. "Do you love her?"

"I've only known her a short time. Love is…big."

Kir nodded knowingly. "That it is. Blyss is a tough person to understand. She's made an odd life choice, but I love her no matter what. She's my blood."

"Do you think she would have chosen differently if, I don't know, she hadn't such a traumatic first shifting experience?"

"I remember that incident. It did scar her. I wish I had been in school at the time, but I'm ten years older than her and at the time was already out working with the Enforcers. And our mother has never been a hands-on compassionate sort of woman. That incident definitely shaped Blyss into what she is today. I can't say I under-stand her choice, though. It offends me that she doesn't want anything to do with our breed. And yet, today I stop by her place and discover her latest lover is a wolf. So she can surprise me."

Thinking about how she had surrendered to their spur-of-the-moment food fight, Stryke had to agree. The woman was indeed surprising.

"I don't want Thrash to hurt her," he said. "We need to find the black diamond. And after that, well…"

Kir cast him a glance. "Well?"

"Just well. I intend to head back to Minnesota once I know Blyss is safe. I've been tasked to start my own pack by my father. So…I'm in the market for a wife. But if I had a reason to stay in Paris awhile longer? Well then."

"I get the wife search. I'd love to marry a werewolf, but the only way that will happen around here is usually arranged."

"My grandfather is in an arranged marriage. They are still madly in love."

"Good to hear. I'll remember that should I ever be faced with the situation. I like you, Saint-Pierre. If you have a chance, I'd like to introduce you to my pack. You'd get along with my best friend Jacques."

"That would be cool. I'd like to learn more about the Enforcers. I graduated from the police academy back home, but when it came time to get a job I realized I couldn't do it. Entry level was desk work. I couldn't bring myself to work with humans, even though they surely need the help as much as we do. I want to work with my own kind, protecting them. We need it."

"You could start an enforcement agency back home."

"It's an idea. Might be the thing to help build a new pack, as well. The place is right up there." Stryke pointed out the club with the black metal door.

"Yep. Been inside that club too many times to admit to. But only for a case, never because the skeevy vampire chicks turn me on." He winked and got out of the parked car. The streets were crowded with young human partyers, but Stryke sensed paranormals mingled among the mix.

"The club usually only allows in paranormals," Kir said as they strode toward the doors. "But they admit pretty human women for the vamps to feed on. The humans aren't aware, but then again, some are and return for the bite. Fang junkies."

"When Blyss and I were here the other day it was dead. We didn't find anything, but the scent trail from

Hawkes Associates was unmistakable right until I reached the main room inside."

"Then we need to go deeper," Kir said.

The bouncer was different than the one who had let Stryke in previously. The bruiser sporting deadly studs—on his forearms, not his leather vest—looked Kir and Stryke up and down, then nodded and opened the door. Demons could scent out any breed, including humans.

"So the devil Himself owns this place?" Stryke asked as they strode down the dark hallway.

"Don't say that name again," Kir cautioned as they paused before the main dance floor. "Say it three times and you've invited that bastard for lunch."

"Got it. I think the back rooms are beyond the stage over there." Stryke sniffed. "I can pick out the familiar scent. I don't think they're here. It's lingered that long. Definitely leads back that way."

"Then let's follow your nose. Take the lead, man."

They pushed through the crush of dancers and to the darkened depths that led through the doorway and turned into a maze of dark hallways. When Stryke sensed someone walking toward them, he slipped behind a black velvet curtain and Kir followed. They waited until what smelled faery to Stryke passed and then sneaked out.

Stryke followed the demonic scent he'd originally picked up at the wedding and at Hawkes Associates. It was barely there, but cloying enough that he didn't feel he was wrong. It wasn't difficult to hold the scent either, despite the thump of drums in his heart, and the rush of adrenaline passing through the dance floor had ignited in his system.

When they landed upon a dead-end wall painted with

glow-in-the-dark graffiti, Stryke stepped onto a metal plate and jumped, testing the floor. "A door," he decided. "Going down."

Knowing the devil Himself owned the place and finding a door going down didn't sit well with him. Stryke reminded himself he wasn't here to play scared. In fact, he had wanted to find danger here in Paris. And here it was. "Shall we?"

"After you," Kir said with a glance the way they had come.

A steel staircase descended straight down within a tunnel, so Stryke could stand upright, stepping down and balancing himself with his hands against the curved steel wall before him. It was claustrophobic, but he felt cooler air rising from below. After descending about thirty feet, he sensed he was close to landing.

Both men arrived on a solid dirt floor and stood underground in the dark, surrounded by steel walls and an icy chill. The thumping beat from the overhead club was now but a murmur inside Stryke's veins.

"It's been built up," Kir noted. "Most tunnels under the city are carved out of the limestone. Interesting."

They sniffed to take in the surroundings.

"This way," Stryke said, veering left. Kir followed. "Just ahead. The scent grows stronger."

A dim light marked a room that was closed off by iron bars. The bars were spaced so wide that Stryke and Kir were able to slip through them and look about. Everything was dark and either steel or blackened metal. The walls were impressed with markings, as was the ceiling. Looked tribal, or at the least, some definite design. Stryke noticed that the floor featured a geometric design, fitted in the dirt floor with black metal ribbons, that traced to the center of the room—where the silver scepter had been placed in a keyhole that looked as though it had been made specifically for it.

"Why does this remind me of every horror or creature flick I've ever seen?" Stryke commented.

"If that doesn't give you the creeps, check that out."

Kir gestured to the wall behind them. In the dimness beyond closer-spaced iron bars were living beings. In cages. Glowing red eyes peered out at them. Four pairs.

"This can't be good," Stryke said. "They've begun to collect the demons for the sacrifice."

Chapter 15

The apartment felt vast and empty now that the men had gone. It was almost as if each had lifted up his own air and carried it out with him. And the air that surrounded Stryke Saint-Pierre was fresh and new and yet it occupied so much space, Blyss could feel his absence painfully.

As she finished cleaning up the food from the floors, walls and counters, she lamented such strange emotions. What was that about?

She didn't miss men. She used men.

Since her early twenties, when she had decided to live as a human among humans—and knew it would require a certain income as werewolf daughters were rarely taught marketable job skills; yes, the medieval ways still ruled in most packs—she had trained herself to carefully select a man as her lover, someone who possessed esteem, money and who got bored quickly. Blyss didn't want to become *the girlfriend*. She enjoyed being the lover. Besides, it was dangerous when men started to develop feelings toward her. She preferred to take the jewels, thank them with a sexy weekend and then stride out of their lives.

Until Stryke had pushed her up against the wall and changed her mind.

Everything about the man was nothing she had ever been interested in. And yet it didn't matter to her at all that he wasn't rich. She preferred his down-home sensibility and everyman qualities. It didn't matter that he'd never bring her a five-hundred-euro bottle of champagne. He liked to lick the cheap stuff off her skin. And that was a thousand times more satisfying.

It might not even matter that he was werewolf.

Maybe?

Blyss sat back against the kitchen counter. She'd scrubbed the floor clean. She tossed the sponge in the bucket of dirty water. She couldn't remember when she'd last done manual labor. It should appall her. Yet she could only feel a sense of satisfaction as she looked over the gleaming marble floor.

Leaning forward, she studied her reflection in a beam of moonlight that mirrored the marble surface. What she saw was a woman who tried to wear her mask with perfection so others would never see the ugly creature lurking beneath.

"But he's not ugly," she whispered.

In fact, she was curious about Stryke's wolf. She wanted to see him shifted, both as a four-legged wolf and as the powerful werewolf that walked as a man on two legs. She wanted to smell his carnal desire for her.

To feel his power and know his strength. She wanted to be owned by Stryke Saint-Pierre in every way possible.

And she realized what hidden part of her actually felt those desires. Her wolf. It had to be. Because the socialite Blyss Sauveterre, masquerading as a human woman, would never consider a werewolf anything but a foul and disgusting creature.

She glanced around the counter and up the side of the stainless-steel fridge where the iPad hung on a rack; it served as her digital calendar. Less than three days before the full moon. It hadn't been a year since she'd last shifted to werewolf. She didn't need to make the shift this month. But she would be forced to if *Le Diabolique* was not found and she could not hand it over to Ed.

Maybe she didn't need the crutch of the pills anymore? Could she…accept her werewolf?

She shook her head, catching a spill of hair against her palm. "What am I thinking? Just because a handsome wolf has snuck into my heart doesn't mean I need to start thinking crazy."

Because without the pills she would revert to werewolf and would need to shift. Every month.

She pressed a palm over her heart. Indeed, Stryke had found a way inside, beneath the mask and into her soul. She felt him there. Wanted to keep him there.

Which complicated things.

Why was she listening to her heart instead of the exacting, rational, and yes, even conniving, socialite who knew what had to be done to survive?

If she was honest with herself, it felt good to allow her heart the lead. She hadn't done so—well, ever. And she missed Stryke. She needed him here, holding her, kissing her, calling her glamour girl.

So what did that mean?

"I think I'm in love," she whispered.

And the realization hurt something far more fragile than her heart. It wounded her very soul.

They decided to leave the caged demons as they were. They appeared drugged because none tried to fight and speak to them. There was no sign of the diamond. Kir walked around the scepter placed in the center of the floor. They couldn't touch it without something to protect them from the silver.

Stryke pulled off his shirt and wrapped it about the scepter, but try as he might, it would not budge. "It's as if it's been riveted into the floor."

"Leave it," Kir said.

They left the underground demon lair with the intention of tracking, but the scents stopped outside the club.

"We'll check back when we learn more," Stryke said.

"I'll check the database and get back to you."

Instead of having Kir drop him at his place, Stryke said he wanted to check in with Blyss and help her clean because he was pretty sure she might be baffled by the whole cleaning process.

Kir chuckled knowingly and said he'd be in touch. He would check his sources regarding local demon nests and call if he found a lead.

Meanwhile, Rhys called. Stryke answered his phone while standing inside the main door that led to the courtyard before Blyss's building. "Rhys, what's up?"

"Tor has more items that need a pickup. Listen, I know this isn't the glamorous security detail I had offered you, but the work does come up occasionally."

"It's cool, Rhys. I'm glad to help out. Is it something I need to dash off to right now?"

"No, actually Tor wants to catalog the items first. I told him to give you a call when it's ready. Probably tomorrow."

"Sounds good. More demon stuff?"

"No, this is related to the *sidhe*. Not sure what it is exactly. Are you still tracking the scepter?"

"I found it, but wasn't able to retrieve it. Just got back from following a lead that took us below Club l'Enfer. It was like wandering through the bowels of hell down there."

"Be careful, Stryke. You're treading Himself's territory."

"Yeah, but tell me why the dark bad guy would have an interest in releasing an all-powerful demon from some big diamond? I mean, wouldn't that be competition?"

"Does sound odd. You suspect it was demons who stole both the scepter and the diamond?"

"Ninety-nine percent sure. I tracked their scent both from your office and the wedding. Definitely demon."

"They could be working on their own. Independent of...you know who." As Kir had stated, it was never wise to mention Himself's name more than once. "The only demon I know right now that has any control over the local denizens is Edamite Thrash."

"Yeah, he's oddly involved in all this, but I don't think he stole either of the items."

"He surely sent lackeys."

"Maybe." Then why even press Blyss to bring him the diamond if Thrash had others steal it for him? Didn't make sense. "I've hooked up with Blyss's brother, Kir Sauveterre."

"Ah yes, from the Valoir pack. Good bunch of wolves. They enforce in the city, yes?"

"Yes, they do. Sounds like a cool job. We need to organize something like that in the States. Anyway, I'll wait for Tor's call. Thanks, Rhys. Let me know if you get any ideas about this situation. The clock is ticking. I have a sense it's all going down on the night of the full moon."

"Doesn't give you much time. I should mention, I've a cabin about an hour out of the city you can use on the night of the full moon if you're still in Paris then. Leagues and leagues of forest surrounding it. All private land. You interested?"

"Hell yes. Thanks, Rhys. You've been so generous, I'm not sure how I'll ever repay you."

"You already are, Stryke. Talk to you soon."

He knocked on Blyss's door and opened it, calling out to her. A gorgeous vision in white came running down the hallway. Stryke immediately sensed danger and grabbed her, hugging her against his chest, as he scanned the hallway behind her. Instincts lifted his head, sniffing for danger.

"What is it?" he asked. His heart thundered, yet he didn't sense another presence in the apartment.

"I missed you," she said.

"What?"

He lifted her and she wrapped her legs about his hips as he strolled down the hallway into the spotless kitchen. She'd cleaned up herself? He walked into the living room and sat with her still attached to him.

"What's wrong, Blyss?"

"Nothing's wrong. And everything's wrong." She hugged up to him and tilted her head against his shoulder. "I missed you desperately."

"Is that the part where nothing is wrong or everything is wrong?"

"It's both." She bracketed her hands aside his head to stare into his eyes. "The whole time you were gone I could only think of you. I didn't even mind the cleaning part. I actually found it rewarding. But my thoughts were on you. If you were safe. If you and my brother were getting along. If you would return to me. You came back to me."

"I wanted to make sure you were okay." And see if she needed help. Which she had not. And she'd been thinking of him the whole time? "You were worried I wouldn't return?"

She nodded. "You've changed my heart, Stryke." She hugged him again, this time tightly. "I think I love you."

"Whoa." While having a woman declare her love for him was an amazing thing, Stryke couldn't imagine she was thinking straight. Must have inhaled fumes from the cleaning spray. "What happened to down with the wolves? I'm pretty sure werewolf isn't tops on your list of potential love interests."

"It doesn't matter to me what you are. Oh, I know this sounds crazy. You don't have to love me back. I just wanted to say it, to feel it on my tongue. And it felt great. It feels right."

"Glamour girl." He tilted his forehead against hers. "I do love your surprises."

"Did you find out anything?" she asked.

Much as he wanted to bask in her confession, Stryke nodded. "Kir and I found a lair. Inside were caged demons. And the scepter. We tried to take the scepter, but it was fixed into a weird mechanism."

"What about *Le Diabolique*?"

"No sight of it. I'm thinking the only way to find that might be to set a trap. Locate one of the twelve demons on the list Libby gave us and sit in wait for whoever comes for it. But even that is an iffy plan. Who's to say the guy in charge will go for that particular demon? Much as I hate to admit it, I'm at a loss what to do. But your brother is looking into his contacts."

"I'm glad the two of you get along."

"Kir's a good guy. He invited me to come meet the pack."

"Valoir is a noble pack that goes back for half a dozen generations. They are good people." She sighed. "If you can overlook my mother. But even she has some favorable moments, I'm sure."

"I don't want to meet anyone from Valoir without you at my side."

"Then I'm afraid that will never happen."

"Hey." He traced a curl of dark hair that tickled along her cheek. She was so soft and smelled like precious things. "I don't want to force you to change or to be something you're not. But you did make an exception for me."

"I have. I think I even want to meet your wolf."

"Really? What have you been smoking, Blyss? Must have been some strong chemicals in those cleaning products. You've had a drastic change of heart."

"I think you got inside me."

"Well." He pumped his hips against her legs. He did have an erection, but that was impossible to avoid when holding her.

"In more ways than the physical," she reiterated. "And I have to face the fact that you might never find the diamond. In a few days the world I've created for myself might forever change. I may have to face my own wolf."

"I'm doing everything I can to stop that from happening, lover."

"And why are you doing that? You, the man who told me he wants to settle down with a wolf and raise a pack of his own. You can't possibly fall in love with me. And I've told you happily-ever-after is out of the question. Why are you helping me, Stryke?"

Why, indeed? *Did* he feel more for her than lust and adoration? Could he possibly be falling in love with the wrong woman? The one woman who was completely the opposite of his ideal mate?

No. He wasn't stupid. He'd entered into this relationship knowing full well it could never satisfy him. It was a fling. In a few more days he'd leave Paris for home, destined to pine for a werewolf wife who may never become reality.

But until then.

"You deserve kindness," he said and kissed her nose. "And I want to see you happy. Even if that means you'll never howl again."

She tilted her head against his shoulder. "I haven't howled for a long time."

"If you get your supply restocked before the full moon, you won't shift?"

She shook her head.

"So you don't need sex the days before and after the full moon?"

All werewolves felt the compulsion to shift the day before the full moon, the day of and the day following. Generally, they tried to shift only one day a month. The werewolf needed that release. But as well, to shift more often was risky. Living among humans required a delicate balance between their wereself and the animal within. And the only way to calm the inner wolf on the days before and after the full moon was to have sex until satiated. It was a nice bonus.

"I don't need to satiate my wolf," Blyss said. "But I would love to be there to help you satisfy yours."

Score! Maybe he wouldn't need the cottage in the woods Rhys had offered, after all. But there was still the night of the full moon. He had to shift. Stryke would never deny that instinctual desire.

"I'll take you up on that offer," he said. "But tell me this. What if you don't get your pills?"

"Then my wolf will come out, and…I'll have to face it."

He hugged her against him, feeling her tiny shiver. She didn't want that. He would love to see her unleashed and wild. But he knew such a release wasn't in Blyss Sauveterre's nature. If he respected her, he'd allow her to be the woman she felt she needed to be.

He tilted his back against the sofa cushion and closed his eyes. It was nice sitting here with her, holding her, feeling her heartbeats against his chest. Comfortable.

A wrong comfort.

So why did it feel so right?

Stryke woke with Blyss in his arms. They'd crawled into bed with a few kisses, but hadn't undressed because sex hadn't been important. Closeness had been. He must have slept the whole night with her hand clasped in his.

Generally he tossed and turned. Last night had been peaceful.

What was up with him and his inability to simply walk away from this impossible woman? He liked her. He needed to remain cautious with her. He understood the reasons for why she did what she did. And that allowed the caution to slip away. He wanted to hold her whenever she would allow it. And snuggle up to her and feel her delicate warmth relaxed against him.

Could he be falling in love? He'd fallen in love a few times. With human women. It had happened quickly, and he'd enjoyed the feeling, but inside he had always known that it could never last. Love didn't have to mean forever. People came together all the time, fell in love and then drifted apart. It was how the world worked. And he'd known from the start this particular relationship had an expiration date.

Sure, werewolves married human. But it took a strong human woman to accept a man who, once a month, shapeshifted into a man/wolf creature and who liked to race through the forest, howl at the moon and even track, kill and eat small animals.

And there were his werewolf's heightened sexual desires. He simply demanded more from a woman in bed. Of which, Blyss had responded beautifully. It was probably because she was wolf. Sort of wolf. Even though she took pills to suppress the wolf, her true nature had to exist within her. There was no changing that.

Was there?

He'd love to bring out the wolf in her. But he didn't want to force her. So that meant he had to accept her as she preferred to be. He could do that. Maybe. Could he? Did he have a chance at a long-term relationship with this woman?

He stroked her hair down her back. Soft morning light glittered on her pale skin.

He suspected even if things did work out with them, it could never last. His home was in Minnesota. Her home was Paris. She'd made it very clear she wasn't up for the country cottage and the kids.

Or the happy ending.

Though maybe one or two kids? They could grow up bilingual and have the manners of a city slicker yet the instincts and call to the wild.

What was he doing? Already planning children with her? If Blyss could read his thoughts she'd laugh and toss back her gorgeous tousle of hair.

No, she was one classy glamour girl. Wolf or not, she belonged at cocktail parties dressed in fabulous gowns and dripping with diamonds. He could never give her the luxury, of which she expected and thrived upon.

So he wouldn't allow his heart to make the leap. That big leap into love that he knew lingered so close. It would be difficult. He was more suited for difficulties such as facing down demons with claws bared and yeah, even the occasional couch-talk-down with a brother who had just been dumped and wanted to punch everything in sight.

He leaned in and kissed the line of Blyss's shoulder blade through the white blouse. She smelled like a flower, of which he would never learn its name. The whole room smelled like a garden. He wondered if whatever flower it was would grow in Minnesota. If so, he'd plant a whole field for her in hopes to win her everlasting affection.

"Morning already?" she whispered and rolled onto her back.

He kissed her forehead and swept away the hair from her face. She wasn't wearing makeup and her green eyes sparkled as if stars. He liked her natural and soft. Unguarded. She seemed more vulnerable, yet also stronger. Because this was simply Blyss unhampered by the mask of makeup and jewels.

"You're beautiful, glamour girl," he said. "I like waking up next to you."

"Could you imagine waking next to the same person for decades?" she whispered, closed her eyes. "I can."

"I can, too." He turned onto his back, staring up through the windows. Clasping her hand, he held it over his stomach. "I might have to run out to do a job for Rhys today. But if I'm not busy I'd like to hang around here. If that's cool with you?"

"I do have some business at the gallery. Insurance stuff regarding *Le Diabolique*. But that can wait until you leave. I'd offer to make you breakfast and we could have a romantic tête-à-tête, but I suspect there's nothing in the fridge."

"Not after yesterday. I'll run out for those *pains au chocolat* that all the women seem to like. Maybe some chai, too. I miss that stuff. Usually drink it every day at home."

"Tell me about your life back in Minnesota. I don't know much about you."

He kissed her and sat up, stretching out a kink with a twist of his back. "I'll fill you in on all the boring details over breakfast. Mind if I hop in the shower quick?"

"Go ahead. Grab some fresh towels from the closet. I'm going to linger in your warmth."

She spread a hand across the sheet where he had sat. Stryke wouldn't have been surprised if a purr had accompanied her kittenish move.

"You make lingering look so damn gorgeous." He strolled into the closet and at sight of the regimented contents let out an appreciative whistle. "Wow."

"Oh, that's the wrong closet," Blyss called. "The towels are in the other one on this side of the bed."

"No kidding?" He took in the rows and rows—and rows—of shoes in the closet that was as large as a living room. The woman had a serious shoe addiction. He backed out, the awe setting him slightly off-kilter as he stumbled into the bedroom. "You have a room just for shoes."

She nodded and tucked the sheet up around her smile.

"How many do you own?"

An innocent shrug. "Hundreds?"

Again he couldn't resist a whistle. Women and their shoes. It was some kind of sacred thing he would never understand. Shaking his head, he found the right closet, grabbed a towel and headed into the bathroom.

An hour later, they sat in the living room finishing off the flaky pastries. The patisserie had also offered chai with fresh cream, much to Stryke's thrill. He'd brought some for Blyss, who had never tried it.

"Good stuff, right?" He liked his spiked with extra clove.

"*Exquis.* You've made me a convert from coffee."

"I'll show you how to make it homemade. I have a secret spice blend recipe that will knock you off your feet."

She bobbed one of her crossed legs, the pink marabou-fluffed slipper dusting the air. Totally *Green Acres.* But he wouldn't tell her that. He didn't mind looking at those gorgeous ankles and the pretty things with which she liked to decorate her feet.

"So you wanted to know about my exciting life?" he prompted.

"It has to be more interesting than mine. Trust me, it may look glamorous, but I can only drink so many glasses of champagne and chatter about the latest designer's affair with a supermodel so many times before I want to gag."

"Try chopping wood and digging six-foot-deep holes in the ground for a fence I've been putting in around my property."

"Don't they have a machine that can do that for you?"

"Sure, but I like the manual labor. And...I've not a job, so it keeps me busy."

"You've no desire to hold a job?"

"Not really. I shouldn't say that. I did attend the police academy. Had big dreams of protecting and serving and all that jazz."

"But?"

"But the idea of starting out behind a desk and answering phone dispatch calls turned me off real fast. And I realized I couldn't be happy wearing a gun at my hip and protecting humans. I'm more interested in working with my own breed. No offense against humans. I get along with them fine. Have to. But your brother's job does interest me."

"Perhaps you could establish an enforcement team back home?"

"Your brother suggested the same thing, and I'm liking the idea. As soon as I get that fence in. Gotta keep the coyotes out of my chicken coop."

"Really? You don't get along with that breed?"

"Not the mangy bunch I've got lurking about the farm. Tried scaring them off with my werewolf one night and they ran, but came right back. Idiots. But I won't trap them. That's cruel. Once I get the fence up I'll hang some bright flags on it and that'll keep them away."

"Living on a farm sounds like a lot of work."

"Probably a lot less work than trying to keep up appearances for the rich and snooty," he commented without thinking. And then he did think. "Oh. Er, I, uh..."

Blyss sighed. "I get it. But rich and snooty is all I know."

"I'm sorry." His cell phone rang. Saved by the bell. An unknown number. "Excuse me. I should check this."

Blyss finished the last sips of chai as he talked.

"Hey, Kir, good to hear from you. What's up? A lead? Yes, I can meet you. Uh, not my place. You can pick me up at your sister's place. See you in ten."

He hung up.

"I suppose Kir is over the moon that I've a werewolf lover," Blyss commented, but she said it with a smile.

"I think he's too polite to make a comment like that. He cares about you, Blyss."

"I know that. I wish I could see him more often, but he has to come to me. I won't go near the pack. So what are you two up to now?"

"Kir has a lead on demon activity. We're going to drive over and check it out. You okay to be alone?"

"Of course," she answered quickly. "But will you call me later?"

"I will." He kissed her and then lingered at her mouth, his lips barely touching hers. "You taste like chai. Mmm, I could drink you. Can we do a date night? After I get back from this, and I might have that thing to do for Rhys, but later, can we do something together?"

"What did you have in mind?"

"I still haven't found time to see the Eiffel Tower."

"How about a dining cruise? You board right in front of the tower, eat and drink as you cruise down the river. Then you arrive back at the tower just as it lights up for the evening. It's a little touristy but I've always been fascinated by the idea of cruising the Seine at night. I'll make a reservation."

"Sounds cool. I'll see you later. Do I have to dress up?"

"A suit might be— Uh, no. Just be yourself." She hooked a finger under his jeans' waistband. "I like you in jeans. Especially when they sit low and show your muscles."

"But a suit would be more appropriate?"

"Those cruises are filled with all sorts, from locals looking for a fancy evening out to tourists in jeans and sweatshirts. I'll even dress down. Nothing sparkly or glittery. Promise."

"I kind of like you sparkly. Make the shoes sparkly, okay?"

"Now, that I can manage."

His kiss wrapped about her heart with a tangible hug. Blyss didn't want the feeling to end, so she followed him down the hallway, lips locked and feet stumbling as he walked backward. Stryke's back hit the front door. Blyss stepped up on tiptoes and tasted him deeply. She never wanted to lose the taste of him.

Her werewolf lover.

Chapter 16

The lead Kir had provided led the men to traverse the sewers of Paris. Stryke shook his head at his incredible luck. He'd seen some seedy parts of the city while here. Guess the City of Love wasn't so romantic once you peeled back its layers. But he didn't mind. The aqueducts were fascinating. He knew they'd been in existence for centuries and was instantly thankful for modern-day plumbing.

They walked along the river, underground, the city above them. The stone aqueduct ceiling arched over this narrow section that was more sewer than actual river, as Kir explained.

"These aqueducts maze all under the city," Kir said, noting Stryke's interest. "And don't get me started on the underground tunnels that twist and twine some seven stories below the city."

"Really? Deeper than the demon lair we found? That's cool."

"There's a whole legion of humans that call themselves cataphiles, who explore, party and even live beneath the depths of Paris. Some of the demons who are incapable of pulling on a humanlike glamour also live underground. You don't want to mess with those horns."

"I imagine not. So this is a gang of demons you've heard that are stealing valuable artifacts?"

"We call them denizens," Kir said. "Large groups of demons that follow one particular leader. Like a vampire tribe or a werewolf pack. This particular denizen is headed by a wraith."

"Is a wraith actually a demon? I thought wraiths were ghosts or spirits." Stryke ducked to pass under a particularly low section of ceiling formed by arched limestone.

Kir came out on the other side and stopped before a rusted iron door that had a big red symbol drawn on it.

"A wraith demon moves like a ghost but it's solid and deadly. It's powerful and wields some wicked talons. No lower jaw, either," Kir added. "Nasty things. So you got any weapons on you? Salt?"

Stryke shook his head and chuckled. What kind of idiots walked into a demon nest unarmed? "You got me, man. I'm so unprepared for this mess I stumbled into in Paris."

"I suspect you probably didn't stumble so much as fell under my sister's allure. You must really like Blyss to be doing this, Saint-Pierre."

"It might be more than that."

"Right. You said you're looking to start a pack. You think hooking up with a werewolf who denies her heritage is such a wise move?"

"I know Blyss likes her men rich and *human*. But right now I've got her attention and we're having some fun together. She deserves whatever I can do to help her out of this situation."

"Damn, I wish you lived in Paris. You'd be good for my sister."

"I don't think she'd care for my idea of living in the country. In fact, she's already made it very clear she would not."

"She is abrupt." Kir rapped the door, avoiding the red marking. "This is a demon sigil drawn in…" He sniffed at the red mark. "…human blood."

"Nice," Stryke said with no appreciation whatsoever.

"I think it best if we stay as far from the nest as possible but get close enough to see if we can pick up a scent trail," Kir said. "You'd recognize the scent, yes?"

"Of course. I'm still thinking about our lack of weapons, though. How to fight a demon?"

"Move fast, and if you can help it, don't bite them. Demon blood won't kill us but it is nasty."

"Got it. So are we going to shift?"

"Much as I'd like to, I think it's wiser to keep our wits about us."

"Yeah? My wits are fine when I'm shifted. If we're overwhelmed, I've got your back, but it's going to be in werewolf form. I can promise you that."

"Deal."

"You want to lead the way?"

Kir stepped aside and gestured toward the door. "I thought I'd give you that pleasure since you're the guy with the nose."

"Sure thing." Stryke tilted his head side to side, snapping the kinks out of the muscles. With a shrug of his shoulders he bolstered up his courage.

Thing was, all the courage in the world wouldn't save him from a creature who served a wraith or even the devil Himself. He flexed his fingers, feeling the tingle of his werewolf *right there*. Close, if he needed it. It took only seconds to shift.

"Hey!"

Both men turned to spy a tall, dark-haired man dressed all in black striding down the narrow aqueduct ledge.

Stryke scented him before he recognized the hematite glint at his temples. "Thrash." He fisted a palm and set back his shoulders.

"Dial it down," Kir cautioned as he stepped around Stryke and offered his hand.

Edamite Thrash shook Kir's hand and the two greeted one another as old friends.

What. The. Hell?

Blyss paced in the kitchen, unsure what to do with herself. Something felt off about the diamond situation. *Le Diabolique* had been missing for days now, and the original owner had not checked to reclaim the borrowed property.

In fact, she was baffled why the police and detectives hadn't knocked down her door yet. And then she realized she couldn't quite place a name to the person who had loaned her gallery the diamond.

Where had it come from? Had the owner known it contained a demon? Maybe that person had wanted it to be stolen and eventually unleashed on the city?

Crazy thoughts. But really, when one had possession

of a diamond that contained a demon, could anything be more crazy?

"I need to check the paperwork."

And while most of the gallery's paperwork was digitized and accessible from her home computer, this particular acquisition was not in the records. Further weirdness.

So she dashed on some eyeliner and lipstick, slipped her feet into a pair of red leather Jimmy Choos and headed off to the gallery to try to figure out this mess.

"You're working with the wrong side, Sauveterre," Stryke said as he strode up to Thrash and Kir. "This asshole kidnapped me the other day and he's extorting your sister."

"Yeah, about that." Kir punched the demon in the jaw.

"Seriously?" Stryke asked as Thrash shook off the iron-fisted hit with a red-eyed smirk. "So why the friendly handshake? You knew what he was doing to Blyss."

"Ed and I go way back. He's okay," Kir said. "Except when he screws with my sister."

"Hey!" Ed put up his palms to ward off the next imminent hit. "Kirnan, you know I respect Blyss. I would do anything for her. She came to me. We've had this business arrangement for years. I am helping her."

"Helping her?" Stryke wanted to be the next in line for the punch. "If she doesn't pay you half a million by the full moon you've threatened to kill her family. That would be your family too, Kir."

This time Thrash's body soared with the punch that Stryke delivered. The demon's head and shoulders hit the limestone wall and he collapsed in a heap before the men.

Stryke rubbed his knuckles and cast Kir a sidelong glance. "Your priorities when it comes to friendship are questionable."

"I know he's been supplying Blyss," Kir said. "I didn't realize he was making threats. He's..." The werewolf bowed his head and said in tight tones, "...sort of family."

"What?"

Kir rubbed his jaw, thinking for a moment as the demon shook his head, attempting to pull out of the bruising punch Stryke had delivered him.

"Blyss doesn't know this," Kir said, "but years ago, when my father was forced out of the pack because he was having an affair with a vampire..."

"Yeah?"

"Me and the old man had a good long talk. He's into more than vampires. Demons are his first choice when it comes to women."

"Don't tell me. He had an affair with Thrash's mom?"

Kir nodded. "Long time ago. We're half brothers."

"Yikes." Stryke didn't know what to say to that one.

"We've been—well, I wouldn't call it friends, but it's something—since learning about one another. We keep each other up on the weird and wacky family we've been meshed into. But we decided to keep it from Blyss. She likes to stay as far away from the paranormal realm as possible. She hates being a wolf. Can you imagine what it would do to her if she learned Thrash was her half brother?"

"Apparently Thrash wasn't going to tell you about

the threat to your family. And I suspect family includes you."

Kir lifted Thrash by the back of his shirt and pushed him against the wall. The demon spat black blood to the side. "What's gotten into you?"

"It's *Le Diabolique*," Thrash said. "I need to keep it out of the wrong hands."

"What?" Stryke shoved a hand against Thrash's shoulder and Kir stepped aside. "Blyss said you wanted to release the demon within the diamond."

"Great Beelzebub, no! That stone imprisons Xyloda from this realm. That demon gets out, I'm finished. I want to keep it out of the wrong hands. I should have never trusted Blyss could handle the snatch. Why the hell did she give it to you?"

Stryke shook his head. "I'm two pages behind you, buddy. This whole affair confuses me. So you want the diamond to keep the demon inside? But right now some demons have both the diamond and the demon scepter. And yesterday, Kir and I found the lair where they're going to perform the release ritual. They've already got demons caged and waiting for the sacrifice."

"Merde." Ed pushed down his shirtsleeves and pressed a thumb to his mouth in thought. His hand, which was concealed by a black leather half glove, revealed dark scrawls on the fingers that looked like tattoos, but Stryke felt sure they were far more evil in nature. "Where was the lair?"

"Beneath Club l'Enfer," Kir said. He met Stryke's castigating expression with a shrug. "Believe it or not, he *is* on our side."

"This asshole had his thugs work me over. Punches intended for your sister. He was going to hurt Blyss."

"I would never hurt her. She's my half sister. I..." The demon shook off what he was going to say. "The pills she takes are expensive, and I do have my own finances to manage. But I had to make the threats to ensure she actually did it. If she doesn't bring me the stone she won't get the pills she so desperately desires. I sure as hell won't lay a finger on any of her family members. Including you, Kir. But without those pills you might have a howling werewolf on your hands in a few days." Ed arrowed his gaze on Stryke. "Bet you'll be thrilled about that, eh, country boy?"

This time Stryke's punch knocked out Thrash and toppled him to the right. The demon's body teetered toward the river. Kir managed to catch his half brother by the wrist as his legs slipped into the Seine.

"I know you're angry," Kir said as he struggled to hold the unconscious demon above water, "but we can work with him. We'll make him pay later for being cruel to my sister, and the threats."

"What? With a brotherly punch? I know how that works."

"Just chill, will you? We can trust him. Right now Thrash is the closest connection we have to whoever might have stolen the diamond. We need him."

"Fine." Stryke bent and reached for the demon's pant leg and helped Kir hoist him onto the cobbled sidewalk. He stepped back and leaned against the wall, catching a palm against his forehead. "If the lair was in the club owned by Himself, why don't we go straight to the source? The devil is obviously behind this. Let's just call him here. The Old Lad, right?"

"Dude, no. Don't say it—"

"Himself!" Stryke called. "We need to talk. Himself!"

"Merde," Ed said as he sat up. "Tell me he didn't say that name three times?"

"You rang?" a sepulchral voice echoed from down the way.

Chapter 17

Before heading into the office, Blyss unlocked the door to the acquisitions closet, which was a small room where she stored all items received before placing them in the gallery. It was built like a safe, with two-foot-thick walls and a digital keypad that was supposed to reset the password every day, which she got updates for on her mobile.

On the night of the Marie Antoinette exhibit, she had slipped in early, replaced *Le Diabolique* with a fake and then placed the real diamond in her desk drawer until she knew she could return later with a dupe. Someone who could carry the diamond out of the museum without a clue.

Stryke was no dupe. But he had, unfortunately, served a purpose. Too well. She never could have anticipated the diamond being stolen from him at the wedding. Or that those who had taken it would be demons.

"Such a mess," she muttered as she stepped into the dark room and flicked on the lights. A Rembrandt sat upon an easel waiting for next weekend's showing. In the center of the room, sitting under a glass case on a pedestal also made of glass, sat…

"Where is it?"

She lifted the glass cube and set it on the floor. Bending before the pedestal, Blyss examined the empty platform, her eye searching for fingerprints. She'd worn black gloves when replacing the real stone with the fake.

Someone had stolen the fake?

"They must have thought it was the real thing. More demons?"

She stood and pressed a hand to her chest. What the hell was going on? And who had gotten into this locked room with no noticeable signs of forced entry?

She turned and inspected the lock and the interior door frame. Pristine. No scratches in the metal sheathing. Her eyes took in the small room from every corner of the ceiling, down the walls and along the baseboards. There were no security cameras. She hadn't felt them necessary in this safe room. A vent near the floor was too small for anyone to access.

Unless they could shape-shift.

Blyss gasped on her own breath. A demon had been here. Had to have been. She sniffed the air, then cursed her inability to detect minute scents that Stryke or any of her breed might do with ease.

Closing the door and marching down the hallway toward the office, she cursed loudly. She did not like losing control. Someone had taken that away from her when the diamond had been stolen at the wedding. And again when stealing the fake.

Alone in the gallery office she paced, hands to hips, her high heels angrily clicking the marble floor. She couldn't call the police. To report a stolen fake? The last thing she wanted was police involvement.

She had planned this carefully. The event featuring *Le Diabolique* had not been announced to the public because she'd never intended to go through with it. Lorcan was the only one she'd needed to fool. And she had. He hadn't asked after the diamond since the night of the showing.

"This should have been so easy."

Could Edamite be behind this? Then why had he insisted she find the diamond and bring it to him?

No, there must be another faction of demons who were also after *Le Diabolique*. How had anyone, beyond Ed, gotten the information that her gallery was to display the diamond?

She sat before the desk and scanned the acquisitions files for the past few weeks. She had been the one to receive *Le Diabolique*. It had been delivered via courier, from the back of a black Mercedes. Such a private delivery method was often utilized with valuable works that the client trusted only to his closest employees.

The courier had unlocked the titanium case from around his wrist and walked inside the gallery. She'd handed him the bill of lading to sign and had signed it herself. In turn, she had signed a form from the courier and...

"Where did I put that form? I did get a copy. It was a yellow piece of paper and had the owner's monogram on it."

She'd noted the elaborate monogram, but at the time, she'd been so nervous about receiving the valuable item she hadn't taken time to really look at it, to determine what letters were woven into the monogram.

She'd become accustomed to overlooking things. Her expectations for all things fine and luxurious had blinded her to details. She could spot a bottle of Krug fifty feet off, but to really say what the label looked like? No clue. Louboutins were a no-brainer. The red sole! But as for the actual design on the main part of the shoe? Just glimpses here and there.

And a sparkling ten-carat diamond always caught her eye, but the setting was never important.

"I can't find it. Maybe Lorcan hasn't transferred it to the digital files."

Her assistant went through the paperwork every few days. And where was Lorcan, anyway? He hadn't called in sick. He simply hadn't shown up for work. Could he be on a bender? She had suspected him of excess drinking or a drug problem because his eyes were often red and puffy and he always had an excuse for a missed morning.

Blyss dialed his number but the phone didn't ring. Instead she got a canceled-number recording.

"Weird."

She had a sneaky feeling she'd never hear from Lorcan again. Had he been in on it? Who was Lorcan Price? She'd thought him merely human. Could he possibly be a paranormal breed? But what? Thanks to the pills she took, she had no way to sense a fellow paranormal. Was it possible he'd been in on the placement of the diamond from the get-go? Could Lorcan be demon?

Had *Le Diabolique* specifically been delivered to her with the hopes it would be stolen because...

"Why?" Blyss asked herself. "It doesn't make sense. Unless Thrash is involved. But then he would have never needed me to steal it in the first place. I don't understand this."

It was as if someone had expected her to take *Le Diabolique* and wanted to make it easy. And with no police investigation to hamper or bring suspicion, then she got off free.

As did the person who had ultimately arranged for this heist in the first place.

That person had to be the one who sought to release the demon from the stone. Yes?

"Makes weird sense."

Then again, why not simply keep the stone and not go through the process of handing it to her gallery? What if she had never agreed to steal the diamond? This made so little sense!

Blyss grabbed her purse and locked up. She hadn't located any clues here. Instead, she'd found only further questions. And a missing fake. Should she call Stryke? He was out with her brother at this moment trying to track *Le Diabolique*. She couldn't provide him any additional information that would help that search.

She'd wait for him to return and tell him her suspicions.

And then she'd tell him again that she loved him. Because more and more she believed what she'd said almost by accident earlier.

There was something about Stryke's kiss that wouldn't allow her to turn away. To instead seek a man who would offer her riches, vacations or false compliments. She wanted Stryke's kiss. Because it tasted like him. Because it tasted like something fine she could never possess. Because it tasted real.

And more and more, she craved real.

* * *

"Who is that?" Stryke asked.

A beautiful redhead in a tight black lace dress strode toward the three men. She wore heels high enough to make a man jump for mercy. And her breasts vied to escape the low neckline. Well, well.

Kir whistled. "I've always loved blondes."

"Blonde? She's a redhead," Stryke muttered with growing interest.

"Gentlemen," Ed said quietly, and with a distinct warning, as he squeezed the river water from his shirt hem. "That's not a woman. The Saint-Pierre idiot just called up the Dark Prince."

"Ah shit." Kir straightened and looked aside to avoid seeing what he knew was illusion.

Those who looked upon Himself saw an image of their greatest temptation.

"What do you mean?" Stryke asked. "She looks like Blyss, but instead with red hair."

"Now is no time to be racking up brother-in-law points," Kir hissed. "Get a whiff of the guy."

Stryke inhaled, expecting some sexy perfume, and instead got a nostril blast of the worst sulfur ever. Hell. He *had* called up the devil Himself.

Heh. He'd called up Himself.

Now, to get down to business.

"Who the hell are you?" The gorgeous woman stood with hands on hips looking too painfully delicious. Her bright green eyes, framed by lush black lashes, took in the trio. Her tongue dashed out to lick red lips. Everything about her was so wrong. "I know the demon Thrash and Kirnan Sauveterre." Her gemstone eyes fixed on Stryke and her teeth actually glinted, as if in a TV commercial. "But you don't belong in Paris."

"I'm Stryke Saint-Pierre."

"Ah." The woman smirked. "I remember a thing with your grandfather Eduoard Credence Saint-Pierre. Something about his daughter, too. Kambriel…" The name sifted from the woman's lips with such lustful reverence Stryke shuddered.

He'd heard about Kambriel's unfortunate stumble upon Himself after moving to Paris to *find herself*, and how the devil had fallen in love with her and seduced her out of her wits. She'd been lost for months in a trippy sort of head game, a virtual slave to the Master of Darkness, until Johnny Santiago had come along and rescued her.

Stryke needed to keep a cool head when dealing with this Demon of All Demons. And that was something he was expert at.

"Why are you after *Le Diabolique*?" he asked the Dark Prince. "Don't you have enough power in this realm? And why unleash another überpowerful demon to torment the humans? You'll get their souls soon enough."

"Insolent!"

If getting sucker punched by a sexy woman wasn't humiliating enough, landing the wall face-first and feeling his nose crunch was. Stryke swallowed blood, grinned and spun around. But, expecting to face off against a gorgeous woman, he abruptly halted his charge when before him stood Himself in his true guise.

The Demon of all Demons was formed all of black muscles and sinew, towering four heads higher than Kir, the tallest of the three men. His shoulders were as wide and bulky as a Barcalounger. Glossy black talons scythed out from the ends of his fingers, putting all horror-movie villains to shame.

At his temples were huge ebony horns just like a matador's nightmare. The demon's red eyes glowed above a haughty stretched-leather smirk that revealed an imperious glint of fangs.

"Now," Himself said in tones that cut like ice down Stryke's spine. "What is this about *Le Diabolique*? I banished the demon Xyloda into that stone centuries ago. Why do you think I would want to bring that bastard out?"

"Because the lair to perform Xyloda's releasement ritual is set up below your Club l'Enfer," Stryke said.

Himself cast a steaming gaze toward Edamite, who, still dripping with river water, bowed his head and stepped back. "I have no intel, Your Darkness," the demon muttered.

Finding his courage, Kir stepped up beside Stryke. "It's true. We saw the lair. Four demons of the twelve required for the blood sacrifice have already been captured. Surely more have been acquired since we've seen the place."

Himself coiled his meaty hands into fists. Behind him, the river Seine actually steamed, mimicking the dark lord's boiling anger.

"We're trying to stop the release from happening," Stryke said, finding his stance and not fearing another hit from Himself. He was still swallowing his own blood from the punch, but at least he was standing and had his wits about him. "If you're not involved, then tell us who is, and we'll take care of it."

"You'll take care of it?" Himself tilted his head at

him, the horns moving dangerously close. One slice from those could take off his head or half his body. "You, a frail werewolf, and his idiot cohorts? Of what value does it serve you to stop Xyloda's release?"

Stryke splayed out his hands before him and offered, "I like my world as demon-free as possible."

Edamite coughed.

Himself sneered. Steam hissed from his black nostrils. But he did not move toward Stryke for another punch.

"So your heroic quest has nothing to do with the tasty bitch who can't decide if she wants to be wolf or human?"

Stryke lifted his jaw. "It has everything to do with Blyss. And she's happy with what she is right now."

"You don't know her very well, boy." Himself eyed Kir up and down and then Ed. "I will not tolerate Xyloda's release. I will end this right now. But the three of you won't escape without proper recompense. I will ensure those who stole *Le Diabolique* are aware of exactly who wished their plot foiled."

Kir and Stryke exchanged looks that said "can't we get a break?"

"That's for the comment about the world having fewer demons," Himself said to Stryke. "If that is all, then, gentlemen, I'll be off."

"I'll go with you," Stryke said, pausing the Dark Prince. "To stop the demons from releasing Xyloda."

Himself tilted his head, considering the offer. "You watch too much television, werewolf. This isn't a supernatural buddy episode."

"Yeah, but I sure as hell wish it was. At least then I'd know a happy ending waited for me. I need to finish what I've started. I promised Blyss I'd take care of matters between her and Thrash regarding that diamond. And until that big black stone is found, it's dangerous."

Himself blinked, and when he eyed Stryke this time his corneas were black around the red irises with a slit of black in their centers. "Your offer amuses me."

The demon king clapped his hands together once, and Stryke suddenly stood in a dark chamber carved from dirt and limestone. Torches lit the vast space, and when he took in his surroundings he found the twelve cages were all filled. And he wasn't sure what number, exactly, *denizens* equaled, but he guesstimated a good twenty to thirty demons standing to one side of the room, each of them lifting their heads to eye Stryke and Himself.

Chapter 18

Stryke muttered to his demonic cohort, "I'm going to need a weapon."

"How about this?"

Stryke's left arm jerked as a medieval mace suddenly appeared in his grip. The spiked ball must've weighed ten pounds. He gave it a test swing and the spiked iron ball almost sliced his leg open.

"Something a little more modern?" he hissed.

Himself shook his head and grumbled, a rattly death thunder that birthed in his throat. The demonic denizen approached with caution.

A Lightsaber with purple beam appeared in Stryke's hand, startled him on his feet. He swung it and it actually made the noise it should. But seriously? "Are you kidding me?"

"Be specific, insolent!"

"Salt and a blade, if you don't mind."

A pistol replaced the Lightsaber, and in his right hand manifested a long, scythed blade that he felt could take off a demon's head with but a slice.

"Nice." Stryke eyed the closest demon, who sported enough hardware in his nostrils, ears and at his temples to make a punk rocker jealous. "Let's do this."

Stryke's blade sliced through a demon's neck. The head toppled, only to reveal yet another demon standing behind him, snarling its wicked double rows of fangs and swinging the silver scepter—which happened to sport *Le Diabolique*.

"A little help here!" Stryke called.

Himself stood off to the side, by a cage, watching as Stryke had taken out half the denizen. At one point when Stryke had been held down on the dirt floor by a nasty demon drooling some kind of caustic saliva onto his neck, he looked up to see Himself studying his talons most intently.

"I thought you said you had this one!" Himself called back.

"I said I wanted to help! I thought I was doing the buddy sidekick role."

"Ah. Always be specific." The Dark Prince stepped into the fray and with but a slash of talon took out the demon wielding the scepter.

Stryke stumbled against one of the cages. The demon within grasped him around the neck. Pointing the pistol over his shoulder, he pulled the trigger. Loaded with salt rounds, it hit its mark. He felt the demon scatter into flakes behind him.

With a clap of his hands over his head, Himself stomped the floor. All standing demons dispersed into flakes of red-ember ash. Demon blood spattered Stryke's face and body. The room went black with the shrapnel. Stryke took aim at one demon standing near the doorway and fired the pistol. Right on target.

Himself turned and nodded acknowledgment. "Good one."

Stryke returned the nod. "Are they all gone?"

The devil swept his hand over the piles of demon ash, and from beneath rose the scepter. And in the center of the room, up popped *Le Diabolique*. Himself snatched both. The scepter, he pointed toward Stryke.

"You want this for a souvenir?"

"I think I'll pick up one of those flashing Eiffel Towers when I get topside, if you don't mind."

"Suit yourself. This is mine." Himself eyed the diamond in the murky darkness. His crimson eyes glowed brightly. He popped the diamond into his mouth and swallowed.

"That's going to give you nasty heartburn."

Himself's chuckle didn't touch levity. "One so heartless as I need not worry. But to show I'm not all treacle and brimstone, I do thank you for alerting me to this anomaly, Saint-Pierre. Ask for one thing and I shall grant it to you."

"Like a wish?" Stryke scratched the back of his head where he was pretty sure demon blood had changed his hair color to black. He eyed the Dark Prince warily. "Are you for real?"

"I invite you to act as my sidekick and you still question me?"

Stryke shrugged.

"I've not the patience for your dally."

Stryke didn't want anything the devil could give him, olive branch or not. Although…

"Can you give me something to make a werewolf completely human?"

Himself actually rolled his eyes. "The woman again? You don't know her very well."

"So you've said. That's what I want," Stryke insisted.

"Very well." Himself gestured dramatically with a sweep of taloned, black-muscled hand, and a glass vial appeared in his grasp. He stretched his arm out over the vast piles of demon ash and the fine particles streamed upward, filling the down-turned vial. A cork stopper appeared in the vial's neck. Black wax melted about the rim. "Here you go."

"This is filled with freaking dead demons." Stryke caught the murky vial. A shake revealed the contents had turned liquid. Of a sudden the contents within the vial glowed red. "What the hell?"

"What is it they say in this abominable realm?" Himself said. "Have a nice day!"

The demon dispersed into ash that then swirled into a black smoke that followed the steel-walled aisle, which led up to the nightclub. And of a sudden Stryke wobbled, arms out to his sides, to catch himself from falling into the Seine.

Kir grabbed him by the front of the shirt and tugged him upright. "That didn't take long. What happened?"

Stryke stood in the aqueduct. No demons. No cages. No devil. Guess his job as sidekick was now officially over.

Edamite peered over Kir's shoulder. "Nice," the demon said from behind them. "Thanks to you, I'll have a gang of pissed-off demons on my ass. Good going, wolf."

Stryke spun about, catching Ed by the throat and slamming him against the stone wall. "I just did what you've been trying to do in a half-assed roundabout way with no success. I went straight to the source. And together we creamed those demons' asses, and the Dark Prince ate the freakin' black diamond. So now you've got what you wanted. No one is going to release Xyloda from the stone. And you're going to do as you promised for Blyss. She owes you nothing. You don't ever speak to her again."

Ed raised his hands up by his face. "The deal was if she brought *Le Diabolique* to me she could have her pills. I don't have the stone."

"But you've the same results."

"Do as he says, Ed," Kir said from over Stryke's shoulder. "Or you'll have to answer not only to Stryke, but as well, me."

Ed fisted the air. "Fine! The things I do for family." He nodded toward the vial Stryke held. "What's that?"

"It's for Blyss. She doesn't need your damn pills anymore. So I don't care if you are her half brother. Stay. The hell. Away from her."

"Did Himself give you that? Is it for Blyss?" Kir asked.

Stryke stuff the vial in his front jeans pocket. "It'll do for her what the pills have done. Only permanently."

"You really want your girlfriend to keep denying her true nature?" Ed blurted out.

Stryke slammed Ed's head against the wall. "None of your damn business, demon."

"Actually, it—"

Stryke growled at the man, and he ceased protest. He turned and strode away, not caring if Kir followed. The deed had been done. The Old Lad would not have another powerful demon running amok on his turf. Of course, Stryke had no idea what to expect from the demons when they discovered who had narced on them.

"Bring it," Stryke muttered. "I want to smash in some demon skull."

"Then you'll need weapons," Kir said as he joined Stryke's side.

"I've got a salt pistol." The thing was still tucked in his waistband. Must have dropped the scythe in the chamber. "You didn't stay behind to talk to your brother?"

"Drop it, Saint-Pierre. You'll never understand how family ties can forge relationships. All may look peachy right now," Kir said, "but you'd be wise to arm yourself. And stay close to my sister."

"That I can promise I will do. I'm heading there right now. We've a date."

"Oh yeah? Somehow I suspect the demon-blood look is not going to go over well with my sister."

Yeah. He'd better head home and shower first.

Stryke's cell phone rang. "Hello?"

"Can you do a pickup?" Rhys Hawkes asked. "In an hour?"

"As soon as I can get to a vehicle I'll be there. Same place?"

"Yes. See you then."

"You're not going straight to Blyss's place?" Kir asked as they landed the surface and the bright evening sunlight made them both blink. "I said you need to protect her."

"I have a quick job to do for Rhys Hawkes. I'll get to her within two hours. You can go check on your sister, you know."

Kir glanced back down the tunnel they'd come from. Stryke suspected he had unfinished business below.

"When you talk to the demon you be sure he keeps his promise to stay away from Blyss."

Stryke wandered off in the direction of the Île Saint-Louis. A half hour later he'd showered, decided the salt pistol was a good accessory to carry with him and headed out to meet Tor for another pickup.

Blyss stood in the shoe closet vacillating over the crystal-laden Louboutins or the black velvet Viviers with the diamonds on the toes.

As a wolf, she'd ruin these precious things. If she shifted all the time, her hair would be a mess. She'd have to shave too often. Her fingernails would be ragged. She'd be a disaster.

Yet if she was a werewolf she could sense Stryke, go for a run in the forest with him. Have werewolf sex with him— What would that be like? Messy. Wild. Weird. Amazing?

She sighed.

"What to do?" She traced a finger along the Louboutins. "I love him. But do I love him enough to change for him?"

Tor presented yet another curious device to Stryke in a wooden box shaped much like a bread box.

"Is it going to jump out at me or otherwise attract demons?" Stryke asked, keeping his hands to his chest because he wasn't too eager to open the box after the surprises he'd found.

"It's *sidhe* related."

"Faeries? So what's inside? A bunch of twinkly dust?"

"Actually, it is." Tor opened the box top and tilted it toward Stryke. Inside, the contents sparkled madly. "It's the remains of a dryad. Can be used in magical spells, alchemical potions, and various rituals and/or occult ceremonies. Lots of power in this purple stuff. Tell Rhys to keep it under lock and key."

Stryke accepted the box with some apprehension. "All that from a bunch of glitter?" He shook his head and whistled. "The things a guy learns. My brother Kelyn…" He suddenly had a desperate thought. "Is this what will happen to him when he dies? He's faery."

Tor shrugged. "I'm no expert on the *sidhe*. Probably. Who knows? How'd you manage a faery in your family?"

"My mother is faery." And then, wanting to see the man's reaction, he said, "Grandpa is a vampire."

"Is that so?" Tor's brow arched.

"He'd never do a thing to attract attention from the Order of the Stake," Stryke clarified. "He fights the good fight. Actually keeps his eye on the local packs who believe they've a right to pit vampires against one another in the blood games."

"Ah. Creed Saint-Pierre. I've heard of him. Good blood."

"Indeed." Stryke tucked the box under an arm. "So that's it?"

The keening wail of something like an insect prompted both men to look toward the heavens.

"Ah, *merde*," Tor muttered. "Demons."

Chapter 19

Stryke saw the demon's face as it leaped and soared toward him—missing the lower jaw. It was one of those nasty wraith demons. Now was no time to bemoan the thing's lack of polite introductions.

Delivering an undercut up into the creature's open maw, he sent it flying up and bouncing over the top of the van.

Tor dived into the back of the van. "I got something!" the Brit called.

"Just stay inside!" Stryke yelled as he bent to avoid the next wraith. Its talons cut through his short hair, sending a chill down the back of his skull. "I got this!"

Pistol in hand, he swung back his shoulder and eyed his periphery. Tor was digging around inside the van. One wraith climbed like a spider over the top of the van, the other—

He smelled the sulfur and turned to catch the demon

square against his chest. They both landed on the cobblestones. Stryke kicked up his knee, but didn't land any particular body part. He grabbed for hair. There was no hair. Something viscous dripped onto his chin and neck. It was coming from the bottom half of the demon's face, which wasn't there.

"You ugly—"

The demon's screech drowned out his oath. And when it spoke the voice was garbled and bubbly. "You sent Himself after us."

"You bet." The Dark Lord had warned he'd let those who wanted the diamond know whom to blame for Himself's discovery of their plot. That was fast. "But if they could only manage to send two of you…"

"We are diversion," his attacker garbled. A swipe of its talons cut across Stryke's collarbone.

Stryke shifted his hand, calling out his claws, and returned the slash with a hearty swipe that cut through the demon's chest and face, rendering it to a goopy, sputtering corpse. He rolled out from under the mess as it collapsed and looked up in time to see Tor dragging what looked like a chain saw down the center of the other demon. But there was no mechanical noise, save for the demon's screams.

The demon dropped in a messy pile and Tor stepped back, wielding the chain saw proudly.

"What is that thing?" Stryke asked, jumping up and leaping over the piles of demons. He shoved the pistol into the waistband of his jeans. "Looks like a chain saw, but it's silent?"

"Yep, it's modified. Easier to sneak up on the enemy that way. Picked this up from a witch years ago. It's especially helpful when attacked in the city and you don't want to draw human attention." Tor cast a glance around and landed on the desecrated demon. "Salt rounds?"

Stryke patted his hip where the pistol grip stuck up. "Yep. But it was more satisfying to take the thing out with a talon."

"I bet. Good thing no one spilled the faery dust. But I've still a sticky mess to clean up. Demon blood. It clings like tar."

"Aren't there people you can call for that?" Stryke knew there were those who specifically answered the call for cleanup after a paranormal being was rendered dead.

"I'm that people." Tor set the chain saw in the back of the van and grabbed a white hazmat suit from a hook on the interior wall. "When necessary, I can clean a crime scene in twenty minutes flat. This mess? I'll be finished in ten. A vacuum cleaner will do the job nicely. What do you think they were after?"

The question hit Stryke hard. He knew the answer to that one. Unfortunately.

"The wraith said something about a diversion. Hell. Blyss. They might be after her, as well." He grabbed the wooden box full of faery dust. "I gotta go." Turning and racing around the side of the van, he paused and backtracked. He tapped the chain saw. "Mind if I borrow this?"

"Go for it. Uh, and if you need cleanup? Give me a call."

"Thanks, man!"

Stryke landed in the driver's seat of the car and tossed the wooden box aside along with the chain saw and the pistol. Bringing up the GPS on his phone, he hoped to find his way to Blyss's place before it was too late.

* * *

By the time Stryke landed in the lush garden court-yard before Blyss's apartment, the scent of sulfur filled his nostrils. Chain saw ready—and so strangely quiet—he sneaked up behind the demon who strolled through the hedgerow toward Blyss's front door. He stepped quickly.

The demon turned toward him. Same missing lower jaw. A wraith.

Stryke winked. Then he dragged the chain saw down the demon from head to gut. Black blood spattered him and the wall outside Blyss's door. But remarkably, the demon didn't shriek. If the neighbors had been watching... He glanced about. Curtains before all the windows.

"Paris. Whoda thought the city of love would be teeming with nasties?"

Tugging out his cell phone, he dialed up Tor. He could be there in fifteen minutes.

Stryke knocked and tried the door. It was open, so, leaving the chain saw dripping with black blood outside, he slipped inside the foyer and closed the door as Blyss's arms wrapped about his neck.

He turned to catch her kiss. "You're happy."

"Because you're finally back. Oh. You smell like..." She tugged him down the hallway and into the kitchen light. "You have black stuff all over you. Demons?"

"Had a bit of a snag with a pickup for Hawkes Associates but it's all good." And before that? She didn't need to know.

"Is it?" Her green eyes watered and he could read her apprehension in the wobble of her lower lip.

"You bet it's good because I'm here now and you are

one gorgeous bit of glamour girl. Did you make dinner reservations?"

"I did. Really? It's…good?"

"Yep." He hugged her. To tell her the truth would only worry her more.

"I think I have a shirt for you to borrow."

Stryke followed her into the bedroom and tugged off his demon blood–soaked shirt while Blyss disappeared into the clothes closet. "Do I want to know how you always seem to have spare men's clothing?"

"Probablement pas!" she called out.

He didn't know what that meant but guessed she'd told him to mind his own beeswax. He wasn't willing to explain about how his day went either, so he'd leave it at that. As far as Stryke was concerned, Blyss no longer had anything to worry about. Her world could return to normal. Or however she defined normal.

And he…well, he'd take each minute as it came and hope for the best.

Heading into the bathroom, he washed his face and squeezed the demon blood out of his hair.

Blyss sipped the white wine and admired its quality. Normally she would send back anything that wasn't exquisite. This wasn't even close to divine, but it sufficed. She hadn't expected much from this river cruise. Thus, her expectations had been wildly exceeded. She sat across the table from a handsome man who only had eyes for her. He wasn't even watching the landmarks they passed by as their boat cruised down the Seine.

"You're missing all the good stuff," she said to Stryke, who finished his salad.

"The good stuff is right in front of me. And I'm not talking about the food. You look amazing tonight."

She wiggled on the chair and touched her hair. She'd pulled it back into a chignon and tucked a diamond clip above her ear. She'd almost gone with the black silk dress but at the last minute had switched to a light pink, airy, summer chiffon dress with matching Louboutins covered in pink crystals. *Keep it simple,* she'd coached. Yet one must always include sparkles when possible.

"You clean up nicely, as well," she said. "Your jeans didn't get any blood on them?"

"Not that I noticed." He tugged at the borrowed tie— so she had a few men's shirts and ties in her closet—and Blyss again noticed the bruise on the side of his neck.

She'd wanted to ask him about his afternoon and the very obvious smell of sulfur on him when he'd arrived, but when he'd come out of the bathroom mumbling something about both of them having secrets to keep, she'd let it go.

Of course, she didn't want to keep her secrets anymore. She had to tell him about the missing fake, but right here on the crowded dining boat was not the place.

The waiter stopped by and served them coq au vin with steaming rosemary bread, and slipped away as quickly and silently as he had appeared. The evening was dusky, though the city lights shone along the shore and glittered on the river, vying with the bright beam of moonlight that dashed across the waters.

"Things didn't go well this afternoon with my brother?" she asked.

Stryke tilted back the remainder of wine, then poured another full serving before leaning forward, checking around that the other diners were all busy chatting and oohing and aahing over the sights, then said, "I called out Himself."

Blyss gasped.

"I know," he rushed out. "Not the sharpest knife in the bunch, this country hick from Minnesota. But at the time it seemed like the quickest way to get to the end point. We've been trying to find the demons who stole *Le Diabolique*. If the lair was found beneath the nightclub, then I assumed he was involved. So why not go directly to the source? But get this. It was news to him."

"Stryke." She placed a hand over his. "I have to tell you about what I found, or didn't find, today while searching the gallery records for info about *Le Diabolique*."

"I wish you wouldn't have gone out. It's dangerous right now, Blyss. That demon by your— Er. Forget it. I'm still worked up over this afternoon. I don't think you have anything to worry about anymore. We talked to… you know, the big dark prince. He didn't want Xyloda released either. So…we took care of it."

"Really? Wait. You said 'we'?"

"Yeah, me and the dark prince are tight." He chuckled and rubbed his jaw. "Kidding. I am so not friends with you know who. But it's over, Blyss. You don't have to worry anymore."

"Then that clears up almost everything."

"Almost?"

She sat back against the chair, no longer hungry. It was amazing that Stryke had found a way to ensure the demon never be released from *Le Diabolique*. That negated her worries about the missing fake. Because it was worthless to whoever had taken it, anyway.

But what was she to do about Edamite Thrash and

her very obvious missing supply? The full moon was in two days.

"There's still Ed," she said softly.

Stryke stood and took a step around to squat beside her chair. He clasped her hand and kissed it. His touch always lured her heartbeats to a slower, more relaxed pace.

"We ran into Thrash today," he said. "Your brother has— Well, that's for him to talk about with you. Suffice, Ed's problem was solved today. He actually wanted to ensure the demon was never released. Can you believe that?"

She could actually. There was something about Ed that wouldn't allow her to label him *full-blown villain*.

"Thrash is satisfied," Stryke said. "He's not going to bother you anymore."

"But he's— Stryke, he is my supplier."

"Yeah, about that. I've a surprise for you. It'll give you the human life you want."

"I don't understand."

"I want to hold off on the surprise. I'll explain it all later." He stood and bent to tilt her face to look at him. "You're going to be fine."

And he kissed her softly and lingered there, as if they were the only two on the boat. He was the only sustenance she needed, and she wanted to tell him that to show him how much he meant to her. But he stood and slid around to sit again. He forked in some chicken and smiled widely. The hero had saved the day. A job well-done, indeed. And she had done nothing to deserve such a favor.

"Thank you" was all Blyss could manage to say without crying and smearing her mascara and turning into a perfect mess. "I love you for that."

He winked at her. "Tomorrow night is the night before the full moon."

"Is that so?" She sensed his teasing tone and wanted to go with the playful mood instead of sinking into the worry that had been niggling at her calm. "I hear your sort require a lot of sex to satiate the need for…" She looked aside before leaning closer and whispering, "…your wild to come out."

"True. Very true. Did I mention that Rhys Hawkes has given me the key to his country cabin for the next few nights? I was thinking of heading out there tomorrow night. Call it a vacation away from my vacation. You interested? Uh, I mean, for tomorrow night. I won't ask you to come along with me on the night of the full moon."

She lifted her goblet and he met hers in a clink. "I'm in for tomorrow night."

The dining boat docked below the Eiffel Tower. By the time they'd climbed up the concrete stairs to street level, the tower twinkled madly with hundreds of thousands of white LED lights and the crowd clapped and cheered.

"Wow." Stryke clasped Blyss's hand and walked toward the massive Iron Lady, head tilted back to take it all in. "This is incredible. I suppose you've seen it so much it doesn't even register on your awe scale."

She snuggled next to him and kissed his jaw where the stubble tickled her mouth. "I've never seen it with you. That makes this a special moment. Come on. Let's stand underneath it."

"Cool. Can we go to the top?"

"Sure, if you want to wait in line."

He stretched his gaze to follow the line that marked around two sides of the tower base. Easily four hundred people waiting, even at ten at night. Probably hours before anyone got to the top.

"Seriously? That's the line?" he asked, his eyes falling to her shoes. "I think I'll pass." He eyed the underside of the tower. His hand clasping hers, he wandered to the left, then stepped back a few paces. "Right here. We're dead center underneath this monster."

"I think you're right." She tilted her head back and looked up into the intricate iron lacing that designed the monument. Exquisite artwork. She was thankful this monument had not been torn down, as was the original plan when it had been built merely as part of a grand exposition in the late 1800s. A breeze brushed the pink chiffon against her legs and tickled through her hair. Never had she felt so light.

"Can you imagine what it was like to build this thing?" Stryke asked. "I mean, what was it, the nineteenth century? No advanced technology. Probably no cranes to hoist up the heavy pieces. Amazing. Come here."

He sat on the ground and patted the concrete beside him.

Blyss tugged at the hem of her pale pink skirt.

He tapped the toe of her shoe. "Yeah, Sparkles, you're going to get a little messy again." He winked, and her heart fluttered in response.

She sat beside him and together they lay back and admired the tower while tourists wandered around them. The night was bright and bustling with people, but Blyss felt the world slip away and in that moment she and Stryke were the only two that existed.

He pulled her hand to his mouth to kiss it, and she nuzzled her head against his shoulder. Who cared if her dress got dirty or her shoes scuffed? All that mattered was she was exactly where she wanted to be right now. Next to a man who had teased her out from behind the mask.

Yes, she felt vulnerable to think that. Because she had let down some of the glamour and just wanted to be with him. Simple. Nothing complicated.

But everything right. Or as right as it could be. Because indeed, she was light.

She wondered if she would ever get a refill of pills from Edamite. Were things settled with him? Not hardly. If not, she would remain the same breed as Stryke—forced to accept her werewolf—but she could never be the woman he desired because she'd always regret her lost humanity.

She wanted to be everything for him.

"What are you thinking about?" he suddenly asked.

"Besides that I hope no one steps on us?"

"Yes, besides that."

"I think I'm lucky that I chose you that night at the gallery. I'm sorry for all the horrible things that have resulted because of that choice. But for all the good, I am thankful. And you are the good."

She twisted up to kiss him, and there beneath the Eiffel Tower, oblivious to the world, they made out like teenagers.

Chapter 20

Once at home, Blyss unzipped her dress as she walked down the long hallway, through the kitchen and veered toward the bedroom. Stryke followed. He'd kicked off his shoes by the door. He tugged the shirt over his head in the kitchen. By the time he'd reached the bedroom door, the zipper on his pants was open.

Blyss stepped out of her dress. Clad in pink lace bra and panties, she wandered toward the bed. She stood there, bathed beneath the moonlight, her fingers gliding along her pinned-up hair.

"Let me watch you take it down," Stryke said in a desire-tinged voice that hardened her nipples in anticipation.

She pulled out the diamond clip and slowly unraveled her hair from the chignon. It tickled across her shoulders and down her back, but knowing her lover watched made the move intensely erotic. Gliding her fingers down her sides to her hips, she tugged at the panties, slipping them down a bit…

She turned to find Stryke leaning against the wall, his gaze fixed on her. He nodded, and she wiggled the panties down and dropped them to her feet, where she stepped out of them, her Louboutins clicking the marble floor.

Turning, she toyed with the snap between the bra cups. She walked toward him, lowering her lashes in a teasing glance. Once unclasped, she quickly peeled aside the cups, flashing him, then as quickly held the lacy bits over her breasts.

"You think so, huh?" He gestured she come closer. Oh, that knowing smile! "I want another peek."

Blyss stepped closer. "Say *s'il vous plaît*."

"What does that mean?"

"Say it, and you'll know."

"See voo plate."

"Oh, darling." She stroked his cheek, following the line of the soft stubble. "Your French is terrible."

"Guilty. But I don't need words to please you." He drew his fingers up her thigh and over to her mons, where he moved lower, deeper.

Blyss sucked in a breath. She tilted her head and closed her eyes at the delicious sensation of his finger entering her. He turned her chin to face him.

"Look at me, glamour girl." Now he slicked over her clit slowly, achingly. "Don't look away."

In his eyes she found an intensity that would have made her wolf howl with delight. It certainly made the woman she was shiver and coo.

Hands still at her breasts, she released the lacy cups and then caressed them while Stryke coaxed her body toward release with his fingers. The focus in his eyes heightened every sensation. It was difficult to look at him, and yet she couldn't look away. That would be a betrayal, a refusal to give him all that she could. And she wanted to. She needed to.

Tomorrow night he would need her to satiate him. And she would do that. Because he could touch her very soul. And she never wanted him to stop.

Gasping as the hum at her loins began to ripple outward, gripping her muscles and promising exquisite release, Blyss moaned and tilted her forehead against Stryke's.

And as she came, she whispered, "I'm yours."

He wanted to melt into her. To kneel before her and worship her. To tie her up and keep her only for him. To set her free and watch her spread her wings. He wanted to never forget the feel of her body shuddering against his as she came. And he must never forget the sound of her whimpers and the clutch of her fingers against his shoulders as the tremendous release captured her.

He didn't want to share her with anyone else. Ever.

Be damned his plans to leave Paris with fond memories of an amazing fling. He wanted to make this woman his. His bondmate. Maybe even his wife.

Yes, even if she chose to live life as a human as opposed to the true wolf she could be. Stryke couldn't see any other way to keep her. So he'd surrender his need to love a werewolf, to love and raise the big family. He'd sacrifice it all for Blyss. Even the pack.

"Let me love you," he whispered in her ear as she shivered against him. "Always."

"Yes. *Jamais.*"

"No one else," he said as he lifted her and carried her to the bed. "Only me."

She pulled him on top of her and pushed down his boxer shorts. "Only you. I don't want any other man, Stryke." She kissed him and then pushed him to roll onto his back so she could straddle his hips. "I don't want any other wolf."

Dipping her head, she licked down his stomach and then took his erection into her mouth. He raked his fingers through her luscious hair and followed her rhythm as her head dipped up and down. She devoured him, nipping gently and then laving him from tip to root.

As he rode the wave of orgasm she clung to his body, her heat insane and the stroke of her fingernails over his skin only prolonging the pleasure. Finally he exhaled, his energy spent and his body lax.

He'd meant it when he'd asked her to love only him. He'd worry about real life—the fact he didn't even live on the same continent as her—in the morning.

Stryke woke to the patter of the shower in the bathroom. Lavender permeated the room. Combined with the lingering tendrils of Blyss's flower perfume, it made for a heady atmosphere. He sat in the queen's chambers, her willing subject, waiting for her beck and call.

With a smile, he got up and pulled on his pants. The glass vial the devil Himself had given him dropped to the floor. He'd almost forgotten about it. After they'd returned to her apartment—well, his mind had been elsewhere. And over dinner he hadn't wanted to spoil the romantic mood.

"She'll be pleased."

And for a moment Stryke struggled with tossing the

vial outside in the nearest garbage can, thus forcing
Blyss to face her werewolf. She'd never have to know
he'd held a definitive fix for what most bothered her.

He rubbed a palm over his face and shook his head.
"She's gotta do what she needs to do to be happy."

Because he'd decided last night that he could be
happy with her no matter what. Really, he could.

Mostly. He chose to ignore that niggle of doubt that
said perhaps his happiness wasn't worth the effort of
tossing the vial.

He clutched the key to Blyss's happiness.

The shower stopped. Blyss's humming made him
smile. But too quickly the smile slipped away. He shook
the little glass container. Just demon ash? Or something
so powerful even he would regret ever giving it to her?

"Morning, lover."

He turned and held out the vial toward Blyss. Because
if he didn't do it now he'd lose the courage.

She wore a sheer black robe that did not hide the gorgeous body beneath. His eyes veered to her breasts, and
even as she took the vial, he pulled her to him and bent
to bite gently through the sheer fabric at the full swell
of her breast.

"What is this?" she asked.

"From Himself."

"What?"

And for the first time he considered that what gleamed
red inside the glass vial was devil magic. The darkest
form of magic in existence. Did he want to let Blyss take
her chances with it?

He had no right to deny her.

"The Dark Prince offered me anything I wanted
after I'd told him about the missing diamond and we…"

Nope. Wasn't necessary to detail his adventures as Himself's sidekick. "I asked for something that a werewolf could take to become completely human."

She clutched the vial against her chest. "Really? But that's... Wow. But what about you?"

"I don't want a thing. My needs are simple. And this way, if you drink the stuff, it's permanent. You'll never have to deal with Thrash again. In fact, I told the asshole to stay the hell away from you."

"You always think of me. That's so..." She gasped. "Thank you, Stryke."

"You deserve whatever makes you happy."

He kissed her. And her lips tasted bittersweet. Suddenly life tasted the same.

He could do this. He wanted to do this. With Blyss.

"You going to take that before I push you onto the bed and make you messy again?"

"Yes, sure. I'll be right back."

He winked and strolled away, wincing as he imagined her pulling out the cork stopper and tilting back the vile concoction. He'd found the wolf he had hoped to find to make him happy.

Too bad she couldn't face that truth.

It was afternoon when Stryke kissed Blyss and bid her *au revoir*. He intended to pick her up and they would then drive out to the country cabin Rhys Hawkes had loaned him for the weekend. Blyss wanted to pack a few things for the day and he was going to the apartment to grab some things, as well.

She closed the front door and realized with a start that she'd forgotten to tell him about the missing transfer records for *Le Diabolique*. And the missing fake.

Not that it mattered anymore. She now had the key to making her life exactly as she wished it.

She wondered if Edamite had forgiven her debt to him. Because she did still owe him the five hundred thousand for this past year's supply. And since when were Ed and Kir friends? She vacillated over giving her brother a call, but the glass vial on the counter called to her.

Tomorrow night was the full moon. When she stopped her pills once a year for the shift, she usually stopped taking them the day before. So today would be appropriate. But it had been only ten months since she'd shifted. She didn't need to do so this month.

The contents of this vial would forever make her human? That was all she desired. She teased at the cork stopper, which was sealed with black wax. She ran her fingernail along the wax, but didn't press hard enough to crack it.

She set the vial on the counter. She'd tuck it in her bag and take it along to the cabin. Right now she had to find something in her closet that could possibly be worn in the country. In a cabin. In the middle of nowhere. That probably didn't even have internet.

"I wonder if there is even plumbing?" She shuddered to consider they could be going rustic tonight. "I hope Stryke realizes the sacrifice I'm making by roughing it. This may be harder than facing my werewolf."

Now, what sort of shoes did one wear to venture into the country?

Chapter 21

Rhys had loaned Stryke an Audi coupe and the keys to a country cabin. The man's kindness was impressive. And they weren't even related, only by the new distant ties that Stryke's aunt had forged with Rhys's grandson, Johnny Santiago. Stryke had yet to meet Rhys's wife, Viviane.

Viviane, a vampire, was supposed to be crazy. Apparently in the eighteenth century she'd been buried alive in a glass coffin by a nasty vampire, and Rhys had only found her two hundred and fifty years later. That would be enough to drive anyone crazy. And talk about holding the romantic torch for over two centuries? Cool.

He glanced at Blyss, who followed the streaks of rain that beat down the car windows with a manicured fingernail. A downpour had rolled into Paris as they'd exited the city periphery and it was difficult to see driving along the dark country roads. Blyss's lips curled into a smile.

"What are you thinking about?" he asked as he slowed the vehicle to follow the GPS's blinking directions to turn. He had to keep an eye on the screen because the French instructions could not be adjusted to English.

"About all the sex I'm going to have with you tonight." She shot him a flirty shimmy of shoulders and a wink. "I've always wanted to have sex in the rain."

"Even this monsoon? Maybe we can find a place on a porch or under an overhang. Wouldn't want you to muss your hair."

"Oh, please. You like me messy."

"I do. I'd love to lick more food off you too, if you want to make that happen."

"All I've brought along is wine, cheese and bread. I suppose I should have packed more if you intend to stay the entire weekend."

He planned to bring her back to town tomorrow and then drive out to spend the full moon by himself. He'd shift, and all would be well with his werewolf.

"I'll pick up some food when we return to town. Rhys did say there was meat in the freezer and some stock in the cupboards. I guess he owns a handful of properties in and around Paris. This cabin he mostly lets friends use. The man is generous."

"Half wolf and half vampire, right? I couldn't imagine having a hunger for blood."

"One of my brothers has such a hunger. Blade is faery and vampire."

"Quite the mix. Has he ever bitten you?"

"Once, when we were teenagers. It was more a tussle

kind of thing. But he spat it out and walked away. Blade is kind of…intense. He's the black sheep of the family if there ever was one. Been through a hell of a lot."

"Handsome, too," Blyss commented. "But everyone in your family is attractive. Your sister's hair was pink."

"Because she's half faery. Make that *faery* now. She sacrificed her wolf because there was something wacky going on with her body. Her two sides were fighting one another, so she had to choose one over the other."

"Living among humans, I've forgotten all the interesting situations and people our breed encounters. I confess the wedding made me nervous."

"I sensed that."

"I've completely forgotten how to be a werewolf. Not that that's a bad thing."

"You said you shift once a year?"

"Yes. It hurts. I don't like it."

"It actually physically hurts you?"

"Yes. Probably because I don't do it often enough. I know it's not supposed to be painful."

"I love shifting," Stryke said. He slowed, noting their destination was a mile ahead. "Great way to stretch the muscles and invigorate my whole system. I bet if you did it more often it would stop being painful."

"Probably." She tilted her head against the window. She didn't like talking about it, so he'd leave it be. For now. Because even if he thought he could overlook her weirdness, he knew, in his heart, the bigger discussion was necessary if he meant to think long-term about their relationship.

"There's a light ahead. Must be the place. Rhys said the garage is separate from the house, so we'll park and then you'll have to dash through the rain."

"I can handle a little water."

The car headlights beamed onto the garage door. Stryke found the door opener and pressed the button. Inside the three-car garage sat a four-wheeler and a couple of mountain bikes. Once parked, they got out and he retrieved their bags from the trunk. Blyss had packed a large suitcase for her one-night stay. He wasn't even going to question. Not after stumbling into the shoe closet.

Standing inside the garage, they assessed the hundred-yard walk from there to the house. Grassy and muddy and slick from the rain, the land rose to an incline closer to the house.

"I'll run these up to the house, then come back and carry you," he suggested.

"You don't think I can walk on my own?"

"Not in those heels and that mud. Unless you want to give it a try?"

She tapped her heels together. "I'll wait here for my knight to come rescue me."

"I like the sound of that. Give me a few minutes." He grabbed the suitcases. "I'll be back."

Blyss leaned into the mist that sifted into the garage. Cool on her nose and lips, it made her smile. Or probably the smile was because she was to spend the night in a romantic cabin with the man with whom she had fallen in love.

She pulled off her shoes and clutched the heels with one hand. "Manolos for a cabin adventure? What was I thinking?"

Should have worn the riding boots and a comfortable pair of jersey leggings. But she felt wrong when not wearing a dress. It was her uniform of sorts. A dress was feminine and sexy and so not rough and wolflike.

Ah, well, she didn't intend to stay dressed long.

"Whoa!" Stryke slid down a slant of dirty land and caught himself by slapping his palms against the garage door wall. "That mud is slippery. The cabin looks amazing. There's a fire started and everything."

"Really?"

"It's an electronic fireplace. I think Rhys sent a maid in to gussy up the place for us. Very cool. As for getting you up to the cabin, you are going to get wet."

She tugged him to her. He was soaked to the skin and smelled like wild spring. "Doesn't take much to get wet around you, *mon amour.*"

The man beamed and he leaned in to kiss her, crushing his wet clothes against her body. She couldn't complain. Tonight, she was in for the whole messy adventure.

Stryke swept her into his arms. "Ready?"

She tucked her shoes against her chest. They were going to get wet, but there was nothing she could do about it. Thank goodness they were patent leather. "Ready as I'll ever be."

He dashed out into the rain. Cold, pounding, it beat about them as he seemed to be racing directly into the storm. A few times his footsteps slipped. His body wobbled, but he maintained balance. Eyes closed against the downpour, Blyss clung to his wet shirt and biceps. They were halfway to the cabin when a big splash of muddy water preceded Stryke's shout. This time when he wobbled he went down.

Blyss fell out of his arms. The shoes flew. And she landed on palms and knees in thick, slippery mud.

"Ah shit, I'm so sorry!" But the chuckle that followed didn't jibe with Stryke's apologetic words. "Told you it's slippery out here. Blyss? Are you okay? You're not hurt?"

"I'm… I don't know." Kneeling there, she tried to get her bearings. Her fingers curled into cold wet mud. Something gritty irritated her knees. She tasted dirt in her mouth. And her precious shoes were not to be seen. "This is horrible."

"I'm sorry, sweetie. Let me lift you carefully—"

"Back off, wolf." She shoved a muddy hand at him, landing on his face. She hadn't intended to do that. Didn't want him to think it a slap. "Oh, no, I didn't mean…"

And then something shifted inside her. The pristine, primped socialite fell off her pedestal and landed in the mud—and laughed. She lowered her head and curled her fingers deeper into the mud and laughed louder.

"Really?" Stryke sat and wiped at the mud on his face. "You think that was funny?"

"*That* wasn't funny." She grasped at the oozy mud and flung a wad at Stryke's chest. His stunned expression was exactly as she'd intended. "But that was."

"You think so?"

He raked up a slosh of mud and trailed his palm along her bare leg to her thigh. It didn't feel any nastier than the cold rain or the gritty mud beneath her knees. Blyss shifted in an attempt to shake his touch away, but her knees slid and her shoulders went down. She landed her back in the mud.

And Stryke landed on top of her, hands to either side of her head. Mud from his cheek spattered her nose and lips. She spat it out and cried out in disgust.

"Too late now, glamour girl. You're going to get messy."

"I already am!" she pleaded as his muddy hands moved over her hips and up to her breasts, where he pulled down her dress and caressed her bare skin. The cold shock of his touch tightened her nipples and the slip and slide of their bodies in the mud made their dalliance more fun than she would have expected.

"You're merciless," she gasped, but followed with a wad of mud to his neck. It oozed down his shirt, which he pulled off and tossed aside.

The sight of his bared muscles dripping clean with rain enticed her. She kissed his cool/hot skin and gently tugged his nipple with her teeth. "Mercy, you are beautiful."

His hand slapped her thigh and slid up under her dress, lifting it to expose her panties, which were soaked in mud. The ooze between her legs was not the sexiest feeling, but the roaming hands that lifted her to sit atop his thighs were.

She kissed his muddy mouth and tasted dirt and rain and summer grass. Definitely a unique taste experience, and the intensity of his want would not allow her to stop.

"You know," he said as he kissed down her chin and to her neck. "There's something about you getting all messy and horny at the same time. When you let down your defenses you get wild."

"You like me this way."

"I love you this way. Wild and unrestrained. You don't care what others think of you or what you look like. It's sexy."

"It'll be even sexier if we can make our way to a

shower. I'm beginning to feel the mud creep into places I'd rather not feel it."

"There's a shower right inside the back door. It's like a mudroom."

"Well named."

"Right?"

"I never thought I'd ever have the need for something so terribly named as a mudroom, but I am at your mercy."

"Come on." He stood and grabbed her hand to pull her up. She claimed her muddy shoes in the process. "Sorry, but the rescue mission was a complete failure." He stroked a hank of wet, muddy hair from her cheek. "Forgive me?"

Blyss shook her head and held the shoes out at a distance. "Never. I like what you've done to me, Stryke. And despite the mud, it feels good. Unrestrained, like you said. Do you think it suits me?"

"It's an odd fit, but you know what? It does suit you."

And he swung her up into his arms and this time made it to the house without another slip.

The mudroom lived up to its name. After they'd showered and Blyss had headed upstairs to the bedroom to unpack, Stryke wiped down the tiled walls and made sure they didn't leave too much of a mess for Rhys.

Out in the homey kitchen that featured open shelves, log walls and red-checked curtains, he found a basket laden with fruit and wine and a welcome note that clued him there were fresh towels in the bathroom and sheets on the bed. Wine chilled in the fridge. The note was signed by a maid service. Nice.

He could get used to living the high life. An apartment in Paris and a country cabin? Toss in a gorgeous girlfriend and what more could he ask for?

Blyss's purse sat on the counter next to the fruit basket and it was open. He spied the cork stopper in the top of the vial he'd gotten from Himself. His heart dropped in his gut.

A *werewolf* was what more he could ask for. But he'd resigned himself to accepting Blyss for what she wanted to be. She accepted him, country hick that he was.

Blyss wandered into the kitchen wearing her sheer robe and fluffing her wet hair over a shoulder. "All the mud gone?"

"Mostly," he reassured her, turning to embrace her and kiss the crown of her head. "Nice place, eh?"

"It is. Not so backwoods as I'd anticipated. Which is a relief. I want to sit in front of the fire. How about some wine before we tame the beast?"

"The beast? Is that what you think of a guy's werewolf?"

"Well, it is your more beastly side, isn't it?" She trailed her finger down his bare chest. He wore but a towel around his hips. "I'd like to tame it."

She wandered into the living room and toward the fire. Firelight danced through the sheer robe silhouetting her slender frame.

"Taming sounds good," Stryke muttered.

He quickly located a corkscrew and opened a wine bottle. Pouring Blyss a goblet and bringing the bottle along for himself, he joined her on the thick white carpet before the fireplace. It was an electronic fire, but it put off some good heat and was probably safer. Though he did miss the smell of smoke and burning logs.

Blyss tilted her goblet against the bottle he held. "Here's to taming your wolf."

Stryke howled, releasing a long and randy call. "Give it your best shot, glamour girl."

"I think I'll start right now." And she tugged the towel from his hips and bent to kiss the head of his extremely hard erection.

Chapter 22

The sun was out. The rain had stopped. The surrounding forest glittered as if it was Faery. Keys in hand, Stryke was prepared to drive Blyss back into Paris when she descended from the upstairs bedroom wearing a sundress and no shoes. Hair darker than the black diamond that had caused him so much trouble spilled loosely over her shoulders and she floated up to kiss him.

"Good morning, *mon amour*."

"Uh, good morning." His sight lingered on the rise of her breasts peeking above the cheery yellow fabric. "You're looking so not ready to head back into the city."

"You want to be rid of me so quickly?"

"Hell no. But I thought… It is afternoon already, Miss Layabed."

"Do not mock my beauty sleep."

"Wouldn't dream of it."

"So…" She sidled up alongside him. She pulled her purse across the counter and sat on a bar stool to sort through whatever it was women kept inside those sacred caches of femininity. "What if I've decided to stay the night with you?"

Stryke couldn't help but gape. The implications should she stay…

"You do understand I'm going to be out running around in the forest tonight? In werewolf form."

She nodded, then pulled out from her purse the glass vial with the black wax seal and placed it on the counter between them.

Stryke bent to peer into the vial at eye level. The red liquid filled it to the top, which didn't make sense. He averted his gaze to Blyss, who nodded in agreement to his unasked question.

"You didn't drink it?" Standing, he stretched his arms along the counter and again eyed the devil's gift. "But that means…"

"I, uh…" She fluttered her lashes and looked aside sheepishly. "…was thinking maybe we could go out together tonight?"

"You mean as wolves?" He straightened. Smoothed a palm down his abs. Scratched his head. "But, Blyss, you said you only have to shift once a year, and that shift wasn't due for a few more months. You don't need to do it. Drink the potion and you'll stay the way you desire."

"I want to do this, Stryke. As painful as it will be to shift, I want to race alongside you and know what it's like to be in the presence of another wolf. A wolf that I can trust. Is that okay?"

"Okay?" He swung around the counter and pulled

her into a hug. "That's better than okay. But are you sure?"

"Positive. I can drink the stuff tomorrow and get right back to where I prefer. But for tonight…I want to do this for me, but I also want to do it for you. Will you let me?"

"I can't wait until moonrise."

Stryke lowered the strap on Blyss's sundress, inhaling her sweet flower perfume as the fabric skimmed her skin. The dress dropped to the summer grass and tickled his bare toes. Naked, she shivered. He sensed it wasn't because she was cold, but rather nervous. The night was sultry and warm, a perfect evening to go skyclad.

That she wanted to shift to be with him as wolves was incredible. But he didn't want to force her to do anything to please him.

He'd already stripped away his clothes in preparation to shift. The summer breeze felt great on his skin, and his erection—unpreventable when standing so close to Blyss.

Now he bent to study her gaze. "You sure?"

"Very sure." She touched his abs and he hissed at the erotic flutter that shivered through his system. "But I don't want you to watch me shift. I don't want you to see me in pain."

"Blyss, if it's going to hurt you—"

She kissed him, stopping his protest. Her mouth was a gift he could never refuse. So sweet and soft. Priceless.

"It only hurts until I'm shifted," she whispered. "Maybe you could go on ahead and wait for me to follow after you?"

"I can do that." He respected her need to protect herself when likely she felt most vulnerable. "But if at any time this feels wrong to you, shift to *were* shape and we'll head back to the cabin, okay?"

"Your werewolf needs to howl at the moon, and I'm going to howl alongside you. Shift, lover. Let me admire you. Then run along and wait for me."

He kissed her, tasting the wine they'd imbibed earlier. The afternoon had been spent on the floor before the fireplace making love, lying quietly beside one another, snoozing a bit. It felt great to hold Blyss and think about spending the night together as wolves. And while he didn't want to know how painful the shift was going to be for her, he also wanted to experience her wild if she was willing to show it.

"I'll wait for you up on that rise in the forest about half a mile north." He pointed in the direction. And then he turned his focus inward and allowed his wolf to take control.

The shift was an exquisite exercise in muscle control and internal command. His bones shifted and shortened. His musculature stretched and snapped to conform to the smaller wolf shape. Fur grew out from his pores and his head changed the most, the maw growing long and his canines lengthening.

When finally he stood on four legs, Stryke was aware of the human female who stood before him. She smelled familiar and a little like a wolf. He knew she was his, but in his wolf mind he had no name for her. What he did know was that he should move along and wait for her elsewhere.

As she bent to stroke her fingers through his fur, he bowed his head and licked at her knee, her leg, the tips of her fingers. Tasted familiar. Tasted safe, like his own.

"I'll be right there" was what the sounds coming from her mouth formed, though he didn't understand them.

Stryke scented a rabbit not far off and his ears swiveled, picking up the movement of dozens of smaller creatures scampering about the earth and within the thick forest undergrowth.

He yipped and dashed off in pursuit of the adventure that could result in a tasty meal.

"That is one gorgeous wolf," Blyss whispered as Stryke loped off into the forest.

His fur was variegated in shades of brown, black and blond. He'd stood high to her waist, and he carried his thick tail proudly upright. A natural pack leader, if there was one.

Blyss had always considered the wolf as repellent as dogs and other animals she didn't want to get too close to. Yes, she had grown up among wolves. Had been accustomed to her parents wandering outside in wolf form, besides having some friends who had already come into their werewolf. Her disgust hadn't developed until her own shift had so awkwardly and devastatingly introduced her to ridicule.

But she was safe here with Stryke. And a giddy hum within her core urged her to crouch on the ground beside her discarded sundress. She wanted this. She needed this.

Closing her eyes and summoning the inner ability to shift, the first painful reactions crackled in her bones. She gasped, her fingers digging into the wet grass and dirt. It wasn't too late to stop. *Keep going. You want to be with him.* Her spine curved unnaturally upward, burning the pain along her length.

She cried out, yet continued. Bowing her head to the ground, she tensed her jaws as every muscle seemed to snap in on itself and tug her skeletal system into a bunch. Flipping onto her back, she released all human thoughts, and as fur covered her body and her legs kicked at air, the wolf whined at the horrible pain.

Finally, the shift was complete and the wolf shakily stood on all fours. The pain had ceased. No one around to fear. To point fingers. She was safe.

She sniffed the air, taking in the lingering scent of what she knew was her partner. And of a sudden, her tail wagged.

The moon was high and full.

The night called to her wild.

The wolves found one another, bumping noses and licking one another's maws in greeting and respect. They nudged their noses against ears, head and body, scenting one another, showing love and care.

Then Stryke dashed off through the forest and Blyss followed close behind.

They chased a rabbit and then a red fox. A few mice were sacrificed in playful dally. The wolves paused near a rocky outcrop and basked in the moonlight, Stryke's head resting upon Blyss's furry flank. And they were taken by the need to mate, and did so, howling their connection to the moon.

They woke on the porch before the cabin, both naked in human *were* form. Moonlight glanced through the oak and maple leaf canopy, dazzling across their skin. Stryke plucked a strand of grass from Blyss's hair and kissed her deeply. She curled up against his body, not being able to recall the pain of the shift, but remembering clearly the freedom and joy she had felt with her lover in their four-legged forms.

"Thank you," she whispered. "For making it so easy to trust you."

"You make a great wolf, glamour girl. I'm pretty sure we had sex."

"I think it was awesome. But you didn't let your werewolf out."

"The night's not over yet. I'll have to give the werewolf reign or it'll be on me all month to do so."

"I wouldn't miss it for the world."

"Really? You going to wolf out with me again?"

"Think you can handle my werewolf, big boy?"

"Bring it."

"Will I…? Will we…?"

He guessed what she couldn't quite put into words. He shouldn't be surprised no one had ever taught her the ways of their breed.

He nodded. "When a werewolf comes upon another of his breed, like a gorgeous female werewolf, he'll feel compelled to mate with her."

"And mating in werewolf form will bond us?"

He clasped her hand. "I don't think either of us is ready for that. Especially not when you've that vial of red stuff sitting inside on the counter. Why don't I head out on my own?"

She nodded. And Stryke exhaled in relief.

Disappointed? Hell yes. He'd love to bond with her. But no, he wasn't prepared to commit to a woman in werewolf form and then forever lose her to the humanity she craved.

He kissed her. "Go inside and snuggle before the fireplace. I won't be more than an hour."

"I'm sorry—"

He kissed her again. "There is nothing to apologize for. I know you. I accept you as you are. Okay?"

"I love you."

"I love you, too."

Morning woke them on the rug before the fire. Stryke had gone out and when he'd returned to the cabin had found Blyss sleeping. They showered together and made love.

Now he turned off the lights in the cabin and checked the fireplace one last time. "All hatches are battened down. You got your purse?"

"Yes."

"Don't forget that vial. It's sitting by the sink."

"Thanks. I'll drink it when I get home. I'm enjoying being able to smell everything turned up to eleven, and I never realized how improved my sight is when I let the wolf out."

"You still think I'm sexy now that you can see better?"

"You're even sexier." She kissed him quickly but took a moment to rub her cheek against his stubble. "Mmm… You're a combination of handsome, sensual and sexy eye candy."

"I don't know what to say to that."

"I'm crazy about you, Stryke. Take it for what you will. Let's stop and pick up some breakfast along the way, yes?"

"Way ahead of you. I'm craving eggs and bacon. Do they make that here in France?"

"A Croque Madame would be delicious."

"A crock of what?"

Blyss giggled. "I did see a McDonald's when we were passing through the suburbs."

"Sausage McMuffin, I'm coming for you!"

The drive-through McDonald's gave Stryke hope that the Europeans had a bit of redneck in them, after all. If he could park the car and shove down some processed food and a tall Coke he was happy. Blyss even took a bite of his sausage-and-egg sandwich and declared it tasty—but now sipped orange juice. Ah well, one did require a certain palate to appreciate the greasy goodness of fast food.

Stryke's thoughts wandered beyond the buzz of traffic zipping by on the ring road. He'd encountered danger in Paris, as he'd hoped for, and had defeated all threats to Blyss. But the thing with Tor and the wraiths the other day wouldn't leave his brain.

"This diversion thing is gnawing at me."

"Diversion?"

He confessed, "The night I showed up at your door with demon blood on me, ready to go on the boat cruise? I'd just killed a demon outside your door."

"What?"

"Earlier, when I met with Tor to pick up some faery dust, we were hijacked by a couple of demons. Only they said they were the diversion. Which is how I guessed you might be in trouble and headed immediately to your place. Caught a demon outside your door."

"Why didn't you tell me that?"

"Wasn't necessary." He balled up the food wrapper and tossed it in the open paper bag on the backseat. "I took care of it. But now that I think of it, if they weren't after me, but instead you, why? Why are demons still after you even knowing you no longer have *Le Diabolique*? What do you have that they want?"

Blyss shrugged. "I have no idea. I've sold all my jewels to pay for the pills. I have nothing of value save this diamond pendant." She tapped the necklace. "Well, and my shoes. But I don't think…"

No, the glamour girl could never part with those precious beauties.

"Think, Blyss. Do you have any friendships or business deals, anything, with demons beyond Edamite?"

"No. Not that I know of. I mean, I could be standing right next to one and I'd never know."

"Right. The pills." He tilted his head against the seat. "Who works with you? Who have you dealt with that might have something against you?"

"No one that I can think of. I'm a socialite. I don't make enemies. I, well, I make love. Except…"

"Yeah?"

"I haven't seen Lorcan in days. You met my assistant. I hired him six months ago. He's always been very attentive and suddenly he's gone. And I was going to tell you about the missing paperwork, but then when you found *Le Diabolique*, I figured it no longer mattered."

"What missing paperwork?"

"I have no records of receiving the diamond. No clue who it came from."

"And your assistant is up and missing?"

She nodded. "Do you think he could be in trouble? The demons could be after him?"

Stryke rapped the steering wheel with his fist. "Whatever it is, I'm inclined to suspect someone out there thinks you have something and they want it."

"I don't have anything. The only thing I took from the gallery was *Le Diabolique*."

"Right. And if demons are still after you, it makes me guess you would have something they want. Demonic."

"Do you think…they want to get rid of me?"

He caught the wobble in her tone and clasped her hand and pulled it to his mouth to kiss. "No, I don't think so. I may be blowing this all out of the water. It's done. *Le Diabolique* is safe and sound in the— Er, wherever the Old Lad has it." Which was in his gut. "And the ones who tried to take it have already had a swing at me and failed. But the missing assistant does bother me."

"It could be Edamite," she decided.

Stryke winced to recall what Kir had told him about Edamite being their half brother. The demon had said he would never harm Blyss. Threaten her, sure. Could he trust the demon had been speaking truthfully?

Hell, if Ed had wanted Blyss out of the picture, he would have succeeded with that task by now.

"You should have a talk with your brother about Ed sometime," Stryke suggested. He navigated the car down the street, heading toward the busy 1st arrondissement, where Blyss lived.

"Why?"

He shrugged. "Just think it would be a good idea. Ed is…more on your side than you know."

"Well, why don't *you* tell me?"

He winced again. Bad move. He didn't want to get stuck in the middle of a forced sibling reunion or rivalry.

"There's your street," he said, relieved for an escape. He pulled before Blyss's building and they strolled through the courtyard. He paused before the door, her suitcases in hand, and sniffed.

"What is it?" she asked as she punched in the digital code.

"Thought I smelled demon. But it's probably leftovers."

"Leftovers?" Blyss wrinkled her nose and did an assessment of the door, wall and ground around them. Tor had done an excellent job of cleanup, Stryke noted. Not a spot of demon blood that he could see.

"Can we go in? These suitcases of yours are heavy."

She cast him a doubtful look before crossing the threshold. So it had been a stupid excuse. He could heft a dozen of these bags and not feel the strain in his muscles. But it wasn't necessary to give Blyss all the bloody details. He'd taken care of the threat. Story over.

Her heels clicked down the hallway, and he followed the sexy sashay of her hips, clad in a narrow yellow dress that hugged all her sleek curves. The swing of her long hair across her shoulders made his mouth water, and he set down the suitcases and went in for the kiss—

"Ahem."

Stryke twisted to spy a strange man in a pink suit standing in Blyss's living room.

Chapter 23

"Lorcan."

Stryke stepped before Blyss, keeping her from approaching the assistant, who stood by the white couch, hands at his hips, the smile on his face as forced as a thief's entry.

"What are you doing here?" Stryke asked. "Do you always break into your employer's home?"

"I came to apologize." Lorcan paced to the side, putting himself a little closer to Blyss, so Stryke was forced to move slightly aside. "I took *Le Diabolique*. I was desperate."

"Oh, Lorcan, but it was a fake."

"Blyss." Stryke was not sensing the man had come to beg forgiveness. Something about the tension in the fisted hands at his sides and the faint but distinct red glow in his eyes. "He's demon."

"Aren't you the clever one?" Lorcan suddenly dropped

the contrite act. "And her." He drew in a breath through his nose. "You're smelling rather wolfish today, Blyss. You finally decide to drop the lie and come clean?"

"What do you know about me, Lorcan?" Blyss asked. Stryke clasped her hand when she stepped up to stand beside him. "Who are you?"

"I've been living among the bloody humans for months in wait of the perfect means to finally gain some power in this city. I need control. More power than Edamite Thrash holds over the local denizens. My denizen was this close—" he pinched his fingers together before him "—to releasing Xyloda. And then the Lone Ranger of Werewolves comes riding in with Himself as his side-kick and spoils all my hard work."

"You were the one after *Le Diabolique*?" Blyss said on a gasp.

"It's gone," Stryke said firmly. "So you can either take the easy way—leave and never return, or…" He flicked out his claws. "…you can do it the hard way."

"I mean Blyss no harm," Lorcan hurried out. "I've seen the error of my ways. I want you to take me back, Blyss. I need the job. I've ransomed my hopes of defeating Thrash at his own game. What do you say? Let bygones be bygones?"

Blyss glanced up at Stryke. He shook his head. No way the demon was telling the truth. "He sent his henchmen after you. They would have killed you."

"Oh, no," Lorcan said. "I don't think I could have killed Blyss. At least, not until I'd learned where *Le Diabolique* was."

Blyss shook her head. "Get out." She stepped forward, gesturing toward the door down the hallway, and in that moment in which her body was positioned slightly closer to the demon than Stryke's, Lorcan grabbed her by the arm and wrangled her into a choke hold.

Stryke growled.

"Come one step closer," Lorcan warned, "and I'll crush her throat." He eased his fingers about her slender neck. "I want the diamond! You were the last to see it. Take me to it, and only then will Blyss be safe."

The bastard didn't know whom he was dealing with. And he would not allow this fool one more moment of contact with his woman.

"Nope." Stryke swept a hand aside Blyss's neck, pushing her away, while at the same time, he brought his other clawed hand down across Lorcan's chest.

The demon screamed, clasping at his chest. Blyss stumbled against the wall.

"I don't make bargains with idiots," Stryke said as the deep cuts in the demon's chest crackled and formed into black crystals that then moved over the pink suit as if eating the creature alive.

Lorcan's body crystallized, burning away the suit, and dispersed across the white marble floor.

Stryke shook his hand and his claws retracted. He grinned over the pile of demon ash. And then he noticed Blyss shivering and balled-up by the wall. He dashed to her and took her in his arms.

"Sorry you had to see that."

"He deserved it. He would have killed me and you."

"You really believe that?"

She shook her head. "No, I don't. You would have protected me, no matter what. He was no match to you. Thank you."

She buried her head against his neck and clutched

him tightly. But she didn't cry. Instead, Stryke thought he could feel her strength permeate his skin and bones, and he inhaled her natural wolfish scent. This woman was strong and brave, and she was more than a simple glamour girl.

"I love you, Blyss. Nothing in this world will come between me and that love. I promise."

"You make it sound like forever," she whispered.

"I want it to be forever."

She looked up at him, her green eyes blinking back tears. "Really?"

"I love you. No matter what. Wolf or human. I'll love you."

"I love you, too. No matter what. But you know what would make me love you even more?"

"Tell me. I'll make it happen."

"Help me clean up this demon mess?"

He laughed and she joined in, and in the middle of retrieving the broom and dustpan and trying to avoid all the black crystals scattered across the marble floor, Stryke's phone rang.

"Rhys, I'm not sure. I'm in the middle of something with Blyss right now. Huh? Oh, no, not that." He winked at Blyss.

She swept the demon ash toward the dustpan. "Go. I've got this."

"I shouldn't leave you."

"Why? Do you think there's still demons out there who want to harm me?"

"No, I just…"

"I'll be fine," she offered. "Go. Come back to me when you can. I'll be thinking of you."

Stryke kissed her long and deep and then glanced

to the pile of demon ash. "I should clean that up for you first."

"No." She pushed him down the hallway. "You know I've been testing my domestic skills lately. This'll be fun."

"Seriously?"

"Stryke, you're needed."

"And it feels like you're trying to get rid of me."

She kissed him again. "Never. I'll be waiting for you in bed."

"I'll hurry back."

Closing the door behind her lover's retreat, Blyss let out a huffing exhalation, then charged into the bedroom and landed on the end of the bed, breathing heavily.

Her spine shifted. Her skin crawled. She moaned at the tendrils of pain that crossed her skin.

"Shit," she hissed, and then her body began to shift.

Stryke had used Rhys's name when holding the phone conversation before Blyss, but that had been a ruse. He had been thinking quick on his feet and hadn't thought it necessary, or wise, to reveal to her who was really on the other end of the line.

Now he shook Edamite Thrash's hand and the demon nodded he follow him down the aqueduct toward the rusted door they had visited previously.

Yeah, he'd shaken the guy's hand. Much as he'd never admit it out loud, Stryke was okay with Thrash. He wasn't okay with how he'd threatened Blyss, but he did believe he would have never gone through with those threats. And the demon had only been trying to keep Xyloda from being released upon this mortal realm.

Something all right about that goal.

Ed stepped through the open doorway, bending as he led Stryke down a tunnel that was all of limestone. Despite the river outside, Stryke swallowed harder the deeper he walked, for the dry air seeped into his lungs.

He was hit by an intense sulfur scent as the tunnel opened into a vast cave. Ed spread out his arms before the empty room. "Wanted you to know that matters have been dealt with."

"I don't understand." He traced his gaze along the walls and up and around the curved ceiling and finally across the floor— Ah. "That looks like a hell of a lot of demon ash."

"I, and my team, slaughtered Lorcan's denizen."

"Nice. How'd you know it was Lorcan?"

"One of his lackeys came to me this morning. I thought you'd appreciate me taking care of the riff-raff."

"I do. Wish you would have called earlier, though. Lorcan was waiting for us in Blyss's apartment."

"Merde."

"He's ash."

Ed smirked and met Stryke's fist bump. "I like you, Saint-Pierre."

"Yeah, well…" Stryke sighed.

"You don't have to say it. I have my own way of doing things. But know I would never harm Blyss or her family. Er, my family."

"I get that. But Blyss still owes you money."

"I'll be fine. Are you going to take care of her? She needs you."

"Not sure Paris needs me, and she doesn't need Minnesota."

"If it's love you should go for it. Not often that comes into a man's life."

"I'll take that into consideration. Thanks, man. I need to get back to Blyss. Left her to clean up Lorcan's ash."

"Blyss does housework?"

"Wonders never cease, eh?"

The doorbell rang and Blyss sat up on the couch. The soft white wool blanket she'd wrapped herself in slipped from her shoulders. She eyed the turned-over coffee table and hastily righted it, setting the books back on top. Cruising through the kitchen, she picked up a tattered magazine and tossed it in the trash.

She glanced about. She'd picked up most of the mess earlier and had swept up Lorcan's remains. *After* she'd come back from the shift to wolf. The new mess had been from her wolf.

She hadn't been able to control the insistent need to shift. The wolf had come upon her so suddenly it was all she could do to keep from screaming at the pain and alerting her neighbors. Thank the goddess the wolf had been contained within her apartment and hadn't tried to get out through a window. She'd been able to come back to human form only fifteen minutes ago and had collapsed on the couch in tears.

Now she checked her face in the refrigerator door glass. She hadn't time to put on makeup earlier—no streaked mascara or smeared lipstick. Her hair needed combing, and other than being naked beneath the blanket, she looked…

"Like hell. He'll never believe me. But I can't tell him. Not yet."

Because she had to be sure. She didn't want to get his hopes up. Or hers.

Stryke rang the doorbell as she swung the door open and leaned out to kiss him. She pulled him inside by his shirtfront, still kissing him and hoping to distract him from asking the obvious questions.

"Mmm, you are happy to see me."

"I am." She tugged him down the hallway.

Stryke slid onto the stool before the counter. "You're wearing a blanket? What do you have on under there?"

"Nothing." She tugged the blanket a little closer. Not feeling the sexy vibes at the moment. "I showered and then lay down for a bit. I, uh, think the weekend tired me out. I was going to get dressed and then you rang."

"You don't have to get dressed. I like you au naturel."

"You like me any way but all dressed up and— Stryke, you used French. You're learning, *mon amour*. So what's up? Everything go well with Rhys?"

"Yep. Another job done all tidy and swept under the rug. And speaking of sweeping… You need me to sweep up a demon for you?" He glanced over his shoulder into the living room.

"No, I got that. Though I've still some cleaning to do. Don't look at the mess."

She cringed at sight of the lamp hanging off the chair arm.

"But how did it get so—?"

Blyss tugged Stryke toward the bedroom. "Come and help me pick out some clothes and shoes."

"Shoes? I have no talent for shoes, glamour girl."

"Sure you do. Just sit there." She pushed him onto the bed. "And I'll model for you." She headed into the shoe closet, glad to have diverted him from the mess out in the living room. The man was keen on picking up the details and sensing when all was not right.

He'd have to go back that way sooner or later. How many pairs of shoes could she model before he figured something was up?

Once inside the closet she felt the strange tug across her shoulder muscles. Hell, the feeling wasn't strange; it was too familiar.

"Not again." She clasped the lip of the closest shelf and breathed shallowly as she concentrated on the sudden twinges to her muscles. Sure sign of an imminent shift. And focusing on the sweet pair of candy-red Viviers wasn't helping to distract one bit.

"I suddenly have the desire for some champagne!" she called out.

"Uh…" Stryke said from the bedroom. "Okay. I'll get some from the fridge."

"All out! You'll need to run to the wineshop down the street."

"Seriously?"

Tensing her gut and clinging desperately to the door frame, Blyss forced on a smile and brushed back the hair from her face. She strode to the closet doorway, blanket clutched before her chest. "If you bring the champagne, I'll find it very difficult to get dressed so quickly."

His eyebrow lifted. That sexy know-it-all smirk curled.

Even as she felt her spine twitch, she ran her tongue teasingly along her lower lip. "I want to celebrate us," she managed to say. "All night."

"The woman has a plan." Stryke stood and approached her.

She put up a palm. "No kisses until you bring the

champagne. I'll be waiting." She tugged off the blanket and tossed it at him. "No touching until you get back."

Her fingernails dug into the door frame on the closet side. He couldn't see her fighting the shift.

"Deal." Stryke tilted a wink at her and strolled out of the bedroom.

Chapter 24

Champagne in hand, Stryke picked up his pace down the cobbled street. It had taken an inordinate amount of time in the wineshop. A two-for-one sale had brought out the French in hordes. And his inability to speak the language had probably made him miss his chance at the register more than a few times. And then there was the spry old woman who had pushed past him with an armload of vino.

Ah well, he'd survived that debacle. And now a gorgeous, and naked, woman waited his return. A woman he had promised to love no matter what. He couldn't wait to snuggle up to Blyss beneath the sheets and drink the champagne from her lips.

Rounding a corner, he was roughly shouldered by a teenager running by. "Hey!" But Stryke didn't pursue because a scream alerted him. "What's going on?" he asked a passing tourist who screamed and clutched his child's hand.

"A monster!" the man said in frantic gasps. "It's a big wolf!"

Heart dropping like a stone, Stryke picked up his pace. A big wolf? Monster? It couldn't be. Not in this city crushed from building to building with people. Suddenly he saw the wolf run across the street and down a narrow alleyway.

Not a wolf, but a werewolf.

A handful of teenage boys followed, curiosity killing their sense of safety.

"Shit." It couldn't be. Could it? "Blyss?"

He'd not seen her in werewolf form. And she had taken the elixir, right?

"Please let her have taken the elixir."

He hastened into a run and rounded the corner, racing up behind the young men. Shoving them out of his way, he pushed hard enough to knock them over, but not break bones. "Stay the hell away!"

"But, dude, it's a werewolf!"

"Movie costume!" Stryke called back.

Ahead, the werewolf howled, obliterating his claim to it being a fantastic movie prop. No werewolf with a sense of self-preservation would ever shift in the city. And if so? They certainly wouldn't run around frightening tourists and inviting the police, or worse, animal control with a tranquilizer gun.

It could be Blyss. Hadn't she taken the elixir Himself had made for her? Did she fear its dark origins? Or had she simply forgotten?

No, that was out of the question. Foremost in Blyss's heart was keeping the illusion of normality that she'd created over the years. Drinking that vial would have been a quick and easy fix. He didn't understand.

Yet she'd pushed him out to get the champagne. He hadn't thought much about it until now. It had been weird, as if she'd wanted to get rid of him. But why? To shift?

"Can't be her," he muttered and pushed harder to gain on the wolf.

They'd entered a residential area. Overgrown shrubbery demarcated some yards. A quiet neighborhood. Not the optimal place for a crazed werewolf to roam. Of course, no place was, unless it was out in a vast forest far from humans.

Just don't howl again, he thought.

The sound of a police siren trilled behind him. A long way off. He couldn't know if it was because of the werewolf—what sane police dispatch was going to answer a call to pursue a werewolf?—or probably it was headed out on a routine call like a burglary or traffic violation.

This had to be the first time Stryke wished for burglary in answer to a multiple-choice question. Because he knew in his heart the werewolf was Blyss. He sensed her now. Could smell her essence. His own wolf stirred in an instinctual need to catch the wolf it recognized as one with whom he'd mated.

The werewolf veered left. Stryke made a quick turn, hoping to head off the wolf. He pushed through a tangle of vines, and seeing the hip-high shrub that delineated a backyard, he leaped and jumped over it, landing deftly on the ground. Realizing the champagne bottle was still in hand, he abandoned it and picked up into the run again. He could hear the wolf's breathing now and sensed it had slowed pace. Pausing to mark the area, determine where next to go. Or perhaps even slowing to rest, take in the surroundings. Seek shelter.

Sneaking under a high-trimmed willow tree, Stryke sighted the sleek black werewolf, who entered a small garden shed without a door. He eyed the house. He saw no clues that residents were inside. The overgrown garden and a couple of plastic bags of garbage sitting on the back stoop also alerted him that perhaps they were gone.

He raced to the shed, and when the werewolf turned to slash its talons at him, Stryke realized he wasn't going to win this one in human form.

Quickly, he shifted, unzipping and shoving down his jeans as he did and tearing off his shirt. The shed was probably ten-by-ten feet square and empty, save for a rack on the wall that held a rusted old bicycle.

The werewolf lunged for him again and pinned him to the dirt ground just as his werewolf fully formed. The werewolves struggled briefly, but Stryke's wolf was able to easily subdue the other, who wasn't so much fighting as acting in self-defense. He sniffed the female and sensed their connection, and as much as the wolf in him wanted to mate, his *were* side pulled more strongly.

Safe was the feeling he knew he had to share. The werewolf needed to feel safe.

Stryke shifted back to *were* shape, clutching the other as she also shifted. They came to *were* form together, lying on the shed's cool dirt floor. Blyss shivered in his arms. She startled and scrambled closer, frantic pants huffing across his chin.

"It's okay, sweetie. I'm here." He pulled her onto his lap and cradled her head against his chest.

"How did I get here? Where are my clothes?"

"You shifted to werewolf shape."

"Mon Dieu."

Why the hell this had happened, he couldn't begin to guess. But now was no time for questions. "Let me take you home."

She nodded and clutched him tighter. "Please."

"I'll get dressed. Then I'll find you something to wear."

He hated leaving her alone and shivering in the shed, but he couldn't walk through Paris with a naked woman in his arms. His jeans had survived the shift. Mostly. One leg was ripped down the inner seam. Nothing he could do about that.

Walking around back of the house, he determined no one was inside, and while he wasn't an expert at picking locks, he did find a low sash window that wasn't locked. And he wasn't sure how much time they had before a curious human found them. Jiggling the wooden frame, he was able to push it up and climb inside.

Elderly people had to live here because he couldn't find anything more suitable than a long, floral robe for Blyss to wear. She didn't complain as he helped her dress.

In fact, she remained quiet, her head bowed. The shift had been unexpected, he decided. She was as freaked about it as he.

"Let's go," he said and swept her into his arms.

Once back at her place, he ran a bathtub full of hot water and helped her get in.

Stryke brewed some chamomile tea he found in the kitchen cupboard. He'd left Blyss to soak in the tub. She had clung to him all the way home, but he'd sensed her need to clean up and pull herself together. To be by herself. He couldn't fathom why she'd been out and about as a werewolf, but he sensed it hadn't entirely been her fault.

Had something gone wrong with the potion Himself had provided? Maybe it was faulty? He should have never accepted a boon from such evil. He blamed himself for anything that may go wrong with Blyss because of the elixir.

And yet, were he a pack leader and had it been one of his pack members who had exposed their breed to the public, he would surely reprimand the wolf. A beating, perhaps from the pack, a show of authority. A female he would assign a less severe punishment.

Could he command a pack and delve out the punishment when the rules were broken? Yes. Because the rules kept them alive. Blyss needed—well, she needed to be human. It was what worked best for her.

What would a pack think if he had a human wife, but also knew that she had been born wolf? That she denied her heritage. It wouldn't go over well. And he would never ask any wolf to accept her as part of the pack family.

He didn't want to lose Blyss.

Did that mean he'd never have a pack? He couldn't let his father down. Or himself. Which meant the next conversation he had with Blyss would prove the toughest ever.

The tea was mixed with a touch of mint, and the cool scent tingled in his nose. He'd made himself a cup, too. The sun had set. Moonlight beamed through the glass ceiling.

Sighing, he picked up the cups and wandered into the bedroom. Blyss sat on the bed, a sheet pulled up about her breasts. She hadn't dressed. She thanked him for the tea and sipped. Earthy scents infused the room.

He wasn't sure how to start the conversation, so he crawled up beside her and nuzzled his face into her hair. She smelled like the exquisite socialite he'd first met in the gallery weeks ago. But her delicate, shivering frame felt defeated and small. As if something had stolen her hope.

After a few sips in silence he made a stab at the truth.

"Blyss, you haven't drunk the red stuff, have you?"

She shook her head, lowered her lashes.

"Is that why you shifted?"

"I think so. I didn't shift on purpose. It came on me so suddenly. I, uh… Earlier today when you were away helping Rhys, I shifted to wolf without volition, as well. It's why I pushed you out of here so quickly when I felt it happening again."

"I did get a weird feeling about that."

"I'm sorry."

"Why don't you drink the elixir and stop it? What happened was dangerous, Blyss. Not only to you but innocent humans. A fully shifted werewolf should not run through the streets of Paris."

"I know, I know."

He traced her cheek, toying with a curl of darkest hair. "I thought you wanted to be human more than anything?"

She stretched her shoulders back, sitting up straighter. The sheet fell away. She was so beautiful beneath the moonlight. He decided this apartment, with the windows in the ceiling, must have been crafted with Blyss in mind. Like a star upon a stage, she was a true glamour girl.

"Things have changed," she said so softly he had to lean forward to hear, and that was saying a lot considering his wolf hearing could pick up a mouse running across wet summer leaves half a mile away.

He took her teacup and set his and hers aside on the nightstand, then clasped her hand and waited for her to explain. For the longest time she held his gaze. Her bold green eyes captured him, teased him, touched him. Revealed her vulnerabilities. For the first time in his life, he could feel tears well behind his eyes.

So this was what it was like to love someone so much that their pain became your own?

Yet beyond her pain he sensed something brighter. Perhaps even hopeful.

"I didn't take the elixir because I thought I could give the werewolf a test-drive," she said. "Maybe try it on and wear it awhile. Get a feel for, well…myself. A lot has changed since that first horrible shift. My life is something I've created down to every last detail, but…" She touched his lips and smiled. "Is the life I've made really the life I was meant to have?"

He kissed her fingertips. She was the only one who could answer that. Hell, he had no clue because he was still making his own life. And he liked the way it was going so long as it included Blyss.

"I figured I could give it a month or two," she continued. "I'll always have the elixir. I can take it at any time. I want to do this for me, but as well, I want to do it for you. I love you, Stryke. And I never felt closer to a person than during the time we spent at the cabin. You make me want to embrace something I've always denied."

Her words were sincere. He believed that she believed what she said 100 percent. But could the glamour girl exist alongside the werewolf? He didn't want her to sacrifice any of the fine things and the lifestyle she had come to love for him.

Because loving him was as far from fancy shoes and diamonds and Paris as she could get.

"Tell me you'll support me," she said. "Please?"

"Blyss, I'm behind you 100 percent. You want to try on your werewolf and take it for a spin? I've got your back. As well as your pretty little tail and those gorgeous claws. But will you promise not to take the werewolf for a run in the middle of Paris during the height of tourist season?"

"That's the one small problem. I can't seem to control the urge to shift. It just…attacks me. I wonder if there's a transition period? I hope that's what this is, because if I can't control my wolf then I might as well drink the Kool-Aid right now."

He stroked her hair and chuckled. "The French have Kool-Aid?"

"Something similar. But will you help me? If I shift again, I don't know what will happen. The wolf I can keep contained in the apartment, but my werewolf is another story."

"Maybe we should head out to the cabin for a couple more days?"

"Can we? Would Monsieur Hawkes mind?"

"I'll give him a call." He kissed her, intending for it to be quick, but Stryke got lost in the sweet taste of his future, and he pushed Blyss back into the pillows and caressed her breasts. "Mmm, I suddenly have the urge to mess you up, glamour wolf."

She propped up on her elbows and pressed a finger over his lips. "You called me glamour wolf."

"That's what you are. You okay with that?"

She nodded. "Very."

A month later, Stryke still hadn't left Paris. And Blyss was over the moon about that. Rhys Hawkes had offered him a permanent job at Hawkes Associates, which he was currently considering. But Blyss knew his home in the States called to him. There was where his family lived. It was where he had made a life, as small and comfortable as it was. It was where his future as a pack leader waited.

And she wanted him to have that future.

As well, Stryke considered the idea of starting an enforcement team such as Kir was a part of. He'd spent more time with Kir and had gone out with the Enforcement team to observe. He always returned to Blyss in a great mood, rambling on how he intended to institute the ideas and procedures when he got back home.

He'd made plenty of friends and gained family here in Paris. But he missed his brothers and sister and his home.

Blyss sensed his heavy heart, and now as she wandered through her apartment, crossing the clean white marble floor and landing in the living room beneath the skylights, she sighed.

Was this her home? Or was it a stage she'd created to suit her desire to live a life as completely opposite of that which her wolf demanded?

Werewolves lived in the city. It wasn't an odd thing. They could even own galleries and host elaborate parties and socialize and own closets full of expensive shoes. She knew that because she'd been doing it for a month.

The wax-sealed vial sat in the medicine cabinet, waiting her complete abandonment of this new lifestyle. Yet it wasn't so different. She'd gained control of her wolf after a weekend at the cabin. It was as though her wild side had jumped forth after being suppressed for all those years. It wanted out and needed to run free. So she had let it out and had spent more time in wolf and werewolf form than in *were* shape.

She and Stryke had been cautious not to bond as werewolves, though. He said it was something sacred, something he would only do if and when they decided that they were the only one for the other. He'd not used the word *marriage*, but Blyss understood. He was old-fashioned that way.

When two werewolves mated, they bonded for life. It was a serious deal. And yet she entertained doing just that with Stryke. She loved him. She wanted to be with him forever.

But his forever tugged him away from Paris. Could she leave the city in which she'd grown up? The city that was as much a part of her soul as her breath?

She'd already made the decision to travel to the States for a few weeks with him over the winter holidays to meet his family. But once there, would he want to stay? Could they manage a life together yet perhaps live in both places? What about a long-distance relationship?

When she'd only recently thought her biggest challenge was accepting her wolf, now she was surprised by the difficulty she faced in merely leaving a city. Her home.

"Come here, glamour girl."

She settled onto the sofa on her lover's lap. His hair had grown since he'd been here and tufted over his ears.

"You have a fancy shindig tonight?"

The gallery, which she was considering selling, was showing a series of Mucha lithographs this evening. Her presence was required, though she trusted her new assistant—Lisa, a human girl from New York City just out of college. She had been vetted by Stryke as human, when she'd introduced the two and he'd surreptitiously sniffed her out. Lisa could handle it. But Blyss did still enjoy the socializing.

"You want to come along?" she asked.

She didn't miss his wince. "How about I head out to the cabin and wait for you? Full moon tomorrow night."

"Sounds like a plan. I'll even pack proper country clothing this time."

He'd spent hours browsing the jewelry shops, looking over every diamond ring, nodding as the salespeople wanted to show him yet another stone in a different cut, or clarity. Or how about a few more carats for the lucky girl?

After two days of shopping for a ring with which he could propose to Blyss, Stryke had given up. Because he realized no diamond could ever satisfy her. Sure, she was all diamonds and moonlight now. He loved his glamour girl when she followed him out to the forest, dropping her pretty silk dress without a care and leaving the diamond on top of that. And then her wild overtook and the moonlight reigned.

No precious stone could ever show her exactly how much he adored her. How much he admired her for bravely accepting her wolf. Or how much he loved being with her.

So when he paused before a shop that sold funky yet modern clothing and jewelry, his eyes landed on a simple ring in the window display. He pressed his palms to the window.

"Perfect."

Chapter 25

Stryke navigated the long country road that wound two miles through a thick forest of pine trees and bare-branched elms to his parents' property. The whole family would be waiting, and he was nervous for Blyss.

Sure, she'd met his brothers and sister briefly at the wedding last summer, but that had been different. Now he was presenting his bondmate to his family. The woman with whom he intended to spend the rest of his life. The woman who wore a wooden engagement ring on her finger because she loved him and wanted to be with him forever.

Okay, so he was nervous, too. He wanted his family to like her. He'd explained everything to his mother over the phone about how Blyss had denied her werewolf for years, and how she only recently embraced her heritage. Surely that news had circulated among his siblings.

It was Malakai Saint-Pierre, his father, from whom he most worried about getting the seal of approval. If his father didn't like Blyss, then she was out, plain and simple. And while he loved Blyss, he respected his father and would likely have a tough decision to make should the pack principal give the thumbs-down. But he couldn't imagine anyone saying nay to Blyss.

As well, when the New Year turned, Kai intended Stryke should make his new pack official by choosing a scion. Trouble wasn't at all bummed that the family pack was being dissolved; he intended to start a pack on his own. But not until he'd thoroughly sown his wild oats. And that guy had a lot of them.

Blade had said *no, thank you* to scion. Kelyn would make an excellent right-hand man but Stryke would give it more consideration. With luck, Blade would change his mind.

He stroked Blyss's cheek now and she smiled at him.

"Pull over," she said and turned on the seat to sit up on her knees.

"We're almost there, glamour wolf. Half a mile—"

"Please?"

She must be as nervous as he was. A few minutes to take a deep breath and chill was a good idea. He shifted into Park and they sat in the Ford truck, the engine idling, the radio quietly broadcasting a country tune.

"They will all love you," he reassured her. "But never so much as I do."

"I'm not worried." She crawled over and straddled him in the tight confines of the cab. "Are *you* worried?"

"My dad's the tough one," he said. "But I know he'll love you."

"It was a good idea to come here for Christmas.

I'm already in love with your state after seeing all this snow."

"You may be the only one who has ever made such a confession."

"Well, I don't have to shovel it. And so you know, I will never shovel snow or do the manual labor in this partnership."

"Wouldn't dream of letting you lift a pretty little finger to do anything but this." He took her hand and kissed her fingertips, one by one. "Sure you don't want a diamond engagement ring?"

"Never. This one is perfect. It's you, wrapped around my finger. I adore it." She leaned in and whispered aside his ear. "I want to give you your Christmas present now."

"Really? You got me something? Blyss, you shouldn't have. Us together is all I want for Christmas."

"Then you don't want this?" She took his hand and placed it over her stomach, which was softly swollen beneath the thick sweater she'd bought yesterday in town at the local thrift store.

"What, sweetie?"

She tilted her head at him and told him to close his eyes. "Now," she said, "concentrate on what you feel. Can you feel it?"

Stryke slid his hand across the soft pink sweater. He could feel her warmth radiate out and into his skin. And beyond the subtle hum of her sensual being, he picked up...

He flashed his eyes open to meet her expectant gaze. "Really? I think I feel a tiny heartbeat."

She nodded. "Our family is already growing."

"Blyss, this is amazing. Really? I'm going to be a daddy?"

"And a very fine dad you will be. We'll raise our family here, in the place that makes you most happy, sending them off to school in the fall and winter, and then in the summer we'll vacation in Paris. Can the pack handle that?"

"They'll handle whatever their leader says they can. You've got great plans. You really think you could live in Minnesota?"

"So long as the summers are in Paris and my shoe closet can be shipped back and forth."

"Why not keep a shoe closet here and one in Paris?"

"I adore you, *mon amour.*"

He bent and hugged his cheek against her tummy and tried to listen for the tiny heartbeat. Detecting it, Stryke smiled. "This little one is going to love his were-wolf mommy."

* * * * *

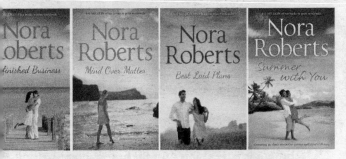
ST_11

MILLS & BOON®

nocturne™

AN EXHILARATING UNDERWORLD OF DARK DESIRES

A sneak peek at next month's titles...

In stores from 17th April 2015:

Wolf Hunter – Linda Thomas-Sundstrom
Possessed by a Wolf – Sharon Ashwood

Available at WHSmith, Tesco, Asda, Eason, Amazon and Apple

Just can't wait?
Buy our books online a month before they hit the shops!
visit www.millsandboon.co.uk

These books are also available in eBook format!

Join our *EXCLUSIVE* eBook club

FROM JUST £1.99 A MONTH!

Never miss a book again with our hassle-free eBook subscription.

★ Pick how many titles you want from each series with our flexible subscription

★ Your titles are delivered to your device on the first of every month

★ Zero risk, zero obligation!

There really is nothing standing in the way of you and your favourite books!

Start your eBook subscription today at www.millsandboon.co.uk/subscribe